THE DE LA SALLE HYMNAL

The
De La Salle Hymnal

For

CATHOLIC SCHOOLS AND CHOIRS

BY THE

Christian Brothors

brothors of the christian schools

KALPAZ

ISBN: 978-93-5128-630-1(PB)

First Published in 1913
Indian Reprint in 2017

Published by

Kalpaz Publications
C-30, Satyawati Nagar,
Delhi – 110052
E-mail: kalpaz@hotmail.com
Website: kalpazpublications.com
Ph.: +91-9212142040

PREFACE

The DE LA SALLE HYMNAL is offered to the Catholic public in the sincere hope that it may be a valuable aid in religious training. In these days of scientific education, it is trite to say that the outward expression of emotion is an effective means of developing that very emotion. The rites and ceremonies of Holy Mother Church have taught this truth from the beginning. It is, then, of great importance that the impression be good and the emotion noble. This Hymnal aims to secure both results. It has retained what was good in its predecessor, the *Catholic Youth's Hymn Book*, while studiously avoiding its defects.

1. The DE LA SALLE HYMNAL conforms to the *Motu Proprio* of Pope Pius X on Church Music.

2. Every tune in the book is either of acknowledged worth as music or has long been associated with Catholic traditions in this country.

3. The editorial file has been applied unsparingly to all the vernacular verses, in order to secure both good English and conformity to the musical rhythm of the hymns.

4. Nearly all the hymns have been written for use by either a unison or a four part chorus.

5. The harmonization, while in full accord with artistic standards, is yet so simple as to fall within the limits of the average children's choir or school chorus.

6. The accompaniment has in every case been adapted to the organ. Piano arrangements have been ruthlessly excluded.

7. The pitch of each hymn has been placed low enough to suit the range of boys' voices and facilitate congregational singing.

To all who have in any way helped in the preparation of this book, cordial thanks are herewith extended; in particular, to the Basilian Fathers of Toronto for permission to use numbers 20, 40, and 215; to the Benedictine Fathers for permission to include hymns by members of their order; to Professor Joseph G Marcks for timely aid and for the use of his own compositions;

to Professor Wenzel A. Raboch both for careful revision of the harmonization of the entire book and for permission to include several hymns and a Mass of his own composition; and to Messrs. J. Fischer & Brother for valuable suggestions, careful supervision of proof, and generous permission to use many of their copyrighted publications.

The Manuscripts of the De La Salle Hymnal were carefully and critically read by a diocesan priest and a religious priest, both of acknowledged authority. We regret that neither, in his modesty, would permit the publication of his name. This book shows the fruits of their generous labor, and to each of them we herewith offer our most sincere thanks.

The numbers contained in the Appendix, while not Church Music in the proper sense of the term, have been included by request as being suitable for reunions of a more or less religious character.

The Index embodies the results of serious effort to trace words and tunes to their source. In this respect the *Catholic Church Hymnal* of J. Fischer & Brother and the *Westminster Hymnal* were both helpful. It is to be hoped that in a later edition many of the present blanks may be filled.

As the singing of hymns is pre-eminently a religious act, the attention of young and the old is called to the Indulgences announced below. May all who use this book experience the hallowed emotions of St. Augustine as he listened to Christian Psalmody, and strive to emulate the example of St. Philip Neri in promoting the effectiveness of Catholic Hymns.

New York, Feast of the Holy Rosary, 1913.

INDULGENCES

Popes Pius VII and Pius IX, by rescripts dated respectively June, 1817, and April, 1858, have granted partial indulgences of *one year* and of *one hundred days* to all the faithful who sing hymns piously in a church or oratory, and to those who teach them so to sing, provided that these hymns be approved by ecclesiastical authority. A plenary indulgence may be gained once a month on the ordinary conditions.

The De La Salle Hymnal has received the requisite approbation.

CLASSIFIED INDEX

	Pages
Advent	1-3
Christmas	4-12
Epiphany	13
Holy Name of Jesus	14-16
Lent	17-26
Easter	27-29
Ascension	30
Pentecost	31-35
Trinity Sunday	36, 37
The Blessed Sacrament	38-57
The Sacred Heart of Jesus	58-62
The Most Blessed Virgin	63-101; 248-251
St. Joseph	103-110
The Guardian Angel	111, 112
St. La Salle	113-119
St. Patrick	120-122, 246
St. Anthony	123
St. Cecilia	123
St. Agnes	125
All Souls' Day	126
Miscellaneous Hymns	127-139
Asperges	140
Vidi Aquam	141
Mass of the Angels	143-152
Mass of St. La Salle	153-166
Mass of the Dead	167-185
Vespers for Sundays	186-197
Vespers of the Most Blessed Virgin	198-211
Vesper Hymns	212-216
Vesper Antiphons	217-221
Benediction of the Blessed Sacrament	222-236
Te Deum	237

ADVENT

SEE HE COMES

1

Slowly
1. See, He comes whom ev - ry na - tion, Taught of God, de - sired to see,
2. See, He comes whom kings and sa - ges, Proph - ets, pa - tri - archs of old,
3. See, the Lamb of God ap - pear - ing, God of God, from Heav'n a - bove!
1. Filled with hope and ex - pec - ta - tion That He would their Sav - ior be.
2. Dis - tant climes and count - less a - ges, Wait - ed eag - er to be - hold.
3. See the Heav'n - ly Bride - groom cheer - ing His dear Bride with words of love.
CHORUS
Sing, oh sing with ex - ul - ta - tion, Haste we to our Fa - ther's Home;
Peace, re - demption, joy, sal - va - tion, Now from Heaven to earth are come.

A GLORIOUS VOICE

At a moderate pace

Ancient Hymn

2

1. A glorious voice sounds through the night, And chides the darkness in-to
2. Now from a - bove the Lamb is sent, To pay thy debt, O pe-ni -
1. light; The mists of sleep are driven a - far, And Christ shines forth the morning star.
2. tent! Weep, and with tears thy praise up-lift In thanks for so supreme a gift.
1. Now from its tor - por leaps the mind, And leaves all taint of earth be -
2. To Fa - ther, Son, and Ho - ly Ghost, The King of Heav'n's im-mor-tal
1. hind; The new-born Planet flames on high, And bids all care and sor - row fly.
2. host! May men and angels praise out-pour For - ev - er and for - ev - er more.

O COME, DIVINE MESSIAH

Slowly and devoutly

French Hymnal

3

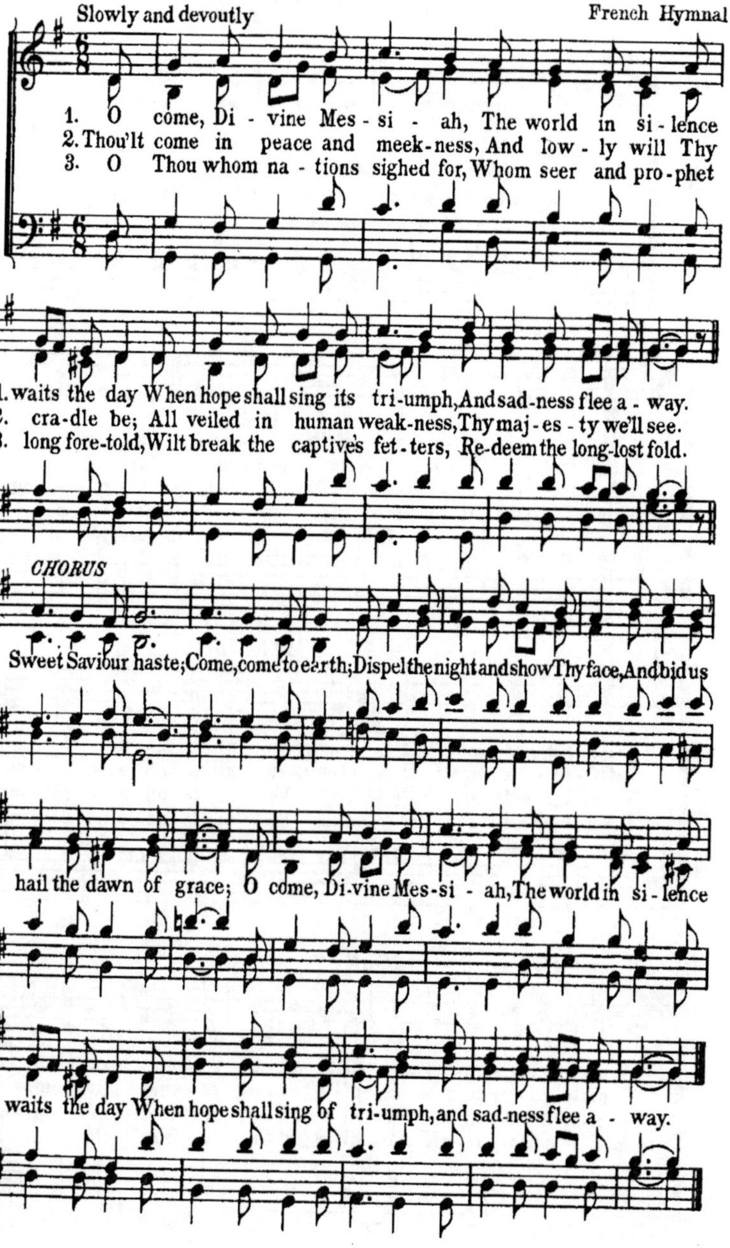
1. O come, Di - vine Mes - si - ah, The world in si - lence
2. Thou'lt come in peace and meek - ness, And low - ly will Thy
3. O Thou whom na - tions sighed for, Whom seer and pro - phet
1. waits the day When hope shall sing its tri - umph, And sad - ness flee a - way.
2. cra - dle be; All veiled in human weak - ness, Thy maj - es - ty we'll see.
3. long fore - told, Wilt break the captive's fet - ters, Re - deem the long - lost fold.
CHORUS
Sweet Saviour haste; Come, come to earth; Dispel the night and show Thy face, And bid us
hail the dawn of grace; O come, Di - vine Mes - si - ah, The world in si - lence
waits the day When hope shall sing of tri - umph, and sad - ness flee a - way.

4

ADESTE FIDELES

Traditional Melody

1. Ad - és - te fi - dé - les, Lae - ti tri - um - phán - tes, Ve -
2. — De - um de De - o, Lu - men de lú - mi - ne,
3. — Can - tet nunc I - o Cho - rus an - ge - ló - rum,
4. — Er - go qui na - tus Di - e ho - di - ér - na,
1. ní - te, ve - ní - te in Béth - le - hem; Na - tum vi - dé - te,
2. Ge - stant pu - él - lae - vi - sce - ra; De - um ve - rum
3. Can - tet nunc au - la coe - lé - sti - um, Gló - ri - a, glo - ria
4. Je - su ti - bi sit gló - ri - a; Pa - tris ae - tér - ni
SOPRANO
SOP.
1. Re - gem an - ge - ló - rum: Ve - ní - te ad - o - ré - mus, Ve -
2. Gé - ni - tum non fa - ctum: Ve - ni - te ad - o - ré - mus, Ve -
3. in ex - cél - sis De - o; Ve - ni - te ad - o - ré - mus, Ve -
4. Ver - bum ca - ro fa - ctum: Ve - ni - te ad - o - ré - mus, Ve -
and ALTO
CHORUS
1. ní - te ad - o - ré - mus, Ve - ní - te ad - o - re - mus Dó - mi - num.
2. ní - te ad - o - ré - mus, Ve - ní - te ad - o - re - mus Dó - mi - num.
3. ní - te ad - o - ré - mus, Ve - ní - te ad - o - re - mus Dó - mi - num.
4. ní - te ad - o - ré - mus, Ve - ní - te ad - o - re - mus Dó - mi - num.

COME ALL YE FAITHFUL

Lerler

5

1. Come, all ye faith-ful, join the march tri-umphant, And hasten, hast-en, to
2. Great God e - ter - nal, Light from light pro-ceeding, How cold and bare is this
3. Dear Lord, we greet Thee, born this hap-py morning; To Thee, O Je - sus, be
ALTO SOLO
1. Beth-le - hem; With-in the crib, there lies the true, the great Messi - ah. Oh,
2. mid-night cave! In fear and love, thrice Ho - ly God, we here a-dore Thee. Oh,
3. glo - ry giv'n; Sal - va - tion comes from Thee, Thou heaven sent Redeem-er. Oh,
SOP. and ALTO
CHORUS
ff
come and let us wor-ship, Oh come and let us wor-ship, Oh come and let us
wor-ship Christ the Lord. Oh come and let us wor - ship Christ the Lord.

ANGELS WE HAVE HEARD ON HIGH

Slowly

Old French Melody

6

1. An-gels we have heard on high Sweet-ly sing-ing o'er the plains,
2. Shepherds,why this ju-bi-lee? Why your joy-ous strains prolong?
3. Come to Beth-l'hem,come,and see Him whose birth the an-gels sing;
4. See with-in a man-ger laid, Je-sus, Lord of Heav'n and earth,
1. And the moun-tains in re-ply Ech-o back their joy-ous strains;
2. Say what may the ti-dings be That in-spire your heav'n-ly song?
3. Come a-dore on bend-ed knee Th'In-fant Christ, the new born King.
4. Ma-ry, Jo-seph, lend your aid, With us sing our Sav-iour's birth.
Glo- - - - - - - -ri-a in ex-cel-sis De-o,
Glo- - - - - - - -ri-a in excel-sis De-o.

CHRISTMAS

SILENT NIGHT

Slowly and tenderly

F. Gruber

7

mf
pp
f
1. Si - lent night, sa - cred night, Beth-lhem sleeps, yet what light
2. Si - lent night, sa - cred night, Shepherds first see the light,
3. Si - lent night, sa - cred night, Son of God! Oh, what light
1. Floats a-round the ho - ly Pair. Songs of an - gels fill the air;
2. Hear the Al - le - lu - ias ring, Which the an - gel cho - rus sing:
3. Is - sues from Thy man-ger bed O - ver realms with darkness spread;
f
p
1. Strains of hea-ven-ly peace, Strains of hea-ven-ly peace.
2. Christ the Sav-iour has come, Christ the Sav-iour has come.
3. Thou in Beth-le-hem born, Thou in Beth-le-hem born.

CHRISTMAS

O HOLY NIGHT

Adam

8

1. O ho-ly night! the stars are bright-ly shin-ing, It is the
2. Led by the light of faith se-rene-ly beam-ing, With glow-ing
1. night of the dear Sav-iour's birth. Long lay the world in sin and sor-row
2. hearts by His cra-dle we stand. So led by light of star so sweet-ly
1. pin-ing, Till He ap-pear'd, and the soul felt its worth. A thrill of hope the
2. gleam-ing, Then came the wise-men from th'Ori-ent land. To see the King who
1. wea-ry world re-joic-es, For yon-der breaks a new and glorious morn.
2. made earth's low-liest choic-es, Yea, chose His throne a man-ger all for-lorn.
Fall on your knees! O hear the an-gel voic-es! O night di-vine! O

ff
night when Christ was born! O night di-vine! O night, O night di - vine!

THE SNOW LAY ON THE GROUND

Old English Carol

9

1. The snow lay on the ground, the stars shone
ni - te ad - o - ré - mus Dó - mi - -
2. 'Twas Ma - ry, daugh - ter pure of ho - ly
laid Him in a stall at Beth - le - -
ni - te ad - o - ré - mus Dó - mi - -
3. Saint Jo - seph too was by to tend the
An - gels hov - er'd round and sang this
ni - te ad - o - ré - mus Dó - mi - -
4. And then that man - ger poor be - came a
come, then, let us join the heav'n - ly
ni - te ad - o - ré - mus Dó - mi - -

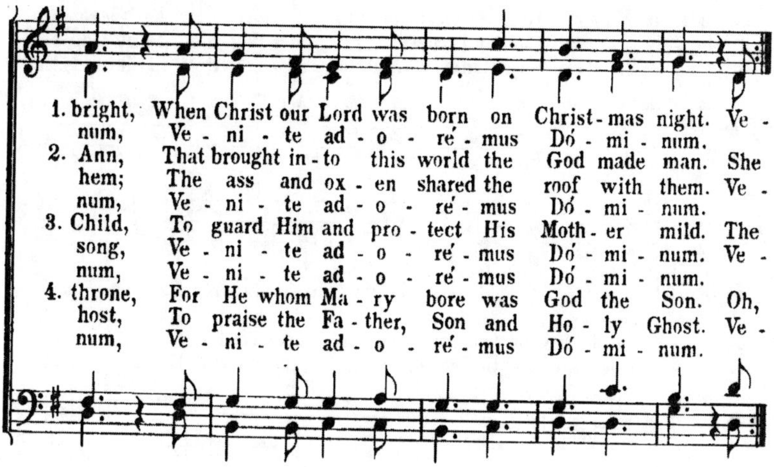

1. bright, When Christ our Lord was born on Christ - mas night. Ve -
num, Ve - ni - te ad - o - ré - mus Dó - mi - num.
2. Ann, That brought in - to this world the God made man. She
hem; The ass and ox - en shared the roof with them. Ve -
num, Ve - ni - te ad - o - ré - mus Dó - mi - num.
3. Child, To guard Him and pro - tect His Moth - er mild. The
song, Ve - ni - te ad - o - ré - mus Dó - mi - num. Ve -
num, Ve - ni - te ad - o - ré - mus Dó - mi - num.
4. throne, For He whom Ma - ry bore was God the Son. Oh,
host, To praise the Fa - ther, Son and Ho - ly Ghost. Ve -
num, Ve - ni - te ad - o - ré - mus Dó - mi - num.

WHAT LOVELY INFANT CAN THIS BE

Slowly and devoutly

Children's Carol

10

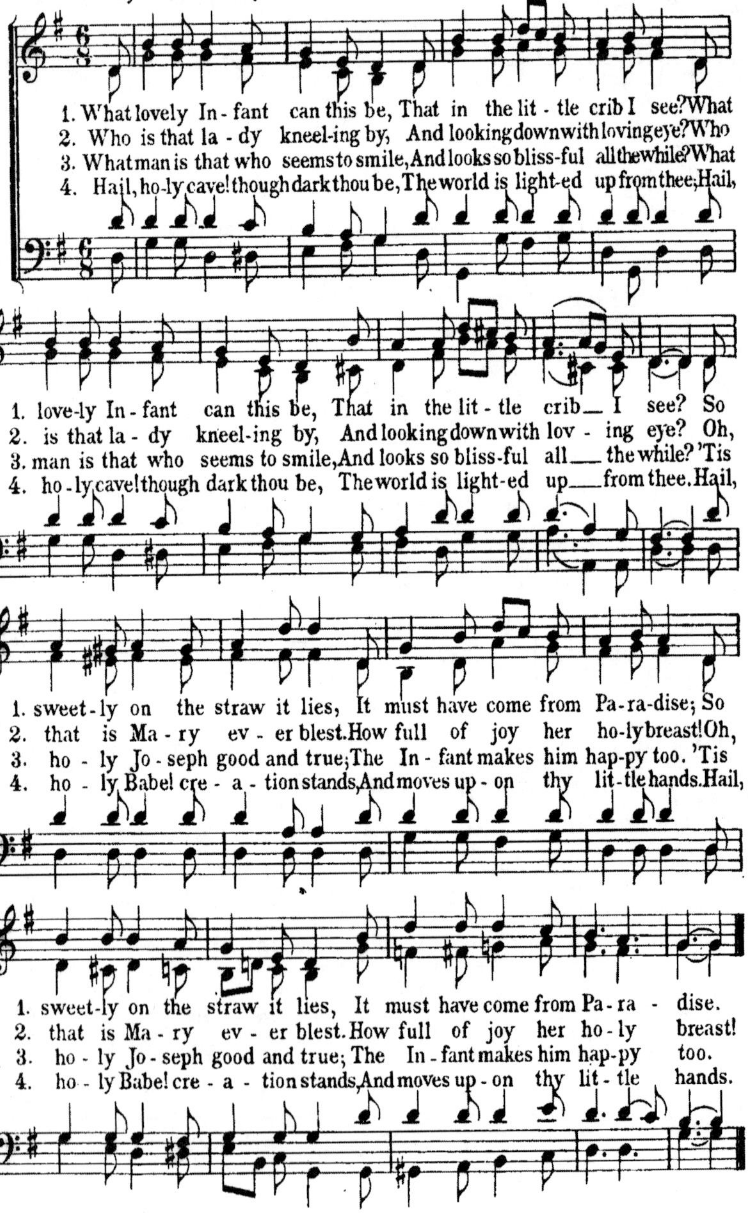
1. What lovely In-fant can this be, That in the lit-tle crib I see? What
2. Who is that la-dy kneel-ing by, And looking down with loving eye? Who
3. What man is that who seems to smile, And looks so bliss-ful all the while? What
4. Hail, ho-ly cave! though dark thou be, The world is light-ed up from thee, Hail,
1. love-ly In-fant can this be, That in the lit-tle crib __ I see? So
2. is that la-dy kneel-ing by, And looking down with lov-ing eye? Oh,
3. man is that who seems to smile, And looks so bliss-ful all __ the while? 'Tis
4. ho-ly cave! though dark thou be, The world is light-ed up __ from thee. Hail,
1. sweet-ly on the straw it lies, It must have come from Pa-ra-dise; So
2. that is Ma-ry ev-er blest. How full of joy her ho-ly breast! Oh,
3. ho-ly Jo-seph good and true; The In-fant makes him hap-py too. 'Tis
4. ho-ly Babe! cre-a-tion stands, And moves up-on thy lit-tle hands. Hail,
1. sweet-ly on the straw it lies, It must have come from Pa-ra-dise.
2. that is Ma-ry ev-er blest. How full of joy her ho-ly breast!
3. ho-ly Jo-seph good and true; The In-fant makes him hap-py too.
4. ho-ly Babe! cre-a-tion stands, And moves up-on thy lit-tle hands.

SEE! AMID THE WINTER'S SNOW

Joyously, Not too fast

11

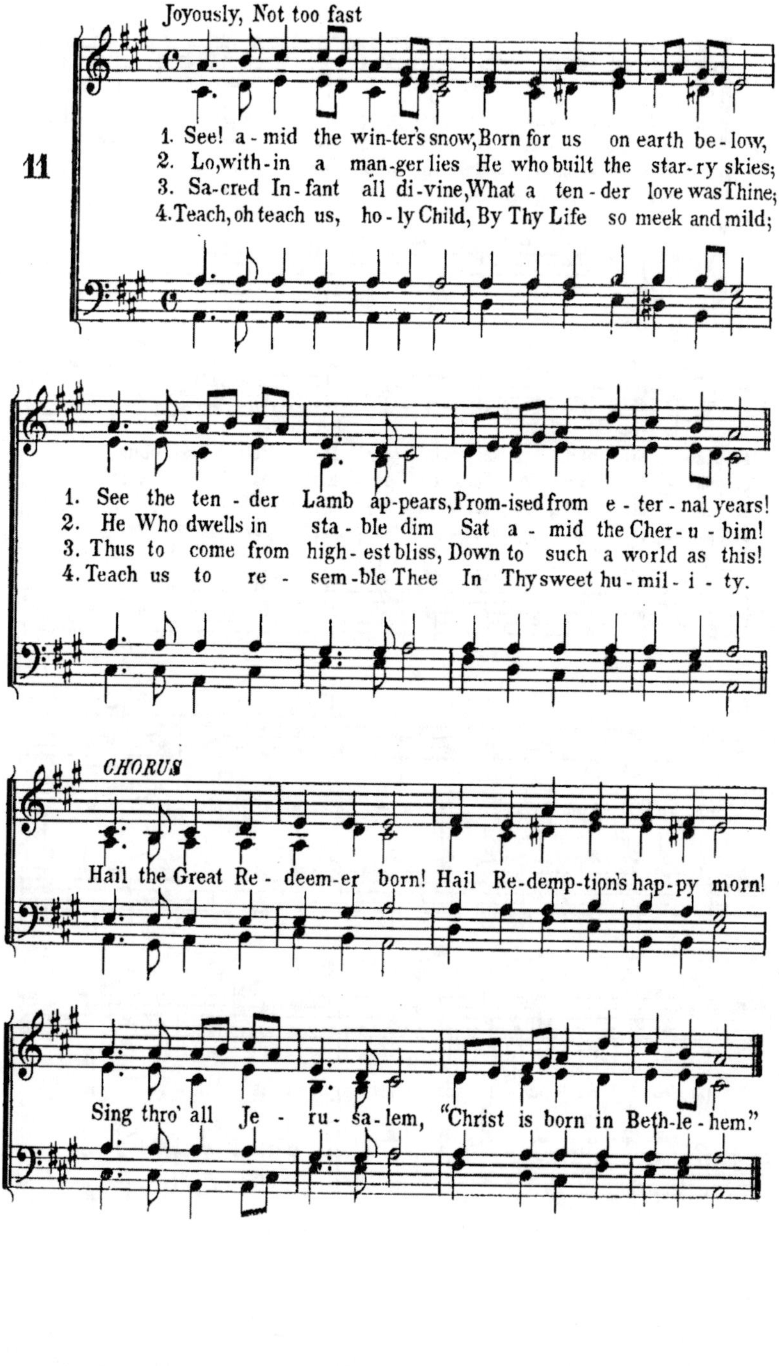
1. See! a-mid the win-ter's snow, Born for us on earth be-low,
2. Lo, with-in a man-ger lies He who built the star-ry skies;
3. Sa-cred In-fant all di-vine, What a ten-der love was Thine;
4. Teach, oh teach us, ho-ly Child, By Thy Life so meek and mild;
1. See the ten-der Lamb ap-pears, Prom-ised from e-ter-nal years!
2. He Who dwells in sta-ble dim Sat a-mid the Cher-u-bim!
3. Thus to come from high-est bliss, Down to such a world as this!
4. Teach us to re-sem-ble Thee In Thy sweet hu-mil-i-ty.
CHORUS
Hail the Great Re-deem-er born! Hail Re-demp-tion's hap-py morn!
Sing thro' all Je-ru-sa-lem, "Christ is born in Beth-le-hem."

CHRISTMAS

IN NATIVITATE DOMINI

12

1. Ré - so - net in láu - di - bus cum ju - cún - dis
2. Pú - e - ri con - cí - ni - te, na - to Re - gi
3. Si - on, lau - da ni - mi - um Sal - va - tó - rem
4. Qui re - gnat in ae - the - re, ve - nit o - vem
SOLI
1. plaú - si - bus, Si - on, cum fi - dé - li - bus.
2. psal - li - te; Vo - ce pi - a dí - ci - te:
3. hó - mi - num, La - va - tó - rem crí - mi - num. Ap -
4. quaé - re - re, Nul - lum vo - lens pér - de - re.
TUTTI
pá - ru - it, Ap - pa - ru - it, quem gé - nu - it Ma - rí - a. Ap -
pá - ru - it, Ap - pa - ru - it, quem gé - nu - it Ma - rí - a.

EPIPHANY

WHAT BEAUTEOUS SUN-SURPASSING STAR

C. Schmidt

13

f
1. What beau-teous sun - sur - pass-ing star, O'er Bethl'hem's lone - ly
2. While thus the star its light im-parts, A ray with - in doth
3. O Je - sus, morn - ing star, our hearts Cleanse with Thy light with-
1. road, Re - veals a ris - ing bright - er far, And shows the cra - dled God!
2. shine, Which leads a few but faith - ful hearts To seek the glori-ous sign.
3. in, And suf - fer not the tempt - er's arts To lure us back to sin.
1. The star from Ja - cob see a - rise, By proph - ets long fore -
2. No dan - gers can their pur - pose shake; Love suf - fers no de -
3. The Light of Gen - tile lands a - dore, The Day - spring from on
1. told; The si - lent night - ly mes - sen - ger, The na - tions East be hold.
2. lay. Home, kin-dred, coun - try, they for - sake; God calls, and they o - bey.
3. high; A - like the Fa - ther ev - er-more, And Spir - it mag - ni - fy.

By permission of J. Fischer & Bro.

HOLY NAME OF JESUS

HOW SWEET THE NAME OF JESUS SOUNDS

W. A. Raboch

14

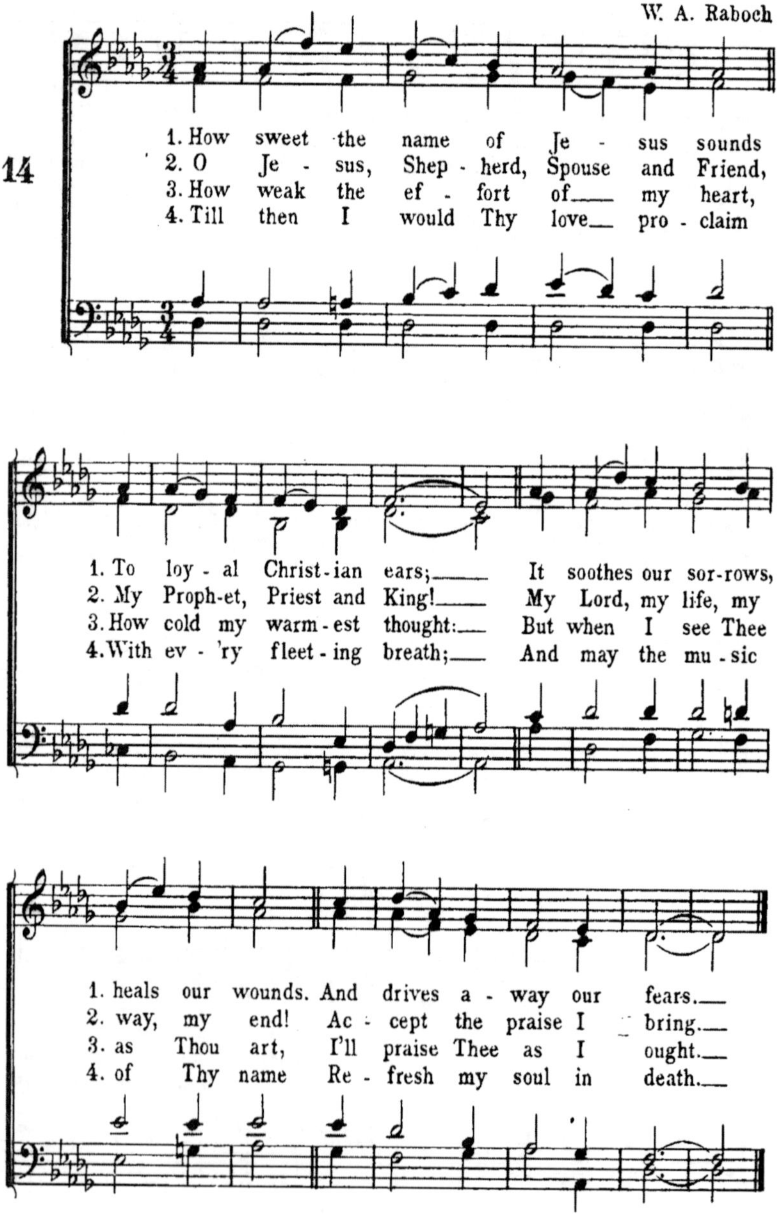
1. How sweet the name of Je - sus sounds
2. O Je - sus, Shep - herd, Spouse and Friend,
3. How weak the ef - fort of__ my heart,
4. Till then I would Thy love__ pro - claim
1. To loy - al Christ - ian ears;__ It soothes our sor-rows,
2. My Proph-et, Priest and King!__ My Lord, my life, my
3. How cold my warm - est thought:__ But when I see Thee
4. With ev - 'ry fleet - ing breath;__ And may the mu - sic
1. heals our wounds. And drives a - way our fears.__
2. way, my end! Ac - cept the praise I bring.__
3. as Thou art, I'll praise Thee as I ought.__
4. of Thy name Re - fresh my soul in death.__

HOLY NAME

O JESUS, DEAR THE THOUGHT OF THEE

15

1. O Je-sus, dear the thought of Thee With sweet-ness fills my
2. O Hope of ev-'ry con-trite heart, O Joy of all the
3. O Je-sus, Light of all be-low, Thou Fount of life and
4. O Je-sus, Thou the beau-ty art Of an-gel worlds a-
1. breast; But sweet-er far Thy face to see, And in Thy pres-ence
2. weak! To those who fall, how kind Thou art, How good to those who
3. fire, Sur-pass-ing all the joys we know, All that we can de-
4. bove; Thy Name is mu-sic to the heart, En-chant-ing it with
1. rest. No voice can sing, no tongue can frame, Nor can the mem-'ry
2. seek! But what to those who find? Oh! this, No tongue, no pen, can
3. sire. May ev-'ry heart con fess Thy Name, And ev-er Thee a
4. love. For Thee I yearn, for Thee I sigh, When wilt Thou come to
1. find A sweet-er sound than Thy blest Name, O Saviour of man-kind.
2. show; For what the love of Je-sus is, None but His loved ones know.
3. dore, And seek-ing Thee, it-self in-flame To seek Thee more and more.
4. me, And make me glad e-ter-nal-ly, With one blest sight of Thee?

JESU DULCIS MEMORIA

16

1. Je-su, dul-cis me-mó-ri-a, Dans ve-ra cor-dis gaú-di-a, Sed
2. Je-su, spes pœ-ni-tén-ti-bus, Quam pi-us es pe-tén-ti-bus! Quam
3. Je-su, dul-cé-do cór-di-um, Fons vi-vus lu-men mén-ti-um, Ex-
1. su-per mel et ó-mni-a, E-jus dul-cis prae-sén-ti-a Nil
2. bo-nus Te quae-rén-ti-bus! Sed quid in-ve-ni-én-ti-bus? Nec
3. cé-dens ó-mne gaú-di-um, Et ó-mne de-si-dé-ri-um: Sis,
1. cá-ni-tur su-á-vi-us, Nil au-dí-tur ju-cún-di-us, Nil
2. lin-gua va-let dí-ce-re, Nec lít-te-ra ex-prí-me-re: Ex-
3. Je-su, no-strum gaú-di-um, Qui es fu-tú-rus praé-mi-um; Sit
1. co-gi-tá-tur dúl-ci-us Quam Je-su, De-i Fí-li-us.
2. pér-tus po-test cré-de-re Quid sit Je-sum di-lí-ge-re.
3. no-stra in Te gló-ri-a Per cun-cta sem-per saé-cu-la.

CHRISTIANS WHO OF JESUS' SORROWS (No. 1)

Pergolesi

17

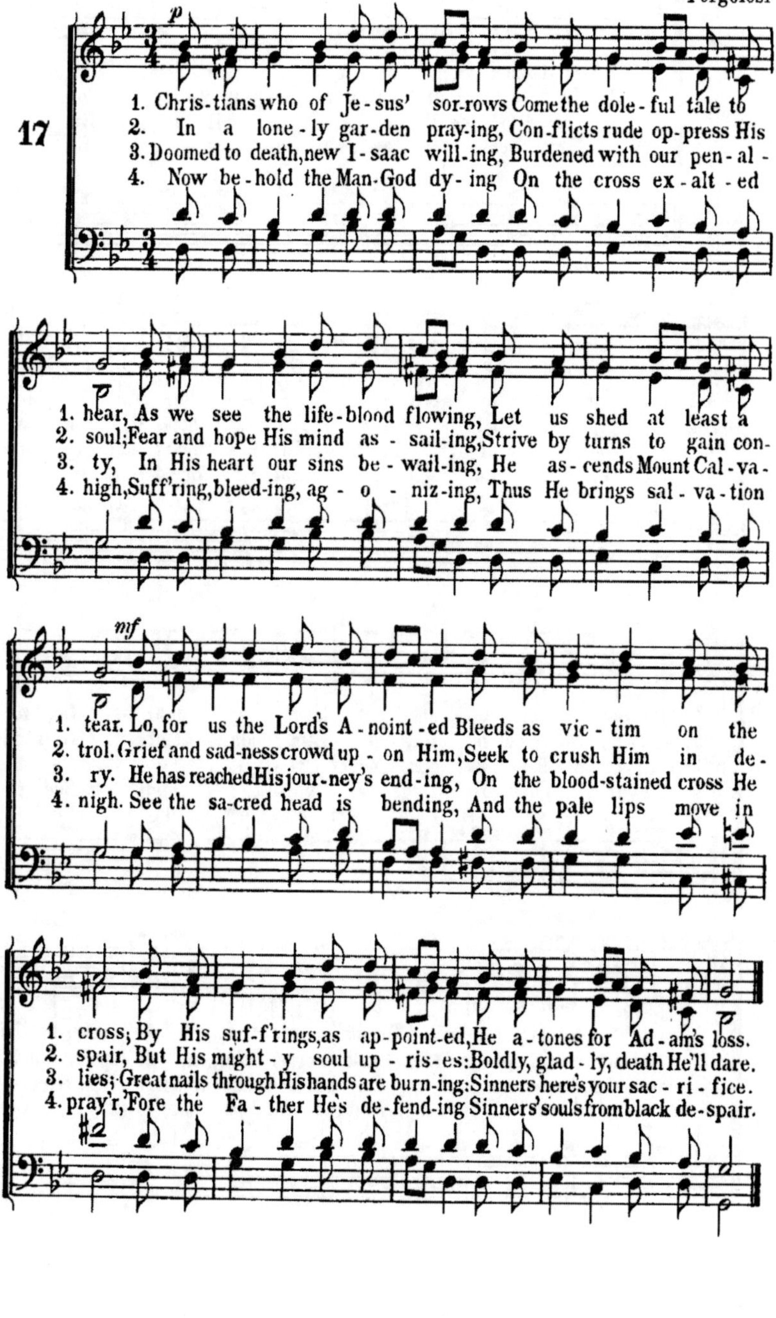
p
1. Chris-tians who of Je-sus' sor-rows Come the dole-ful tale to
2. In a lone-ly gar-den pray-ing, Con-flicts rude op-press His
3. Doomed to death, new I-saac will-ing, Burdened with our pen-al-
4. Now be-hold the Man-God dy-ing On the cross ex-alt-ed
1. hear, As we see the life-blood flowing, Let us shed at least a
2. soul; Fear and hope His mind as-sail-ing, Strive by turns to gain con-
3. ty, In His heart our sins be-wail-ing, He as-cends Mount Cal-va-
4. high, Suff'ring, bleed-ing, ag-o-niz-ing, Thus He brings sal-va-tion
mf
1. tear. Lo, for us the Lord's A-noint-ed Bleeds as vic-tim on the
2. trol. Grief and sad-ness crowd up-on Him, Seek to crush Him in de-
3. ry. He has reached His jour-ney's end-ing, On the blood-stained cross He
4. nigh. See the sa-cred head is bending, And the pale lips move in
1. cross; By His suf-f'rings, as ap-point-ed, He a-tones for Ad-am's loss.
2. spair, But His might-y soul up-ris-es: Boldly, glad-ly, death He'll dare.
3. lies; Great nails through His hands are burn-ing: Sinners here's your sac-ri-fice.
4. pray'r, 'Fore the Fa-ther He's de-fend-ing Sinners' souls from black de-spair.

CHRISTIANS WHO OF JESUS' SORROWS (No. 2)

Slowly
1. Christ-ians who of Je-sus' sor-rows Come the
2. In a lone-ly gar-den pray-ing, Con-flicts
3. Doomed to death, new I-saac will-ing, Bur-dened
4. Now be-hold the Man-God dy-ing On the
1. dole-ful tale to hear, As we see the life-blood
2. rude op-press His soul; Fear and hope His mind as-
3. with our pen-al-ty, In His heart our sins be-
4. cross ex-alt-ed high, Suff'ring, bleed-ing, ag-o-
1. flow-ing, Let us shed at least a tear. Lo, for
2. sail-ing, Strive by turns to gain con-trol. Grief and
3. wail-ing, He as-cends Mount Cal-va-ry. He has
4. niz-ing, Thus He brings sal-va-tion nigh. See the
1. us the Lord's A-noint-ed Bleeds as vic-tim on the cross; By His
2. sad-ness crowd up-on Him, Seek to crush Him in de-spair, But His
3. reached His jour-ney's end-ing, On the blood-stained cross He lies; Great nails
4. sa-cred head is bend-ing, And the pale lips move in pray'r, 'Fore the

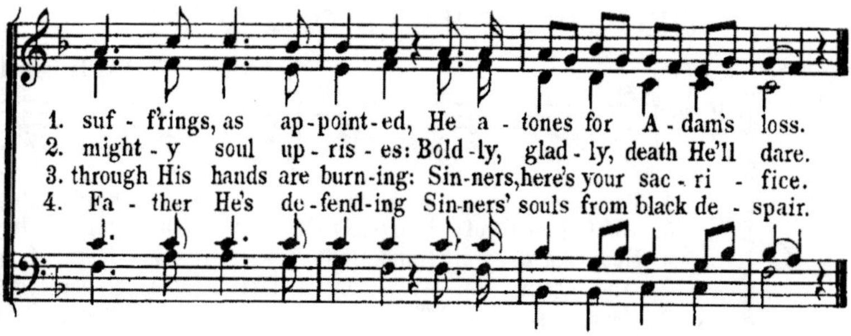
1. suf - f'rings, as ap-point-ed, He a - tones for A-dam's loss.
2. might - y soul up - ris - es: Bold-ly, glad - ly, death He'll dare.
3. through His hands are burn-ing: Sin-ners, here's your sac - ri - fice.
4. Fa - ther He's de-fend-ing Sin-ners' souls from black de - spair.

O COME AND MOURN WITH ME

French Passiontide Melody

19

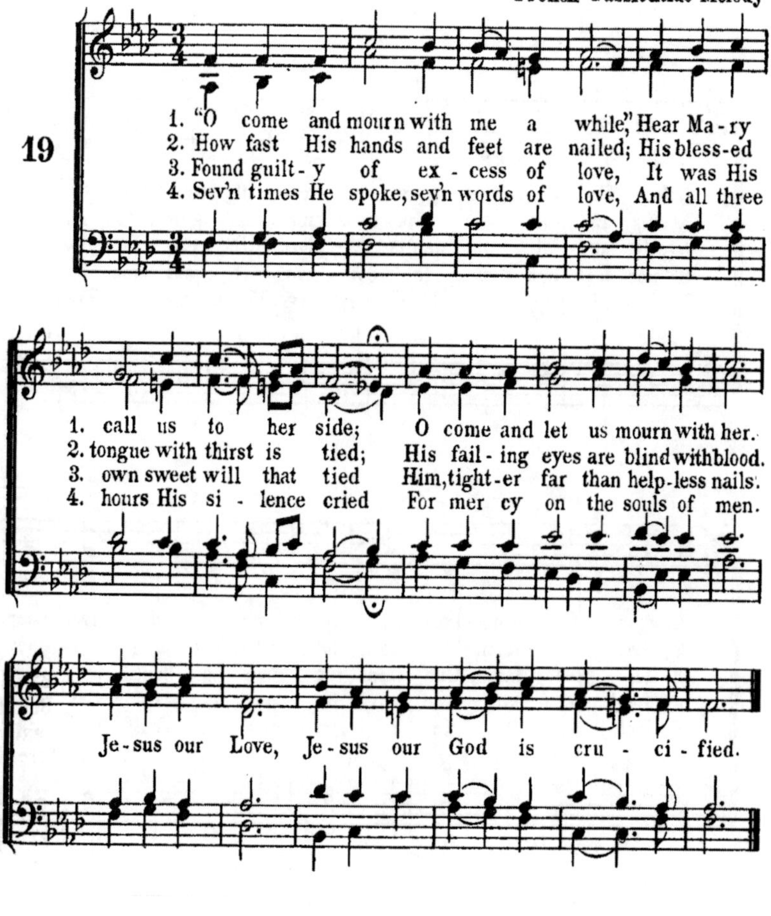
1. "O come and mourn with me a while," Hear Ma-ry
2. How fast His hands and feet are nailed; His bless-ed
3. Found guilt-y of ex - cess of love, It was His
4. Sev'n times He spoke, sev'n words of love, And all three
1. call us to her side; O come and let us mourn with her.
2. tongue with thirst is tied; His fail-ing eyes are blind with blood.
3. own sweet will that tied Him, tight-er far than help-less nails.
4. hours His si - lence cried For mer cy on the souls of men.
Je-sus our Love, Je-sus our God is cru - ci - fied.

THOU LOVING MAKER OF MANKIND

St. Basil's Hymnal

20

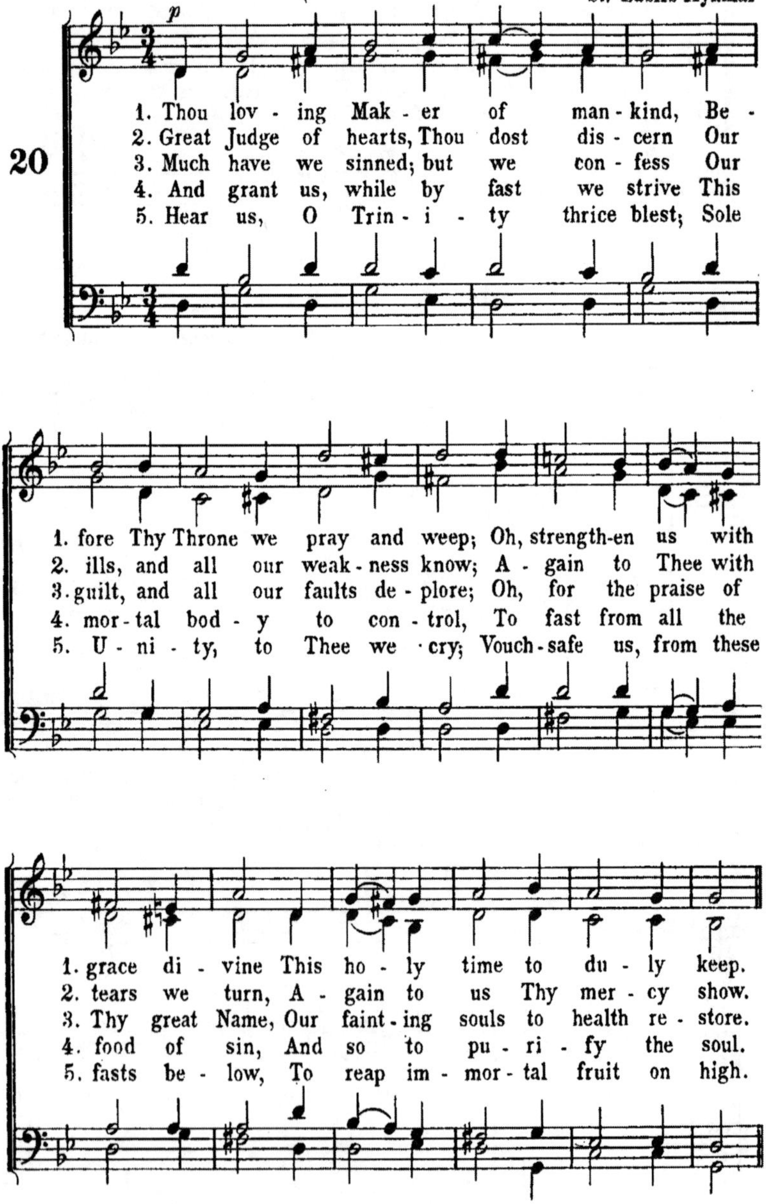
p
1. Thou lov - ing Mak - er of man - kind, Be -
2. Great Judge of hearts, Thou dost dis - cern Our
3. Much have we sinned; but we con - fess Our
4. And grant us, while by fast we strive This
5. Hear us, O Trin - i - ty thrice blest; Sole
1. fore Thy Throne we pray and weep; Oh, strength-en us with
2. ills, and all our weak - ness know; A - gain to Thee with
3. guilt, and all our faults de - plore; Oh, for the praise of
4. mor - tal bod - y to con - trol, To fast from all the
5. U - ni - ty, to Thee we cry; Vouch - safe us, from these
1. grace di - vine This ho - ly time to du - ly keep.
2. tears we turn, A - gain to us Thy mer - cy show.
3. Thy great Name, Our faint - ing souls to health re - store.
4. food of sin, And so to pu - ri - fy the soul.
5. fasts be - low, To reap im - mor - tal fruit on high.

STATION HYMN

M. M. 𝅗𝅥 = 50 From the Schubiger Hymnal

21

1. Thy slay - ers, dear Je - sus, we kneel round Thy
2. When stern just - ice dark - ens Thy path at the
3. Through dark - ness ap - pall - ing come ac - cents of
1. cross, Poor Ad - am's sad chil - dren, we mourn here our
2. goal, Though fin - ished Thy la - bor, com - mend - ed Thy
3. grace. Like him on Thy right, Lord, I'm seek - ing Thy
1. loss, Till words that re - lease us fall soft - ly as dew:
2. soul; With new hope we heark - en to Thy mes - sage mild:
3. Face; And hear Thy sweet call - ing to him and to me:
1. "Kind Fa - ther, for - give, They know not what they do."
2. "Be - hold, son, thy Moth - er; see Moth - er thy child."
3. "This day shalt thou with Me in Pa - ra - dise be."

JESUS! JESUS! BEHOLD AT LENGTH THE TIME

22

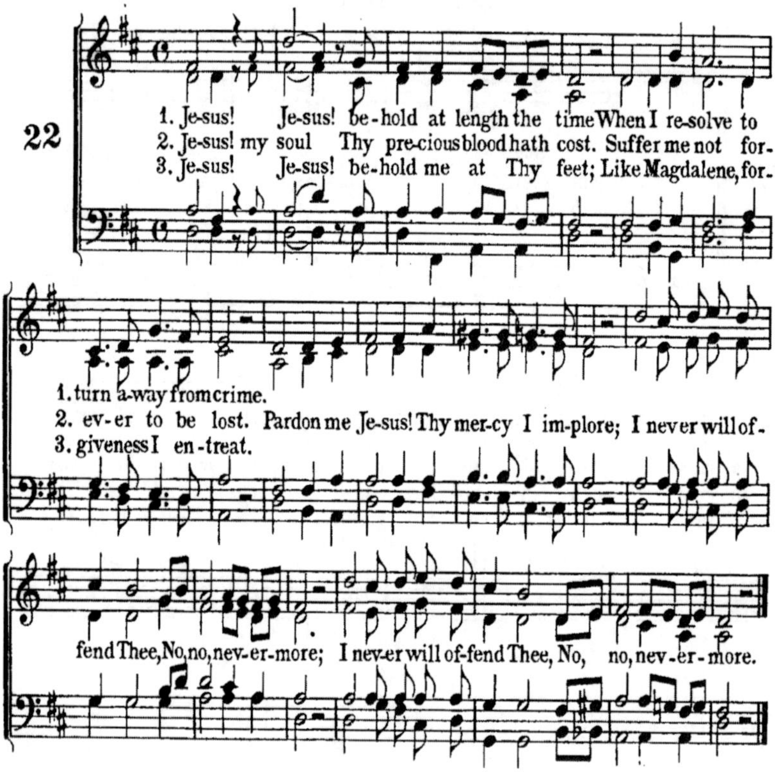
1. Je-sus! Je-sus! be-hold at length the time When I re-solve to
2. Je-sus! my soul Thy pre-cious blood hath cost. Suffer me not for-
3. Je-sus! Je-sus! be-hold me at Thy feet; Like Magdalene, for-
1. turn a-way from crime.
2. ev-er to be lost. Pardon me Je-sus! Thy mer-cy I im-plore; I never will of-
3. giveness I en-treat.
fend Thee, No, no, nev-er-more; I nev-er will of-fend Thee, No, no, nev-er-more.

STABAT MATER

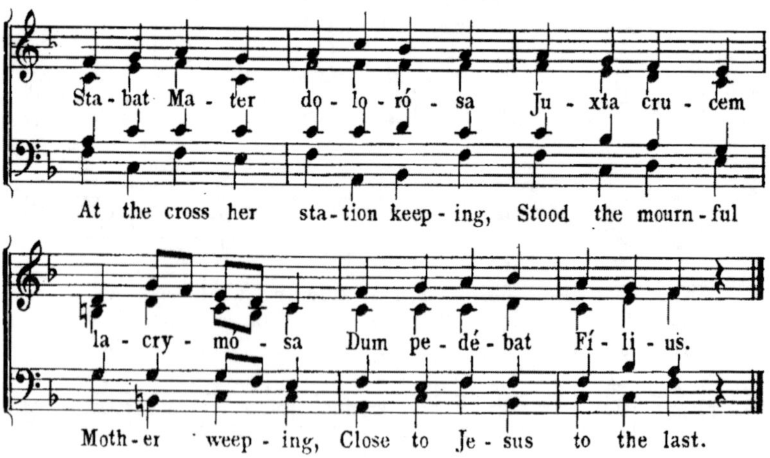
Sta-bat Ma-ter do-lo-ró-sa Ju-xta cru-cem
At the cross her sta-tion keep-ing, Stood the mourn-ful
la-cry-mó-sa Dum pe-dé-bat Fí-li-us.
Moth-er weep-ing, Close to Je-sus to the last.

23 STABAT MATER Nº 1

English Version

1.

At the cross her station keeping,
Stood the mournful Mother weeping,
Close to Jesus to the last;
Through her heart, His sorrow sharing,
All His bitter anguish bearing,
Now at length the sword has passed.

2.

Oh how sad and sore distressèd
Was that Mother, ever-blessèd
Of the Sole-begotten One!
How she stood in desolation,
Gazing at the desecration
Of her dying glorious Son!

3.

Who could mark, from tears refraining,
Christ's dear Mother uncomplaining,
In so great a sorrow bowed?
Who, unmoved, behold her languish
Underneath His cross of anguish,
'Mid the fierce, unpitying crowd?

4.

For His people's sins rejected,
She, her Jesus, unprotected,
Saw with thorns, with scourges rent,
Saw her Son from judgment taken,
Her Beloved in death forsaken,
Till His spirit forth He sent.

5.

Fount of love and holy sorrow,
Mother, may my spirit borrow
Somewhat of thy woe profound;
Unto Christ, with pure emotion,
Raise my contrite heart's devotion,
Love to read in every wound.

6.

Those five wounds on Jesus smitten,
Mother, in my heart be written,
Deep as in thine own they be:
Thou, my Saviour's cross who bearest,
Thou, thy Son's rebuke who sharest,
Let me share them both with thee.

7.

In the passion of my Maker,
Be my sinful soul partaker,
Weep till death, and weep with thee;
Mine with thee be that sad station,
There to watch the great salvation
Wrought upon th' atoning tree.

8.

Virgin thou of virgins fairest,
May the bitter woe thou sharest
Make on me impression deep:
Thus Christ's dying may I carry
With Him in His passion tarry,
And His wounds in memory keep.

9.

May His wounds transfix me wholly
May His cross and life-blood holy
Ebriate my heart and mind;
Thus inflamed with pure affection,
In the Virgin's Son protection
May I at the judgment find.

10.

When in death my limbs are failing,
Let Thy Mother's prayer prevailing
Lift me, Jesus, to Thy throne;
To my parting soul be given
Entrance through the gate of Heaven
There confess me for Thine own.

Amen

LENT

O HAPPY TIME OF BLESSED TEARS

J. G. Mareks

24

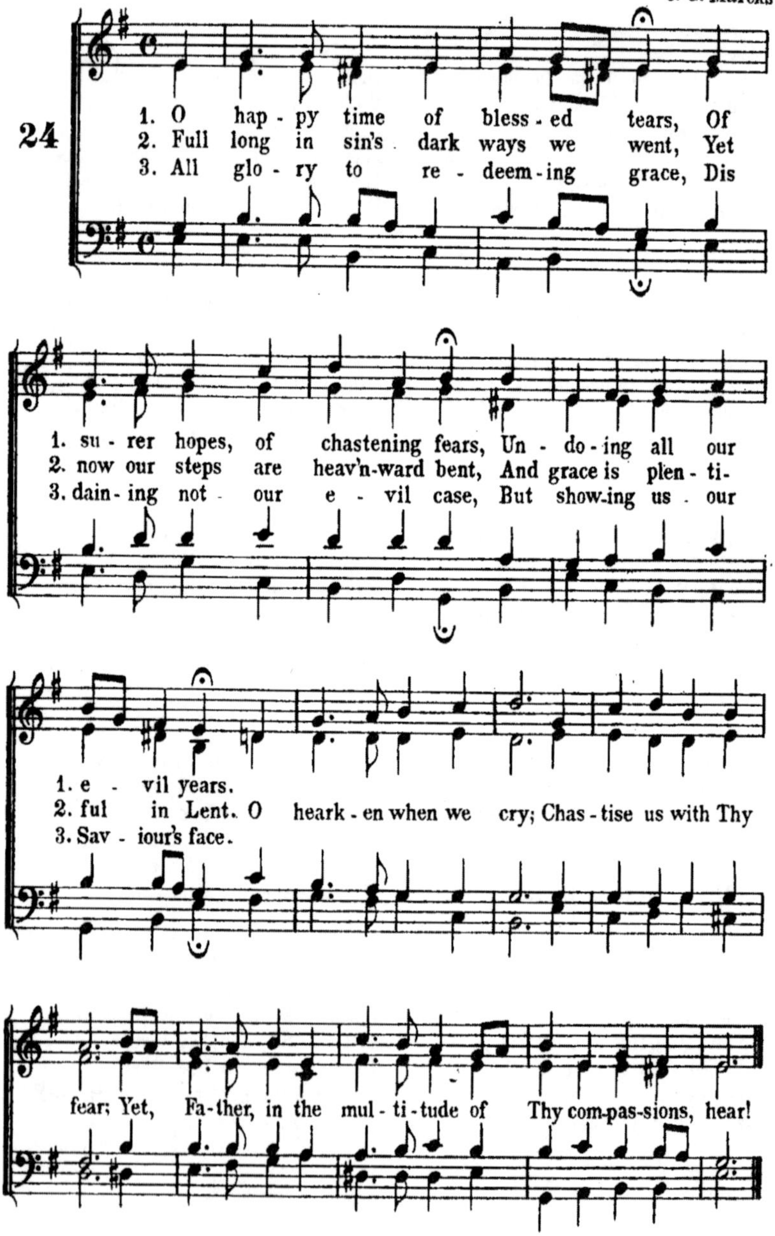
1. O hap - py time of bless - ed tears, Of
2. Full long in sin's dark ways we went, Yet
3. All glo - ry to re - deem - ing grace, Dis
1. su - rer hopes, of chastening fears, Un - do - ing all our
2. now our steps are heav'n-ward bent, And grace is plen - ti-
3. dain - ing not our e - vil case, But show-ing us our
1. e - vil years.
2. ful in Lent. O heark - en when we cry; Chas - tise us with Thy
3. Sav - iour's face.
fear; Yet, Fa - ther, in the mul - ti - tude of Thy com-pas-sions, hear!

STABAT MATER No. 2

25

M.M. ♪ = 132

1. Sta - bat Ma - ter do - lo - ró - sa, Ju-xta cru -
2. Cu - jus á - ni - mam ge - mén - tem, Con-tri - stá -
3. O quam tri - stis et af - flí - cta Fu - it il -
4. Quae moe - ré - bat et do - lé - bat, Pi - a Ma -
5. Quis est ho - mo qui non fle - ret, Ma-trem Chri -
6. Quis non pos - set con - tri - stá - ri Chri-sti Ma -
7. Pro pec - cá - tis su - ae gen - tis Vi - dit Je -
8. Vi - dit su - um dul - cem Na - tum Mo - ri - én -
9. Ei - a Ma - ter, fons a - mó - ris, Me sen - tí -
10. Fac ut ár - de - at cor me - um In a - mán -
11. San - cta Ma - ter, i - stud a - gas, Cru - ci - fí -
12. Tu - i Na - ti vul - ne - rá - ti, Tam dig - ná -
13. Fac me te - cum pi - e fle - re, Cru - ci - fí -
14. Ju - xta cru - cem te - cum sta - re Et me ti -
15. Vir - go vír - gi - num prae - clá - ra, Mi - hi jam
16. Fac ut por - tem Chri - sti mor - tem, Pas - si - ó -
17. Fac me pla - gis vul - ne - rá - ri, Fac me cru -
18. Flam - mis ne u - rar suc - cén - sus, Per te, Vír -
19. Chri - sti cum sit hinc ex - í - re, Da per Ma -
20. Quan - do cor - pus mo - ri - é - tur, Fac ut á -

1. cem la - cri - mó - sa, Dum pen - dé - bat Fí - li - us.
2. tam et do - lén - tem Per - tran - sí - vit glá - di - us.
3. la be - ne - dí - cta Ma - ter U - ni - gé - ni - ti!
4. ter dum vi - dé - bat Na - ti poe - nas ín - cly - ti.
5. sti si vi - dé - ret In tan - to sup - plí - ci - o?
6. trem con - tem - plá - ri Do - lén - tem cum Fí - li - o?
7. sum in tor - mén - tis Et fla - gél - lis súb - di - tum.
8. do de - so - lá - tum Dum e - mí - sit spí - ri - tum.
9. re vim do - ló - ris Fac ut te - cum lú - ge - am.
10. do Chri - stum De - um Ut si - bi com - plá - ce - am.
11. xi fi - ge pla - gas Cor - di me - o vá - li - de.
12. ti pro me pa - ti Poe - nas me - cum dí - vi - de.
13. xo con - do - lé - re, Do - nec e - go ví - xe - ro.
14. bi so - ci - á - re In plan - ctu de - sí - de - ro.
15. non sis a - má - ra: Fac me te - cum plán - ge - re.
16. nis fac con - sór - tem Et plá - gas re - có - le - re.
17. cé in - e - bri - a - ri, Et cru - ó - re Fí - li - i.
18. go, sim de - fén - sus In di - e ju - dí - ci - i.
19. trem me ve - ní - re Ad pal - mam vic - tó - ri - ae.
20. ni - mae do - né - tur Pa - ra - dí - si gló - ri - a. Amen.

GETHSEMANE ET GOLGOTHA

Arr. from P. Conrad Stöcklin, O. S. B.

Slowly and softly M. M. ♩ = 72

26

mf
1. O mon-tes me-mo-rá-bi-les Geth-sé-ma-
2. Il-linc in-dú-tus hó-mi-nem, et no-stra
3. Sit sum-mo Pa-tri gló-ri-a; Sit pa-ti-
1. ne et Gól-go-tha! De-dí-stis, heu! spe-
2. por-tans crí-mi-na, Pres-sus cor-dis an-
3. én-ti Dó-mi-no, San-cto si-mul Spi-
p
1. ctá-cu-la Nul-lis au-dí-ta saé-cu-
2. gú-sti-is Ser-vá-tor su-dat sán-gui-
3. rí-tu-i Sit gra-ti-á-rum á-cti-
f
1. lis, Nul-lis au-dí-ta saé-cu-lis.
2. nem, Ser-vá-tor su-dat sán-gui-nem.
3. o! Sit gra-ti-á-rum á-cti-o!

CHRIST THE LORD IS RISEN TO-DAY

27

With spirit
f
1. Christ the Lord is risn to-day: Christ-ians,haste your vows to pay;
2. Christ,the Vic-tim un-de-filed, Man to God hath re-con-ciled,
3. Christ,who once for sin-ners bled, Now the first-born from the dead,
f
1. Of - fer ye your prais - es meet At the pas - chal Vic - tim's feet.
2. When in strange and aw - ful strife Met to-geth - er death and life.
3. Thron'd in end - less might and pow'r, Lives and reigns for ev - er-more.
1. For the sheep the Lamb hath bled, Sin - less in the sin-ner's stead;
2. Christ-ians, on this hap - py day, Haste with joy your vows to pay.
3. Hail, e - ter - nal hope on high! Hail, Thou King of vic - to - ry!
1. Christ the Lord is ris'n on high, Now he lives no more to die.
2. Christ the Lord is ris'n on high, Now he lives no more to die.
3. Hail, Thou Prince of life a-dor'd! Help and save us, gra - cious Lord!

JESUS CHRIST IS RISEN

English Melody

28

f
1. Je - sus Christ is ris'n to - day, Al - - le - lu - ia!
2. Hymns of praise, then, let us sing, Al - - le - lu - ia!
3. But the pains which He en - dured, Al - - le - lu - ia!
4. Sing we to our God a - bove, Al - - le - lu - ia!
1. Let us, then, our hom - age pay, Al - - le - lu - ia!
2. Un - to Christ, our heav'n - ly King, Al - - le - lu - ia!
3. Our sal - va - tion have pro - cur'd; Al - - le - lu - ia!
4. Praise e - ter - nal as His love; Al - - le - lu - ia!
1. Who did once up - on the Cross, Al - - le - lu - ia!
2. Who en - dur'd the Cross and Grave, Al - - le - lu - ia!
3. Now a - bove the sky He's King, Al - - le - lu - ia!
4. Praise Him all ye heav'n - ly host, Al - - le - lu - ia!
1. Suf - fer to re - deem our loss Al - - le - lu - ia!
2. Sin - ners to re - deem and save, Al - - le - lu - ia!
3. Where the an - gels ev - er sing, Al - - le - lu - ia!
4. Fa - ther, Son, and Ho - ly Ghost, Al - - le - lu - ia!

O FÍLII ET FÍLIAE

SOLO
29
1. O Fí - li - i et fí - li - ae, Rex coe - lé - stis, Rex gló - ri - ae Mor - te sur - ré - xit hó - di - e. Al - le - lú - ia!
2. Et Ma - rí - a Mag - da - lé - ne Et Ja - có - bi et Sa - ló - me Ve - né - runt cor - pus ún - ge - re. Al - le - lú - ia!
3. A Mag - da - lé - na mó - ni - ti Ad ó - sti - um mo - nu - mén - ti Du - o cur - runt di - scí - pu li. Al - le - lú - ia!
4. Sed Jo - án - nes a - pó - sto - lus Cu - cúr - rit Pe - tro cí - ti - us; Ad se - púl - crum ve - nit pri - us. Al - le - lú - ia!
5. In hoc fe - sto san - ctís - si - mo Sit laus et ju - bi - lá - ti - o: Be - ne - di - cá - mus Dó - mi - no. Al - le - lú - ia!
6. De qui - bus nos hu - míl - li - mas De - vó - tas at - que dé bi tas De - o di - cá - mus grá - tí - as. Al - le - lú - ia!
TUTTI Unison
Al - le - lú - ia! Al - le - lú - ia! Al - le - lú - ia!
TUTTI

OUR LORD IS RISEN FROM THE DEAD

30

1. Our Lord is ris - en from the dead, Our Je-sus reigns su-preme on
2. Re - stor'd, re-viv'd, He now a-waits The legion'd Saints in grand ar -
3. Loose all your bars of gold-en light And wel-come Him with joy - ous
1. high; The pow'rs of hell are cap - tive led, No more shall they the cross de - fy.
2. ray; Lift up your heads, ye heav'n-ly gates, Ye ev - er - last-ing doors give way.
3. ring; He claims those mansions as His right, The Prince of peace, The ris - en King.
CHORUS
Who is this King of glo - ry? Tell, o ye who sing His praise so
well. The Lord of hosts, the Lord most high, Al-migh-ty
King o' the con-quered sky, Al-migh-ty King o' the con-quered sky.

COME, HOLY GHOST, CREATOR BLEST

31

Slowly and devoutly
Lambillotte
p
1. Come, Ho - ly Ghost, Cre - a - tor blest,
2. O, Com-fort - er, to Thee we cry,
3. O Ho - ly Ghost, Through Thee a - lone,
4. Praise we the Lord, Fa - ther and Son,
1. And in our hearts take up Thy rest; Come with Thy
2. Thou heav'n - ly gift of God Most High; Thou Fount of
3. Know we the Fa - ther and the Son; Be this our
4. And Ho - ly Spir - it with them one; And may the
1. grace and heav'n - ly aid, To fill the hearts which
2. Life, and Fire of Love, And sweet a - noint - ing
3. firm un - chang - ing creed, That Thou dost from them
4. Son on us be - stow All gifts that from the
1. Thou hast made, To fill the hearts which Thou hast made.
2. from a - bove, And sweet a - noint - ing from a - bove.
3. both pro - ceed, That Thou dost from them both pro - ceed.
4. Spir - it flow, All gifts that from the Spir - it flow.

PENTECOST

COME, HOLY GHOST, CREATOR, COME [1]

Slowly — Holy Face Hymnal

32

1. Come, Ho - ly Ghost, Cre - a - tor, come, From
2. Thou Who art call'd the Par - a - clete, Best
3. Oh, guide our minds with Thy blest light, With
1. Thy bright heav'n-ly throne: Come take pos - ses - sion of our souls, And
2. Gift of God a - bove, The liv - ing Spring, the liv - ing Fire, Sweet
3. love our hearts in - flame; And with Thy strength which ne'er de-cays, Con-
1. make them all Thine own, And make them all Thine own.
2. Unc - tion and true Love, Sweet Unc - tion and true Love.
3. firm our mor - tal frame, Con - firm our mor - tal frame.

SEE THE PARACLETE DESCENDING

Russian Melody

33

1. See the Par - a - clete de - scend - ing,
2. Tim - id souls, no long - er fear - ing,
3. Source of love, our hearts in flam - ing

[1] By permission of J. Fischer & Bro.

PENTECOST

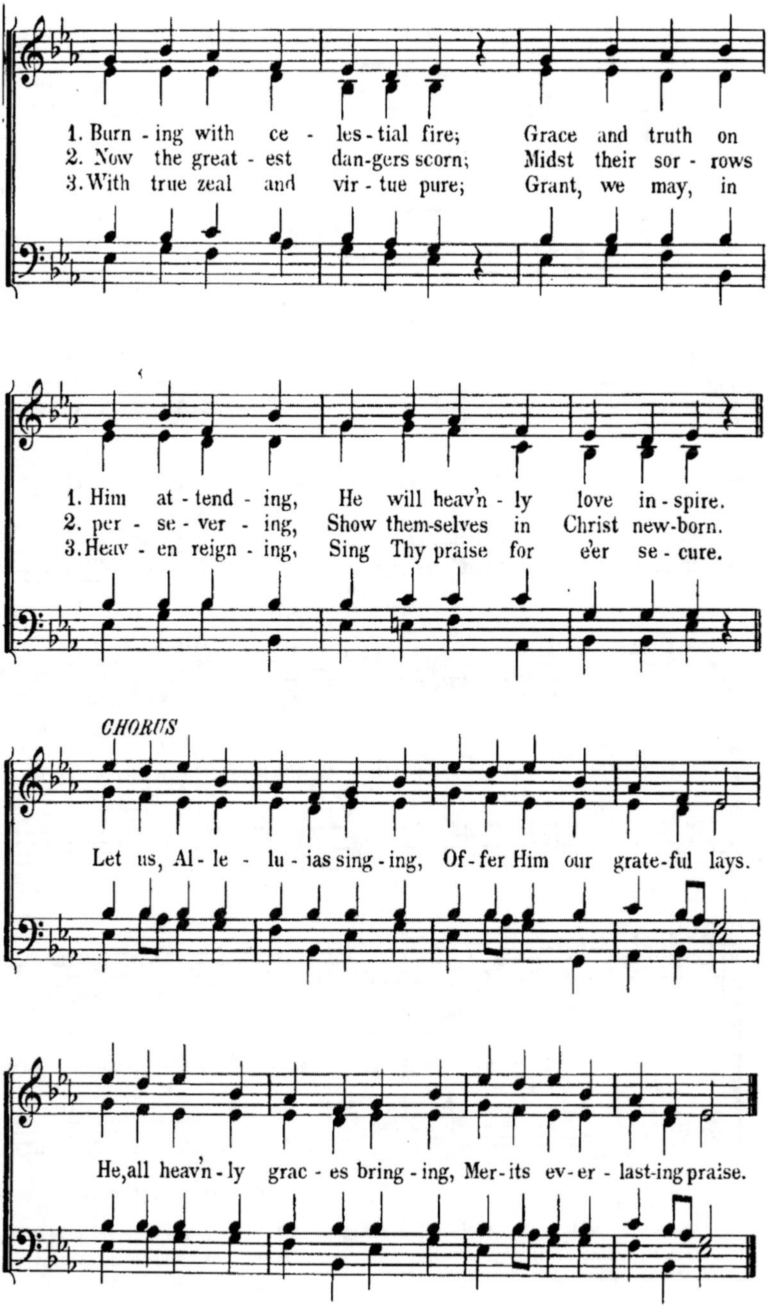
1. Burn - ing with ce - les - tial fire; Grace and truth on
2. Now the great - est dan-gers scorn; Midst their sor - rows
3. With true zeal and vir - tue pure; Grant, we may, in
1. Him at - tend - ing, He will heav'n - ly love in - spire.
2. per - se - ver - ing, Show them-selves in Christ new-born.
3. Heav - en reign - ing, Sing Thy praise for e'er se - cure.
CHORUS
Let us, Al - le - lu - ias sing - ing, Of - fer Him our grate-ful lays.
He, all heav'n - ly grac - es bring - ing, Mer - its ev - er - last-ing praise.

PENTECOST

FOR SOLEMN ADMINISTRATION OF

HOLY CONFIRMATION

Ant. 8
34
Con-fír-ma hoc De - us * quod o-pe-rá-tus es in no - bis,
a tem-plo san-cto tu - o, quod est in Je - rú - sa - lem. V. Gló - ri - a
CHANTERS
Pa-tri et Fí - li - o, et Spi - rí - tu - i San-cto. R. Sic - ut e - rat in prin - cí -
CHOIR
pi - o, et nunc, et sem-per, et in saé - cu - la sae-cu-ló-rum. A - men.

Repeat the Antiphon as far as V

V. Osténde nobis Dómine misericórdiam tuam. R. Et salutáre tuum da nobis.
V. Dómine exáudi oratiónem meam. R. Et clamor meus ad te véniat.
V. Dóminus vobíscum. R. Et cum spíritu tuo.

VENI CREATOR

35

M.M. ♪ = 144

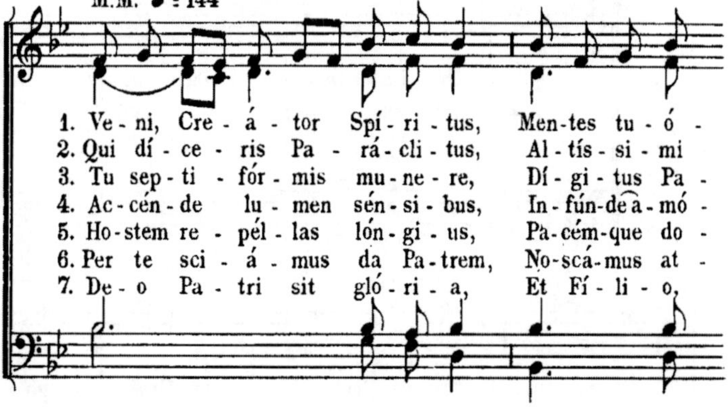
1. Ve - ni, Cre - á - tor Spí - ri - tus, Men-tes tu - ó -
2. Qui dí - ce - ris Pa - rá - cli - tus, Al - tís - si - mi
3. Tu sep - ti - fór - mis mu - ne - re, Dí - gi - tus Pa -
4. Ac - cén - de lu - men sén - si - bus, In - fún-de a - mó -
5. Ho - stem re - pél - las lón - gi - us, Pa-cém-que do -
6. Per te sci - á - mus da Pa - trem, No-scá-mus at -
7. De - o Pa - tri sit gló - ri - a, Et Fí - li - o,

1. rum ví - si - ta, Im - ple su - pér - na grá - ti - a
2. do - num De - i, Fons vi - vus, i - gnis, cá - ri - tas
3. tér-nae déx - te - rae, Tu ri - te pro - mís - sum Pa - tris,
4. rem cór - di - bus: In - fír - ma no - stri cór - po - ris
5. nes pró - ti - nus: Du - ctó - re sic te praé - vi - o
6. que Fí - li - um, Te-que u - tri - ús - que Spí - ri - tum
7. qui a mór - tu - is Sur - ré - xit, ac Pa - rá - cli - to,

1. Quae tu cre - á - sti pé - cto - ra.
2. Et spi - ri - tá - lis ún - cti - o.
3. Ser - mó - ne di - tans gút - tu - ra:
4. Vir - tú - te fir - mans pér - pe - ti.
5. Vi - té - mus o - mne nó - xi - um.
6. Cre - dá - mus o - mni tém - po - re.
7. In sae - cu - ló - rum saé - cu - la. A - men.

V. Emitte Spíritum tuum et creabúntur.
R. Et renovábis fáciem terrae.

O THOU IMMORTAL LIGHT DIVINE

Gounod

36

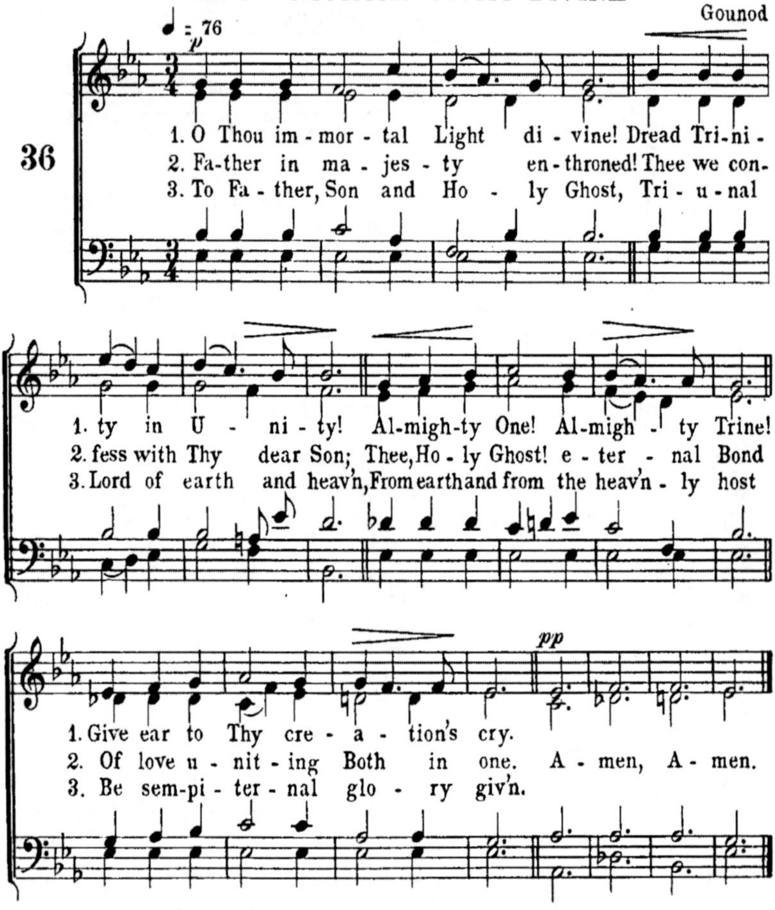
♩ = 76
p
1. O Thou im - mor - tal Light di - vine! Dread Tri-ni-
2. Fa-ther in ma - jes - ty en-throned! Thee we con-
3. To Fa - ther, Son and Ho - ly Ghost, Tri - u - nal
1. ty in U - ni - ty! Al-migh-ty One! Al-migh - ty Trine!
2. fess with Thy dear Son; Thee, Ho - ly Ghost! e - ter - nal Bond
3. Lord of earth and heav'n, From earth and from the heav'n - ly host
1. Give ear to Thy cre - a - tion's cry.
2. Of love u - nit - ing Both in one. A - men, A - men.
3. Be sem-pi - ter - nal glo - ry giv'n.
pp

HAVE MERCY ON US, GOD MOST HIGH

Bro. Luke

37

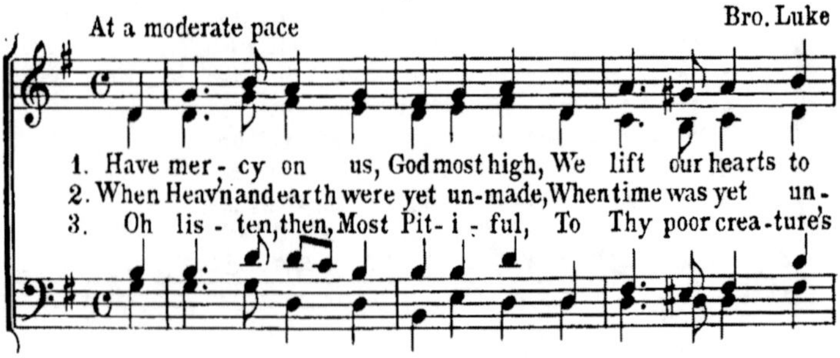
At a moderate pace
1. Have mer - cy on us, God most high, We lift our hearts to
2. When Heav'n and earth were yet un-made, When time was yet un-
3. Oh lis - ten, then, Most Pit - i - ful, To Thy poor crea-ture's

1. Thee; Have mer - cy on us worms of earth, Most Ho - ly Trin - i -
2. known, Thou, in Thy bliss and maj - es - ty, Didst live and love a -
3. heart; It bless - es Thee that Thou art God, That Thou art what Thou
1. ty Most an-cient of all mys - te - ries, Be - fore Thy throne we
2. lone. Thou wast not born, there was no fount From which Thy be - ing
3. art. Most an-cient of all mys - te - ries, Still at Thy feet we
1. lie; Have mer - cy now, most mer - ci - ful, Most Ho - ly Trin - i -
2. flow'd; There is no end which Thou canst reach; But Thou art sim - ply
3. lie; Have mer - cy now, most mer - ci - ful, Most Ho - ly Trin - i -
1. ty, Have mer - cy now, most mer - ci - ful, Most Ho - ly Trin - i - ty.
2. God, There is no end which Thou canst reach; But Thou art sim - ply God.
3. ty, Have mer - cy now, most mer - ci - ful, Most Ho - ly Trin - i - ty.

O JESUS, LORD, MY GOD, MY ALL!

38

1. O Je - sus, Lord, my God, my all! How
2. Had I but Ma - ry's sin - less heart To
3. Oh, see up - on the al - tar placed, The
4. May earth grow flow'rs be - neath His feet, And
1. can I love Thee as I ought? And how re - vere this wondrous gift So
2. love Thee with, my dear - est King, Oh with what bursts of fer - vent praise Thy
3. vic - tim of di - vin - est love! Let all the earth be - low a - dore, And
4. bright - est sun - beams light His way. The Lord of Heav'n we rise to greet, Our
CHORUS
1. far sur - pass - ing hope or thought?
2. goodness, Je - sus, would I sing!
3. join the choirs of heav'n a - bove.
4. Je - sus comes to us this day.
Sweet Sac - rament! we Thee a - dore. O
make us love Thee more and more, O make us love Thee more and more.

IN THIS SACRAMENT, SWEET JESUS

Slowly and devoutly

French Hymnal

39

1. In this Sac-ra-ment, sweet Je-sus! Thou didst give Thy Flesh and
2. Come, sweet Je-sus, in Thy mer-cy, Give Thy Flesh and Blood to
1. Blood, With Thy soul and God-head al-so, As our own most precious food. Yes,
2. me; Come to me, O dear-est Jesus! Come my soul's true life to be. Come that
1. dear-est Je-sus! I be-lieve it, And Thy pres-ence I a - dore, And with
2. I may live for - ev - er, Thou in me and I in Thee; Liv-ing
1. all my heart I love Thee, May I love Thee more and more, And with
2. thus, I shall not per-ish, But shall live e - ter - nal - ly, Liv-ing
1. all my heart I love Thee, May I love Thee more and more.
2. thus I shall not per-ish, But shall live e - ter - nal - ly.

WHEN OUR SAVIOUR WISHED TO PROVE

St. Basil's Hymnal

40

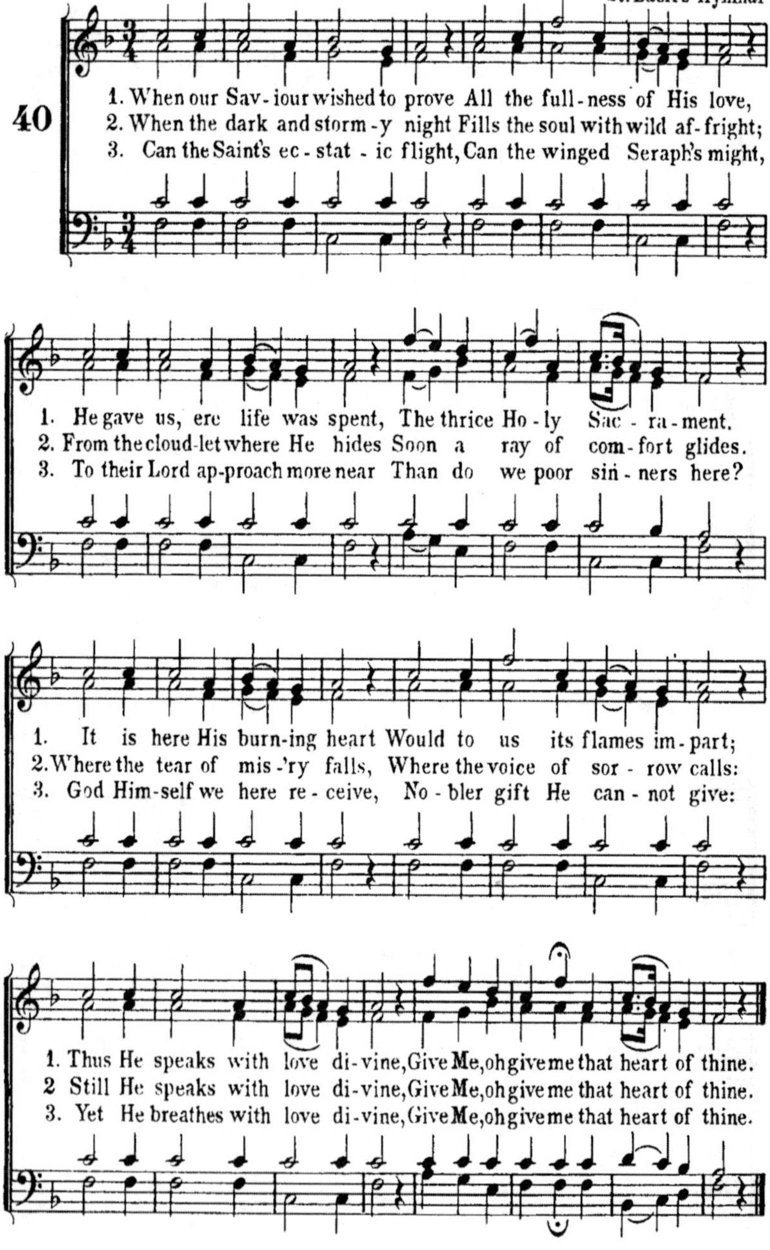
1. When our Sav-iour wished to prove All the full-ness of His love,
2. When the dark and storm-y night Fills the soul with wild af-fright;
3. Can the Saint's ec-stat-ic flight, Can the winged Seraph's might,
1. He gave us, ere life was spent, The thrice Ho-ly Sac-ra-ment.
2. From the cloud-let where He hides Soon a ray of com-fort glides.
3. To their Lord ap-proach more near Than do we poor sin-ners here?
1. It is here His burn-ing heart Would to us its flames im-part;
2. Where the tear of mis-'ry falls, Where the voice of sor-row calls:
3. God Him-self we here re-ceive, No-bler gift He can-not give:
1. Thus He speaks with love di-vine, Give Me, oh give me that heart of thine.
2 Still He speaks with love di-vine, Give Me, oh give me that heart of thine.
3. Yet He breathes with love di-vine, Give Me, oh give me that heart of thine.

JESUS, JESUS, COME TO ME

Devoutly

Prussian Air

41

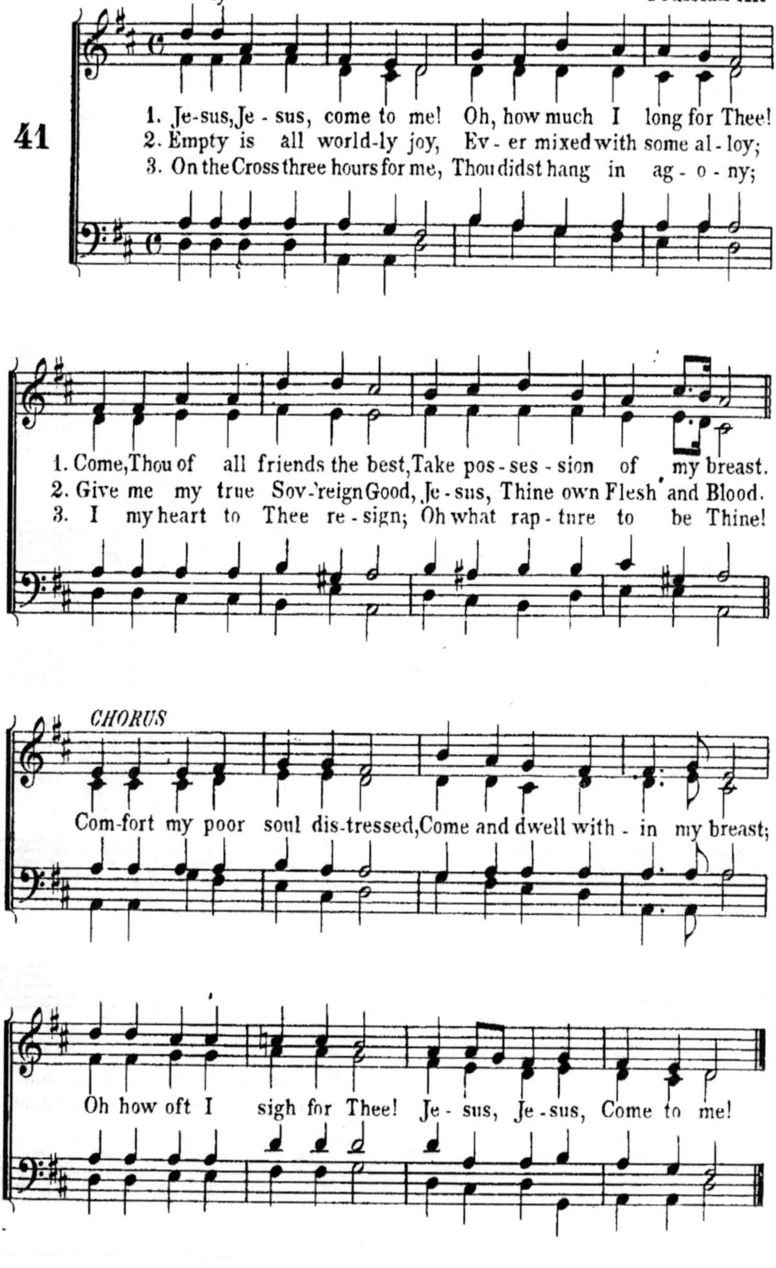
1. Je-sus, Je - sus, come to me! Oh, how much I long for Thee!
2. Empty is all world-ly joy, Ev - er mixed with some al - loy;
3. On the Cross three hours for me, Thou didst hang in ag - o - ny;
1. Come, Thou of all friends the best, Take pos - ses - sion of my breast.
2. Give me my true Sov-'reign Good, Je - sus, Thine own Flesh and Blood.
3. I my heart to Thee re - sign; Oh what rap - ture to be Thine!
CHORUS
Com-fort my poor soul dis-tressed, Come and dwell with - in my breast;
Oh how oft I sigh for Thee! Je - sus, Je - sus, Come to me!

LORD JESUS, WHOM BY POWER DIVINE

Holy Face Hymnal

42

p
1. Lord Je - sus, whom by pow'r di-vine Now hid-den 'neath the
2. O Food that wea - ry pil-grims love! O Bread of An - gel
3. O Fount of Love! O cleans-ing Tide! Which from the Sav-iour's
f
1. out-ward sign, We wor-ship and a - dore, We wor-ship and a -
2. hosts a - bove! O Man-na of the Saints! O Man - na of the
3. pier - ced side And sa-cred heart dost flow, And sa-cred heart dost
p
1. dore, Grant, when the veil a - way is roll'd, Thee face to face we
2. Saints! The hun - gry soul would feed on Thee; Ne'er may the heart un -
3. flow, Be ours to drink of Thy pure rill Which on - ly can our
mf a tempo
1. may be-hold, Dear Lord, for - ev - er - more, Thy - self for - ev - er - more.
2. sol-aced be Which for Thy sweet-ness faints, Which for Thy sweet-ness faints.
3. spir - its fill, And all we need be stow, And all we need be - stow.

By permission of J. Fischer & Bro.

WHEN AT THY ALTAR, LORD, I KNEEL

Devoutly

English Air

43

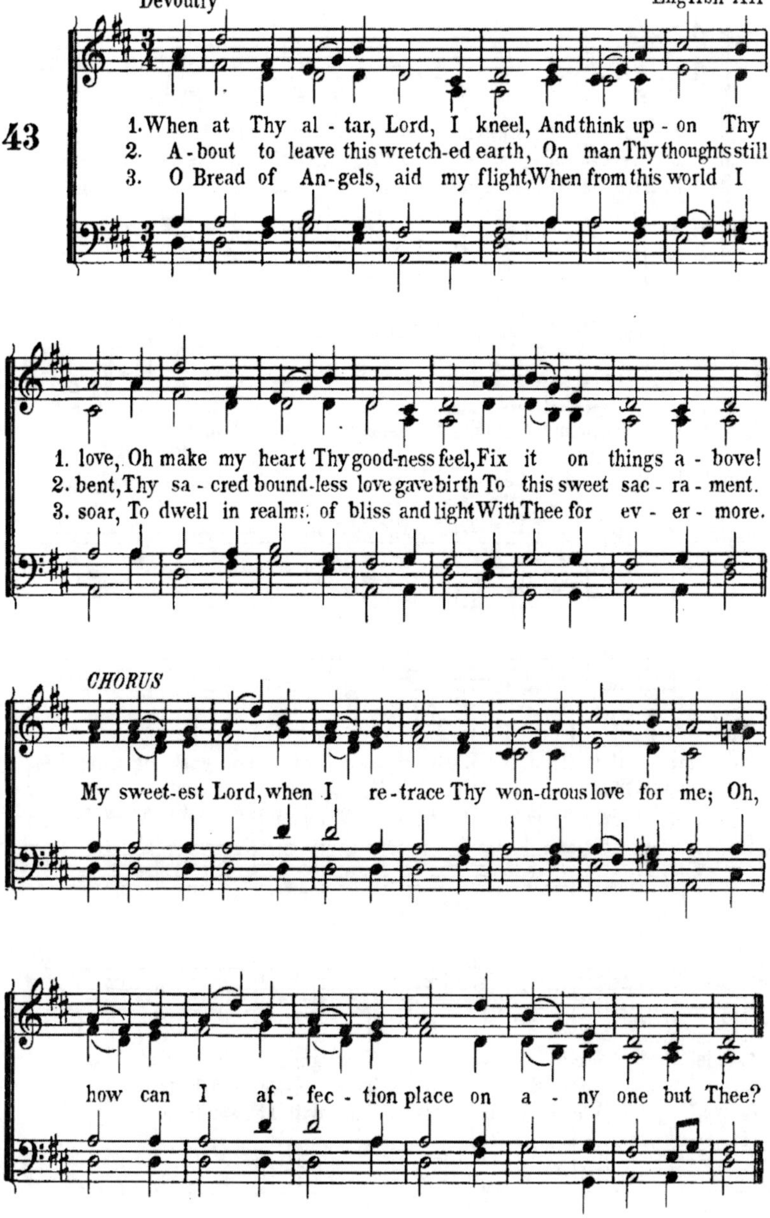
1. When at Thy al - tar, Lord, I kneel, And think up - on Thy
2. A - bout to leave this wretch-ed earth, On man Thy thoughts still
3. O Bread of An - gels, aid my flight, When from this world I
1. love, Oh make my heart Thy good-ness feel, Fix it on things a - bove!
2. bent, Thy sa - cred bound-less love gave birth To this sweet sac - ra - ment.
3. soar, To dwell in realms of bliss and light With Thee for ev - er - more.
CHORUS
My sweet-est Lord, when I re-trace Thy won-drous love for me; Oh,
how can I af - fec - tion place on a - ny one but Thee?

SOUL OF MY SAVIOUR

44

mf
1. Soul of my Sav-iour, sanc - ti - fy my breast, Bod - y of
2. Pas-sion of Je - sus, soothe, Oh, soothe my fears. Sav-iour, Oh
3. Save me, Oh save me from my dead - ly foe, Call me at
1. Christ, be Thou my sav-ing Guest; Blood of my Je - sus,
2. hear my sighs, re - gard my tears; Deep in Thy wounds, Lord,
3. death from off my bed of woe; Call me from time un -
pp
1. bathe me in thy tide, Wash me, ye wa - ters gush-ing from His
2. hide and shel-ter me, So shall I nev - er, nev - er part from
3. to e - ter-nal day, Where I may praise Thee with Thy saints for
1. side, Wash me, ye wa - ters gush-ing from His side.
2. Thee, So shall I nev - er, nev - er part from Thee!
3. aye, Where I may praise Thee with Thy saints for aye!

JESUS, GENTLEST SAVIOUR

45

M. M. ♩ = 88
1. Je-sus gent-lest Sa - viour! God of might and pow'r!
2. Out be-hind the shin - ing Of the fur - thest star,
3. O how can we thank Thee For a gift like this?
1. Thou Thy-self art dwell - ing in us at this hour;
2. Thou art ev - er stretch - ing in - fin-ite-ly far:
3. Gift that tru - ly mak - eth Heav'n's e - ter-nal bliss?
1. Na - ture can - not hold Thee Heav'n is all too strait
2. Yet the hearts of chil - dren Hold what worlds can - not,
3. Ah! when wilt Thou al - ways Make our hearts Thy home?
1. For Thine end - less glo - ry And Thy roy - al state.
2. And the God of won - ders Loves the low - ly spot.
3. We must wait for Heav - en, Then the day will come.

O LORD I AM NOT WORTHY

Burns

46

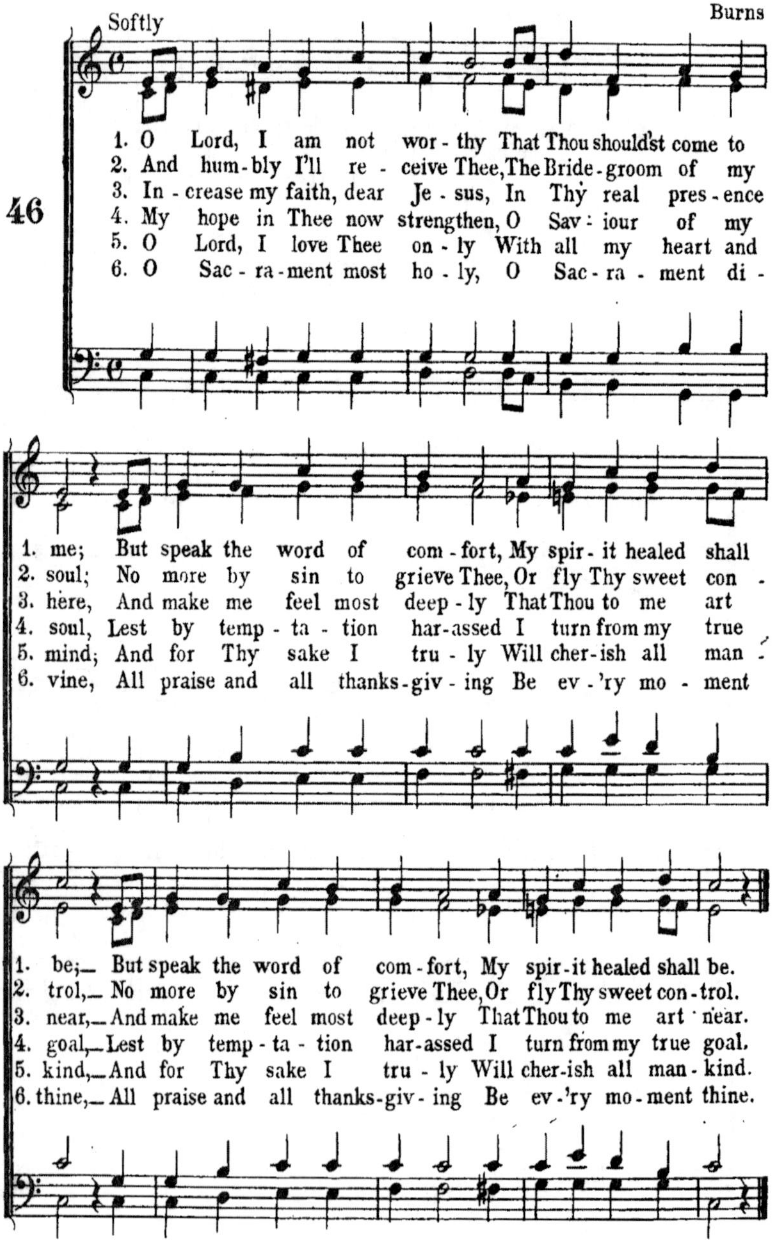
Softly
1. O Lord, I am not wor - thy That Thou should'st come to
2. And hum - bly I'll re - ceive Thee, The Bride - groom of my
3. In - crease my faith, dear Je - sus, In Thy real pres - ence
4. My hope in Thee now strengthen, O Sav - iour of my
5. O Lord, I love Thee on - ly With all my heart and
6. O Sac - ra - ment most ho - ly, O Sac - ra - ment di -
1. me; But speak the word of com - fort, My spir - it healed shall
2. soul; No more by sin to grieve Thee, Or fly Thy sweet con -
3. here, And make me feel most deep - ly That Thou to me art
4. soul, Lest by temp - ta - tion har - assed I turn from my true
5. mind; And for Thy sake I tru - ly Will cher - ish all man -
6. vine, All praise and all thanks - giv - ing Be ev - 'ry mo - ment
1. be; — But speak the word of com - fort, My spir - it healed shall be.
2. trol, — No more by sin to grieve Thee, Or fly Thy sweet con - trol.
3. near, — And make me feel most deep - ly That Thou to me art near.
4. goal, — Lest by temp - ta - tion har - assed I turn from my true goal.
5. kind, — And for Thy sake I tru - ly Will cher - ish all man - kind.
6. thine, — All praise and all thanks - giv - ing Be ev - 'ry mo - ment thine.

SALUTATION OF THE BLESSED SACRAMENT

With flowing rhythm. M. M. ♩= 92

From German Hymnals

47

1. Ho - ly! Ho - ly! Ho - ly! Ho - - - ly!
2. Ho - ly! Ho - ly! Ho - ly! Ho - - - ly!
3. Ho - ly! Ho - ly! Ho - ly! Ho - - - ly!
1. Art Thou Je - sus whose de - light 'Tis to
2. O Host di - vine on the beam, From whose
3. Who this wear - y earth hast trod Son of
1. stay by day and night In this Sac - ra-
2. side in sa - cred stream Wa - ter flows and
3. Ma - ry Son of God, Here up - on Thy
1. ment With Thy chil - dren to the end.
2. blood, Cleanse us in that sav - ing flood.
3. throne Ev - er - more for us a - - tone.

PROCESSIONAL OF FIRST COMMUNICANTS

From the St. Gall Hymnal

48

Somewhat lively
SOLI
TUTTI
1. The bless-ed hour is com-ing, The joy-ous feast draws near, The ban-quet of our Sav-iour U-nites his chil-dren here. To make us one with Him, This feast of love is spread; For in this tear-ful val-ley Our souls to Him are wed, Our souls to Him are wed.
2. While fear and faith and love Lead up-wards to the goal, Let Man-na from a-bove Re-fresh the sin-ful soul. The pow'r of Heaven's bread Must hold us weak-ly mortals; While up to Heav-en's por-tals The pil-grim's path we tread, The pil-grim's path we tread.

VENI, JESU, AMOR MI

Slowly Cherubini

49

p
Ve-ni, Je-su, A-mor mi! Ve-ni, ve-ni, ve-ni, a-mor
Je-su! Ve-ni, Ve-ni, A-mor mi! Ve-ni, O
mf
f
A-mor mi! Ve-ni, Je-su, A-mor mi! Ve-ni, Je-su, A-mor
mf
mi! Ve-ni, Je-su, A-mor mi! Ve-ni, ve-ni, O A-mor
f
mi! Ve-ni A-mor mi! Ve-ni A-mor mi!
p
pp
A-mor mi! A-mor mi!

O MI JESU!

Adapted from Schubiger's Hymnal

50

O mi Je - su! O mi Je - su!
M. M. ♪ = 116
1. O De-us, e - go a-mo Te, nam pri-or Tu a - má-sti me: En, li-ber-tá-te
2. Nil súg-ge-rat memó-ri-a ni - si de Tu - a gló - ri-a; Nil in-tel-léc-tus
3. Pro - té-stor ni-hil vel-le me, ni - si quid sci-am vel - le Te. Quae do-no Tu-o
4. A Te ac-cé-pi, ré-ci-pe, quid e - is ve-lis praé-ci-pe: Gu-bér-na si-cut
5. A - mó-re so - lo do-na me, ut e - go quo-que a-mem Te: Haec dando da-bis
1. pri - vo me, ut spon-te vin-ctus se-quar Te.
2. sá - pi - at prae-tér-quam ut Te cá - pi - at.
3. me - a sunt, haec do - no me - o Tu - a sunt. De-sí-de-ro, mi Je - su,
4. scis et vis, nam sci - o quod a - má-tor sis.
5. ó-mni - a, nam cé - te - ra sunt só - mni-a.
Hoc an-ge-ló-rum e - su, Ut me re-fí-ci-as, Ut me e-nú-tri-as, o Je - su!

QUOD IN COENA

German Melody

51

Slowly
1. Quod in coe - na Chri - stus ges - sit, Fa - ci - én - dum
2. Dog-ma da - tur Chri - sti - á - nis, Quod in car - nem
3. Sub di - vér - sis spe - ci - é - bus, Si - gnis tan - tum
4. Su-munt bo - ni, su - munt ma - li, Sor - te ta - men
1. hoc ex - prés - sit In su - i me - mó - ri - am.
2. trans - it pa - nis Et vi - num in sán - gui - nem.
3. et non re - bus, La - tent res ex - í - mi - ae:
4. in - ae - quá - li Vi - tae vel in - té - ri - tus.
1. Doc - ti sa - cris in - sti - tú - tis Pa - nem, vi - num,
2. Quod non ca - pis, quod non vi - des, A - ni - mó - sa
3. Ca - ro ci - bus, san - guis po - tus; Ma - net ta - men
4. Mors est ma - lis, vi - ta bo - nis; Vi - de pa - ris
1. in sa - lú - tis Con - se - crá - mus hó - sti - am.
2. fir - mat fi - des Prae - ter re - rum ór - di - nem.
3. Chri - stus to - tus Sub u - trá - que spé - ci - e.
4. sum - pti - ó - nis Quam sit dis - par éx - i - tus.

O ESCA VIATORUM No. 1

Cantata Catholica

52

p
1. O es-ca vi-a - tó-rum, O pa-nis an-ge -
2. O lymph-a fons a - mó-ris, Qui pu-ro Sal-va -
3. O Je-su, tu-um vul-tum, Quem có-li-mus oc -
mf
p
1. ló - rum, O man-na coé - li - tum! E- -
2. tó - ris E cor - de pró - flu - is, Te
3. cúl - tum Sub pa - nis spé - ci - e, Fac
f
1. su-ri-én-tes ci-ba, Dul-cé-di-ne non pri-va Cor -
2. si-ti-én-tes po-ta: Haec so-la no-stra vo-ta, His
3. ut, re-mó-to ve-lo, A - pér-ta nos in coe-lo Cer -
1. da quae-rén - ti - um, Cor - da quae-rén - ti - um.
2. -u - na súf - fi - cis, His u - na súf - fi - cis.
3. ná-mus á - ci - e, Cer - ná-mus á - ci - e.

O ESCA VIATORUM No. 2

Schubiger's Hymnal

53

1. O es - ca vi - a - tó - rum! O pa - nis an - ge -
2. O lym - pha fons a - mó - ris, Qui pu - ro Sal - va -
3. O Je - su, tu - um vul - tum Quem có - li - mus oc -
1. ló - rum! O man - na coé - li - tum! O man - na coé - li -
2. tó - ris E cor - de pró - flu - is, E cor - de pró - flu -
3. cúl - tum Sub pa - nis spé - ci - e, Sub pa - nis spé - ci -
1. tum! E - su - ri - én - tes ci - ba, Dul - cé - di - ne non
2. is. Te si - ti - én - tes po - ta, Haec so - la no - stra
3. e; Fac ut, re - mó - to ve - lo, A - pér - ta nos in
1. pri - va Cor - da quae - rén - ti - um, Cor - da quae - rén - ti - um.
2. vo - ta, His u - na súf - fi - cis, His u - na súf - fi - cis.
3. coe - lo Cer - ná - mus á - ci - e, Cer - ná - mus á - ci - e.

VERBUM SUPERNUM

Arr. from Luxemburg Hymnal

54

M. M. 𝅗𝅥 = 60
1. Ver-bum su - pér - num pró - di - ens, Nec Pa-tris
2. In mor-tem a di - scí - pu - lo Su - is tra -
3. Qui-bus sub bi - na spé - ci - e Car - nem de -
4. Se na-scens de - dit só - ci - um, Con - vé-scens
5. O sa - lu - tá - ris hó - sti - a, Quae coe-li
6. U - ni tri - nó - que Dó - mi - no Sit sem-pi -
1. lin - quens déx - te - ram, Ad o - pus su - um
2. den - dus áe - mu - lis, Pri - us, in vi - tae
3. dit et sán - gui - nem, Ut dú - pli - cis sub -
4. in e - dú - li - um, Se mó - ri - ens in
5. pan - dis ó - sti - um, Bel - la pre - munt ho -
6. tér - na gló - ri - a: Qui vi - tam si - ne
1. éx - i - ens, Ve - nit ad vi - tae vé - spe - ram.
2. fér - cu - lo, Se trá - di - dit di - sci - pu - lis.
3. stán - ti - ae To - tum ci - bá - ret hó - mi - nem.
4. pré - ti - um, Se re-gnans dat in praé - mi - um.
5. stí - li - a, Da ro - bur, fer au - xí - li - um.
6. tér - mi - no No - bis do - net in pá - tri - a.

PANGE LINGUA

55

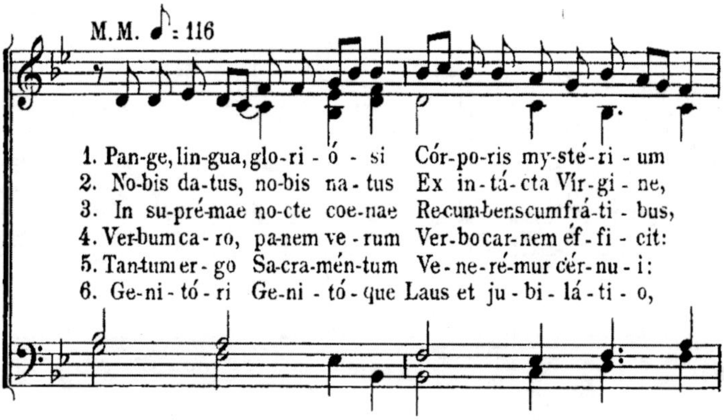
M.M. ♪ = 116
1. Pan-ge, lin-gua, glo-ri - ó - si Cór-po-ris my-sté-ri - um
2. No-bis da-tus, no-bis na - tus Ex in-tá-cta Vír-gi - ne,
3. In su-pré-mae no-cte coe-nae Re-cum-bens cum frá-ti - bus,
4. Ver-bum ca - ro, pa-nem ve - rum Ver-bo car-nem éf - fi - cit:
5. Tan-tum er - go Sa-cra-mén-tum Ve - ne-ré-mur cér-nu - i:
6. Ge-ni - tó - ri Ge-ni - tó - que Laus et ju - bi - lá - ti - o,

1. San-gui-nís-que pre - ti - ó - si, Quem in mun-di pré - ti - um
2. Et in mun-do con-ver-sá - tus, Spar - so ver - bi sé - mi - ne,
3. Ob - ser - vá - ta le - ge ple - ne Ci - bus in le - gá - li - bus,
4. Fit-que san-guis Chri-sti me-rum, Et si sen-sus dé - fi - cit,
5. Et an - tí - quum do - cu-mén-tum No - vo ce - dat rí - tu - i:
6. Sa - lus, ho - nor, vir - tus quo-que Sit et be - ne - dí - cti - o:

1. Fru-ctus ven-tris ge-ne-ró-si Rex ef-fú - dit gén - ti - um.
2. Su - i mo-ras in - co - lá - tus Mi - ro clau-sit ór - di - ne.
3. Ci-bum tur-bae du - o - dé-nae Se dat su - is má - ni - bus.
4. Ad fir-mán-dum cor sin-cé-rum So - la fi - des súf - fi - cit.
5. Prae-stet fi - des sup-ple-mén-tum Sén - su-um de - fé - ctu - i.
6. Pro - ce - dén - ti ab u - tró-que Com-par sit lau - dá - ti - o. A - men.

ADOREMUS IN AETERNUM

Arranged by W.A.R.

56

Ad - o - ré - mus in ae - tér - num sanctís - si - mum Sa - cra - mén - tum.
1. Lau - dá - te Dóminum, omnes gen - tes:
2. Quóniam confirmáta est super nos misericórdia e - jus,
3. Glória Patri et - Fí - li - o;
4. Sicut erat in princípio | et nunc, et sem - per,
1. lau - dá - te e - um, o - mnes pó - pu - li.
2. et véritas Dó - mi - ni ma - net in ae - tér - num.
3. et Spi - rí - tui San - cto.
4. et in saécula saecu - ló rum. A - men.
Repeat Adoremus

I NEED THEE, GRACIOUS JESUS

J. G. Marcks

57

1. I need Thee, gra-cious Je - sus, I need a friend like Thee; A
2. I need Thee, Heart of Je - sus, To feel each anx-ious care; To
1. friend to soothe and pit - y, A friend to care for me. Up -
2. tell to Thee my ev'ry want, And all my sor-rows share. Sweet
1. hold me then, sweet Je - sus, My tot-t'ring foot-steps guide; And
2. Je - sus, keep me near Thee, Close by Thee all the day; Per -
1. though I fall ten - thou - sand times, I fear not, but con - fide.
2. mit me not, e'en though I would, From Thy loved side to stray.

WHEN SOFTLY DAWNS THE GOLDEN LIGHT

With devotion — Oratorian Hymnal

58

1. When soft-ly dawns the gold-en light, And shadows melt o'er land and
2. When all the toil of day is done, And twi-light spreads her pur-ple
3. In joy or grief, in hope or fear, In sin, in suf-f'ring and dis-
1. sea, O sweet and sa-cred Heart of Christ! We con-se-crate our souls to
2. wing, When star-ry vig-ils have be-gun Be-fore the Eu-cha-ris-tic
3. tress, Be-hold a ref-uge ev-er near, To heal, to com-fort, and to
1. Thee. Be-fore Thy al-tar's ho-ly throne, The while we hum-bly kneel and
2. King, As earth's poor lov-ers at the tryst With ar-dor to the loved one
3. bless. In light or dark-ness, life and death, In time and in e-ter-ni-
f
1. pray, We bring to Thee, to Thee a-lone, The of-f'ring of the new-born day.
2. flee, O true and ten-der Heart of Christ, We haste to give the night to Thee.
3. ty, De-vot-ed Heart, with trusting faith We con-se-crate our all to Thee.

O JESUS, JESUS DEAREST LORD

At a moderate pace
59
1. O Je-sus, Je-sus, dear-est Lord! For-give me if I
2. Oh won-der-ful that thou shouldst let So vile a heart as
3. For Thou to me art all in all; My hon-or and my
4. What lim-it is there to Thee, love? Thy flight where wilt Thou
1. say, For ver-y love, Thy sa-cred Name, A thou-sand times a
2. mine Love Thee with such a love as this, And make so free with
3. wealth, My heart's de-sire, my bod-y's strength, My soul's e-ter-nal
4. stay? On, on! our Lord is sweet-er far To-day than yes-ter-
1. day. I love Thee so, I know not how My trans-ports to con-
2. Thine. The craft of this wise world of ours Poor wis-dom seems to
3. health. Burn, burn, O love with-in my heart, Burn fierce-ly night and
4. day. O love of Je sus, bless-ed love! So will it ev-er
1. trol; Thy love is like a burn-ing fire With-in my ver-y soul.
2. me; Dear Je-sus, I have child-ish grown With trust-ing love of Thee.
3. day, Till all the dross of earth-ly love Is burned, and burned a-way.
4. be; Time can-not hold thy won-drous growth, No, nor e-ter-ni-ty!

A MESSAGE FROM THE SACRED HEART

Haydn

60

1. A message from the Sacred Heart! What may this message be? "My
2. A message to the Sacred Heart! Oh, bear it back with speed: "Com
1. child, My child, give Me thy heart–My Heart has bled for Thee." This
2. Je - sus, reign with - in my heart–Thy Heart is all I need." Thus,
1. is the mes - sage Je - sus sends To my poor heart to - day, And
2. Lord, I'll pray un - til I share That home whose joy Thou art. No
1. ea - ger from His Throne He bends To hear what I shall say.
2. mes-sage, dear - est Je - sus, there–For heart will speak to heart.

COR JESU

Frank

61 
rit.
Cor Je-su sa-cra-tis - si-mum, mi-se-ré - re no - bis.

ff
mf
p
Cor Je - su sa - cra - - tís - si- - mum, Cor Je - su sa - cra- - tís- - si - mum, mi- - se - ré - re no- - bis.
Cor Je - su, Cor Je - su sa - cra - tís - si- - mum, Cor Je - su sa - cra- - tís- - si - mum, mi- - se - ré - re no - - bis.
Cor Je - su sa - cra - tís - si- - mum, Cor Je - su sa - cra- tís- - si - mum, mi- - se - ré - re no- - bis.
Cor Je - su sa - cra - tís - si- - mum, Cor Je - su, Cor Je - su sa-cra - tís - si- - mum, Cor Je - su, mi- - se - ré - re no- - bis.

AD SACRATISSIMUM COR JESU

Piel

62

1. O cor Je - su, fons a - mó - ris, Im - ple no - strum
2. En o Je - su, an - he - lán - tem, Ca - ste Te de -
3. Ser - va me in hoc a - mó - re, Ne lan - gués - cam
4. Tu lae - tí - ti - ae es da - tor, Tu do - lén - tis
1. vi do - ló - ris Et cru - ó - re ró - se - o. No-strum De - o
2. si - de - rán - tem Ca - ri - tá - te fér - vi - da: Fac me sem-per
3. in la - bó - re. Clau - de me in pé - cto - re U - bi fór - ti -
4. con - so - lá - tor: So - lo ex Te gaú - di - um. E - ia, á - ni -
1. of - fe - rá - tur Vi - cti - má - que ac - cen - dá - tur
2. Te a - má - re Et a - mó - re con - fla - grá - re
3. ter de - fén - sus Et a - mó - re sim ac - cén - sus
4. mae a - mán - tes, Nunc ve - ní - te cir - cum - dán - tes
1. Pu - ro ae - stu í - gne - o, Pu - ro ae - stu í - gne - o.
2. Tu - a dul - ci grá - ti - a, Tu - a dul - ci grá - ti - a.
3. Tu - o sa - cró vúl - ne - re, Tu - o sa - cro vúl - ne - re.
4. Cor, sa - lú - tem ó - mni - um, Cor, sa - lú - tem ó - mni - um.

LOOK DOWN, O MOTHER MARY

French Hymnal

63

p
1. Look down, O Moth-er Ma - ry, From thy bright throne a - bove; Be-
2. See how we, wretched sin-ners, Now stand be - fore thy Son; Whose
3. O Ma-ry dear-est Moth-er, If thou would'st have us live, Say
4. En-fold us in thy man-tle, And drive a - way our fear. What
1. hold how sore-ly tried are The chil-dren thou dost love; And if thy heart so
2. lov-ing heart dis-clos-es The e - vil we have done. Yet if thou wouldst ap-
3. that we are thy children And Je - sus will for - give. Our sins make us un-
4. e - vil can be-fall us When, Mother, thou art near? O sweet-est, dear-est
1. ten-der With pit - y flows not o'er, Then turn a-way, O Moth-er, And
2. pease Him, Breathe for us but one sigh; Thou on - ly canst ob-tain us Our
3. wor-thy That ti-tle still to bear, But thou art still our Moth-er; Then
4. Moth-er, Thy sin-ful chil-dren save. Look down on us with pit - y, Who
1. look on us no more, Then turn a-way, O Moth-er, And look on us no more.
2. par-don from on high, Thou on - ly canst ob-tain us Our pardon from on high.
3. show a Moth-er's care: But thou art still our Moth-er; Then show a Mother's care.
4. thy pro-tec-tion crave, Look down on us with pit - y, Who thy protec-tion crave.

GLORIOUS MOTHER

64

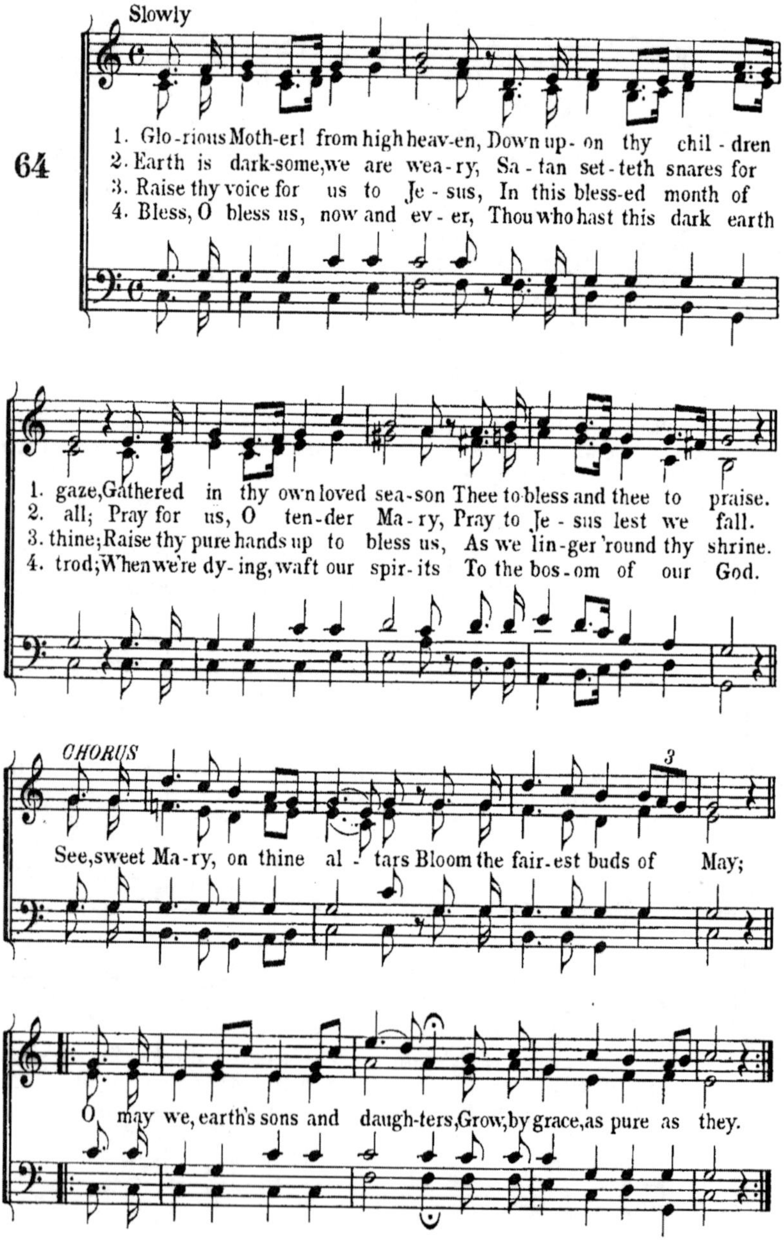
Slowly
1. Glo-rious Moth-er! from high heav-en, Down up- on thy chil - dren gaze, Gathered in thy own loved sea-son Thee to bless and thee to praise.
2. Earth is dark-some, we are wea-ry, Sa - tan set-teth snares for all; Pray for us, O ten-der Ma-ry, Pray to Je - sus lest we fall.
3. Raise thy voice for us to Je - sus, In this bless-ed month of thine; Raise thy pure hands up to bless us, As we lin-ger 'round thy shrine.
4. Bless, O bless us, now and ev - er, Thou who hast this dark earth trod; When we're dy-ing, waft our spir-its To the bos-om of our God.
CHORUS
See, sweet Ma-ry, on thine al - tars Bloom the fair-est buds of May;
O may we, earth's sons and daugh-ters, Grow, by grace, as pure as they.

HAIL VIRGIN, DEAREST MARY!

Rather slowly — Lambillotte

65

mf
Hail, Virgin, dear-est Ma-ry, O gen-tle Queen of May! O spot-less bless-ed La-dy, O gen-tle Queen of May!
Fine
1. Thy chil-dren hum-bly bend-ing Sur-round thy shrine so
2. For thee earth's flow'rs are spring-ing In beau-teous form and
3. We'll gath-er fresh, bright flow-ers, To bind our fair Queen's
1. fair, With heart and voice as-cend-ing: Sweet Ma-ry hear their pray'r.
2. hue; For thee all na-ture's bring-ing Her sweetest charms to view.
3. brow; From gay and ver-dant bow-ers, We haste to crown thee now.

OUR LADY OF LOURDES

66

M. M. ♩ = 84
1. Im - ma - cu - late Moth - er, We come at thy
2. In grief and temp - ta - tion, In joy and in
3. In death's sol - emn mo - ment, O Moth - er, be
1. call, And low at thy al - tar Be - fore thee we fall.
2. pain, We'll seek thee, our Moth - er, Nor seek thee in vain.
3. nigh, As chil - dren of Ma - ry O teach us to die.
REFRAIN
A - ve, A - ve, A - ve Ma - ri - a! A - ve, A - ve Ma - ri - - a!

LOVED HEART, ALL MILD, ALL MEEK, ALL TENDER

67

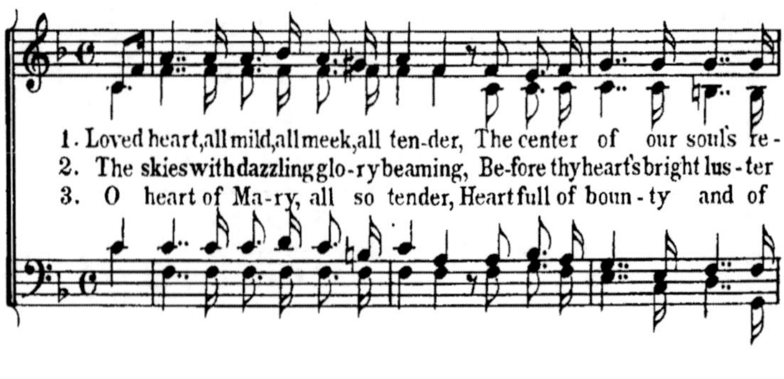
1. Loved heart, all mild, all meek, all ten-der, The center of our soul's re -
2. The skies with dazzling glo - ry beaming, Be-fore thy heart's bright lus - ter
3. O heart of Ma-ry, all so tender, Heart full of boun - ty and of

1. pose, Blest he who rests with-in thy splen-dor Whence peace with
2. pale; The sun with peer-less splen-dor gleam-ing, By thee seems
3. grace, Il - lume us with thy heart's bright splen-dor, Have pit - y
CHORUS
1. light un-ceas-ing flows. Blest he who in thy heart con-
2. cov-ered with a veil. Haste on, O Vir-gin, nev - er
3. on our fall - en race. Be thou our hope, our strength for-
1. fid - ing, Brings thee the hom-age of his lays; Who
2. fal - ter, Bring thou thy off'-ring to his shrine; More
3. ev - er, And screen us with thy grace for aye; And
1. wealth and fame and pomp de - rid - ing, Deems serv - ing
2. grate - ful gift ne'er graced God's al - tar, Than that im -
3. when at last, with life we sev - er, As - sist us,

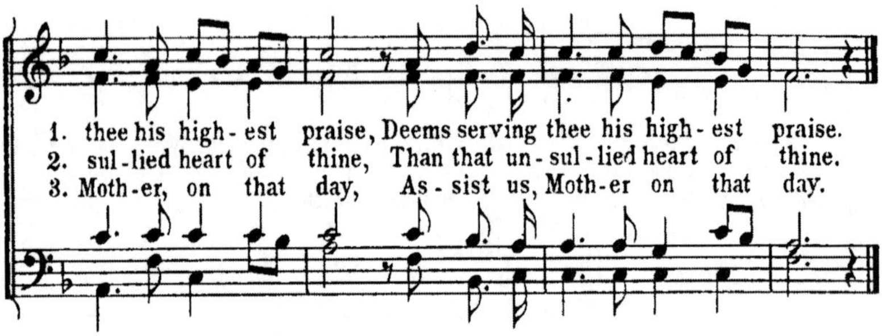
1. thee his high - est praise, Deems serving thee his high - est praise.
2. sul-lied heart of thine, Than that un-sul-lied heart of thine.
3. Moth-er, on that day, As - sist us, Moth-er on that day.

HAIL, QUEEN OF THE HEAVENS

Briskly

68

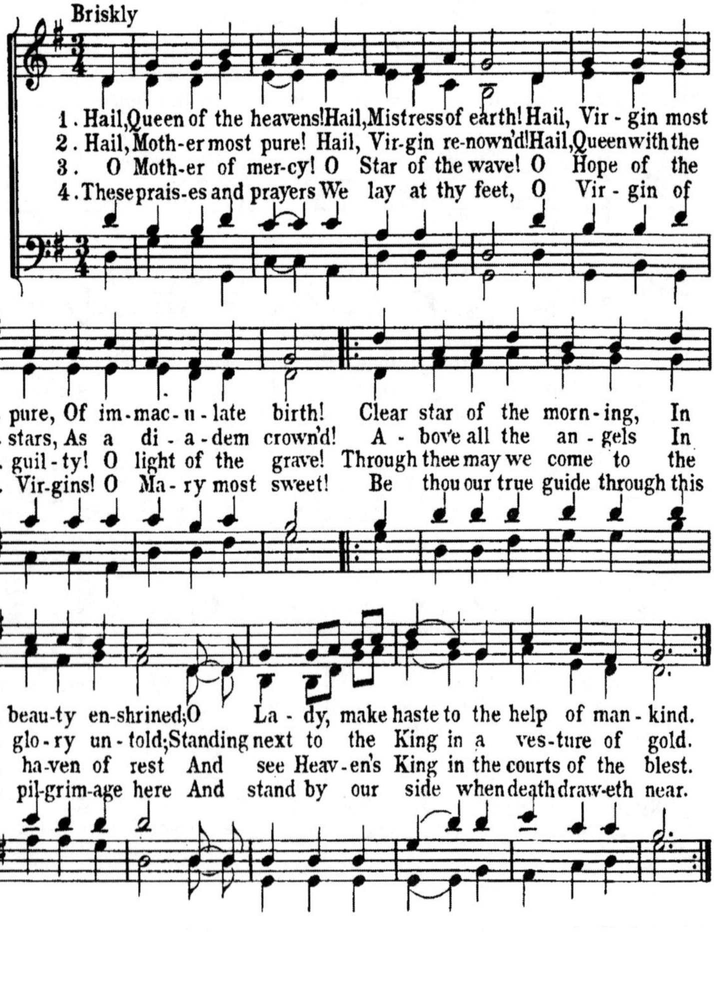
1. Hail, Queen of the heavens! Hail, Mistress of earth! Hail, Vir - gin most
2. Hail, Moth-er most pure! Hail, Vir-gin re-nown'd! Hail, Queen with the
3. O Moth-er of mer-cy! O Star of the wave! O Hope of the
4. These prais-es and prayers We lay at thy feet, O Vir - gin of
1. pure, Of im-mac-u-late birth! Clear star of the morn-ing, In
2. stars, As a di - a - dem crown'd! A - bove all the an - gels In
3. guil - ty! O light of the grave! Through thee may we come to the
4. Vir-gins! O Ma - ry most sweet! Be thou our true guide through this
1. beau-ty en-shrined; O La - dy, make haste to the help of man - kind.
2. glo - ry un - told; Standing next to the King in a ves-ture of gold.
3. ha-ven of rest And see Heav-en's King in the courts of the blest.
4. pil-grim-age here And stand by our side when death draw-eth near.

MEMORARE

Schubiger's Hymnal

69
1. Ma - ry, mild-est Queen, re-mem-ber Nev-er has it yet been
2. Did'st thou e'er re - fuse thy chil-dren Aid in need or help in
3. See us poor re - pent-ant sin-ners Prone, sweet Vir-gin, at thy
1. known That a child who sought thy fa-vor Had un-heard to leave thy throne.
2. pain? Nev-er did a child of thine Tears of an-guish shed in vain.
3. feet! Shall the least of thy poor chil-dren Un-heard leave thy mer-cy seat?
CHORUS
Mild-est Moth-er, at thy feet We poor children humbly pray. O dear
Moth-er of our Saviour, Hearken to our cry this day, Hearken to our cry this day.

STAR OF THE SEA

L. Selle

70

1. O pur-est of creatures! Sweet Mother! sweet maid! The one spot-less
2. Oh, blissful and calm was the wonder-ful rest Thou gav - est thy
3. To sinners what comfort, To an-gels what mirth, That God found one
1. womb where-in Je - sus was laid! Dark night has come down on us,
2. God in thy vir - gin - al breast, For Heav - en He left He found
3. creat-ure un - fall - en on earth, One spot where His Spir - it un -
1. Moth-er, and we Look out for thy shin-ing, Sweet Star of the Sea! Look
2. Heav-en in thee, He shone in thy shin-ing, Sweet Star of the Sea! He
3. troub-led could be, The depths of thy shin-ing, Sweet Star of the Sea! The
1. out for thy shining, Sweet Star of the Sea! Sweet Star _ of the Sea! _
2. shone in thy shining, Sweet Star of the Sea! Sweet Star _ of the Sea! _
3. depths of thy shining, Sweet Star of the Sea! Sweet Star _ of the Sea! _

HOLY MARY MOTHER MILD

W. Dressler

71

1. Ho - ly Ma - ry, Moth - er mild! O dear-est Moth-er!
2. Toss'd on life's tem - pes - tuous sea, O dear-est Moth-er!
3. Bright-est in the courts a - bove, O dear-est Moth-er!
4. Maid - en Moth - er! hear my pray'r, O dear-est Moth-er!
1. Hear, O hear thy fee - ble child, O sweet, sweet Moth-er!
2. Cast thy ten - der eyes on me, O sweet, sweet Moth-er!
3. Joy of an - gels, Queen of love, O sweet, sweet Moth-er!
4. Prove to me thy lov - ing care, O sweet, sweet Moth-er!
O ex - ult, ye Cher - u - bim! And re - joice, ye Ser - a - phim!
Praise her! Praise her! Oh praise our spot - less Moth - er.

FADING STILL FADING

Slowly and tenderly

Wiesenthal

72

mf
1. Fading, still fading, the last beam is shining, A-ve Ma-ri-a, The
2. A-ve Ma-ri-a! oh hear when we call! Moth-er of Him Who is
1. day is de-clin-ing; Safe-ty and in-no-cence fly with the light, Temp-
2. Sav-iour of all. Fee-ble and fail-ing, we trust in thy might, In
1. ta-tion and dan-ger walk forth in the night. From the fall of the
2. doubt-ing and dark-ness, thy love be our light. Let us sleep on thy
1. shade to the bright morning time, Shield us from dan-ger and save us from crime.
2. breast while the night ta-per burns, And wake in thy care when the morning re-turns.
ff CHORUS
A-ve Ma-ri-a, A-ve Ma-ri-a, A-ve Ma-ri-a, au- -di-nos

MOTHER MARY AT THINE ALTAR

Not too fast — Lambillotte

73

1. Moth-er Ma-ry, at thine al-tar, We thy lov-ing children kneel;
2. Thou wilt love us, thou wilt guide us, With a mother's fond-est care;
3. Life's temp-ta-tions are be-fore us, We must min-gle in the strife;
4. So we take thee for our Moth-er, And we claim the right to be,
1. With a faith that can not fal-ter, To thy good-ness we ap-peal.
2. And what-e'er in life be-tide us, We will seek a ref-uge there.
3. If thy good-ness watch not o'er us, All un-safe will be our life.
4. By the gift of our dear Brother, Lov-ing chil-dren un-to thee.
CHORUS
We are seek-ing for a moth-er O'er the earth so waste and drear, And the
dy-ing Je-sus gives us Thee to be our Mother dear, Thee to be our Mother dear.

"AVE MARIA"

With devotion

74

1. Now the live-long day is done, A-ve Ma-ri-a: And the stars gleam
2. So my life will speed a-way, A-ve Ma-ri-a: So will fade my
1. one by one, A - ve Ma-ri - a: Now from out the old church-tow'r
2. lit-tle day, A - ve Ma-ri - a: Moth-er, when my pass-ing hour
1. Tolls the rest-ful ev'-ning hour, Save me from the e - vil pow'r, A - ve Ma-ri-a.
2. Tolls from out the old church-tow'r, Help me by thy grace and pow'r, A - ve Ma-ri-a.

AVE SANCTISSIMA

75

1. A - ve, San-ctis - si-ma! We lift our souls to thee;
2. A - ve, San-ctis - si-ma! Oh hear thy chil-dren's pray'r.

1. O - ra pro no - bis! 'Tis night-fall on the sea. Watch us while
2. Au-di, Ma - ri - a! And take us 'neath thy care. O thou whose
1. shadows lie Far o'er the wa-ters spread; Hear the heart's lone - ly sigh,
2. vir-tues shine With brightest pu - ri - ty, Come and each thought re - fine
1. Thine too hath bled. Thou that hast look'd on death, Aid us when death is nigh;
2. Till pure like Thee. Oh save our souls from ill; Guard thou our lives from fear;
1. Whis-per of heav'n to faith,
2. Our hearts with grac - es fill,
Sweet Mother, Sweet Mother, hear. O - ra pro
no - bis, The wave must rock our sleep. O - ra, Ma-ter, o - ra, Star of the sea.

MACULA NON EST IN TE

76

1. Daugh-ter of the might-y Fa-ther, Stainless Maid-en Queen of
2. Moth-er of the Son and Sav-iour, Of the Truth, the Life the
3. Vir-gin Spouse of Ho-ly Spir-it, Lis-ten to our ear-nest
4. Bright-est Star in heav-en's glo-ry, Let thy splen-dor light our
1. May; An-gel forms a-round thee gath-er: Ma-cu-la non est in te.
2. Way; Guide our foot-steps, calm our passions: Ma-cu-la non est in te.
3. lay; Grant we may thy love in-her-it: Ma-cu-la non est in te.
4. way; Guide and help us, love and bless us: Ma-cu-la non est in te.
CHORUS
Má-cu-la non est in te, Má-cu-la non est in
te, Má-cu-la non est in te, Má-cu-la non est in te.

HAIL, QUEEN OF HEAVEN

At a moderate pace
English Ai
1. Hail Queen of Heav'n, the o - cean Star, Guide of the
2. O gen - tle, chaste, and spot - less Maid, My sin - ful
3. So trav - ers - ing this vale of tears, To thee, blest
4. And while to Him who reigns a - bove, In God - head
1. wand-'rer here be - low! Tossed on life's sea, I claim thy care,
2. soul now prays to thee; Re - mind thy Son that He has paid
3. ad - vo - cate, I cry; As - suage my sor - rows, calm my fears
4. One, in Per - son Three, The Source of life, of grace, of love,
1. Save me from per - il and from woe. Moth - er of Christ,
2. My ran - som from in - i - qui - ty. Vir - gin most pure,
3. And soothe with hope my mis - e - ry. Re - fuge in grief,
4. Hom - age I pay on bend - ed knee; Do thou, bright Queen.
1. Star of the sea, Pray for the wand - 'rer, pray for me.
2. Star of the sea, Pray for the sin ner, pray for me.
3. Star of the sea, Pray for the mourn - er, pray for me.
4. Star of the sea, Pray for thy chil - dren, pray for me.

WITH HOLY CHOIRS OF ANGELS

German Melody

78

1. With ho - ly choirs of an - gels, Come let us join our lays: With songs, O Queen of heav - en, We cel - e - brate thy praise.
2. Be - side thee, Star of morn - ing, Fair na - ture hides her face; And heav-en's bright a - dorn - ing Is thy tran - scen - dent grace.
3. Earth, sin and dark - ness blend - ed Could ne'er thy strength as sail; To bless thee God de - scend - ed, Sweet li - ly of the vale.
CHORUS
Ho - ly Ma - ry, let us praise thee, From thy love we'll ne'er de - part;
Now be - fore thee, we im - plore thee, Come and reign o'er ev - 'ry heart.

MARY, STAR OF THE SEA

B.S.

79

Slowly
1. When ev'ning shades are fall-ing O'er o-cean's si - lent deep, To
2. The noon-day tem-pest o - ver, Now o-cean toils no more, While
1. pil-grims' hearts re - call-ing Their home which an-gels keep; When,
2. peace and joy now hov-er Where all was strife be-fore. Oh
1. rest o'er all de-scending, The just pray God the while That sin-ners, their ways
2. thus may life, in-clos-ing Its short tempestuous day, Beneath Heav'n's smile re -
1. mend-ing, May keep from de-mons' wile.
2. pos-ing, Drive all the storms a - way.
rit.
CHORUS, a tempo
Then Ma-ry, Mother Ma - ry, Thou
bright star of the sea, We'll pray to thee, our Mother, We'll pray, we'll pray to thee.

O HEART OF MARY PURE AND FAIR

Slowly
Piel
80
1. O Heart of Ma-ry pure and fair, There is no stain in
2. As some fair lil-y 'midst the thorns, Thou 'mongst Eve's daughters
3. Dear heart, with-in thy depths so pure, We'll dwell and ne'er de-
4. And when from thy loved heart we'll go To that of thy dear
1. thee; In Ad-am's fall thou hast no share, From sin's taint thou art free.
2. art; Ce-les-tial pu-ri-ty a-dorns Thy chaste and ho-ly heart.
3. part, Till thou our souls hast linked se-cure To Je-sus' Sa-cred Heart.
4. Son, Oh shall we leave thee then? Ah, no; His Heart and thine are one.
O Heart of Ma-ry, pure and fair, No beau-ty can with thine compare! From
ev-'ry stain of sin thou'rt free; Oh make us pure in heart like thee.

HAIL MARY, QUEEN AND VIRGIN MEEK

Bro. Luke

81

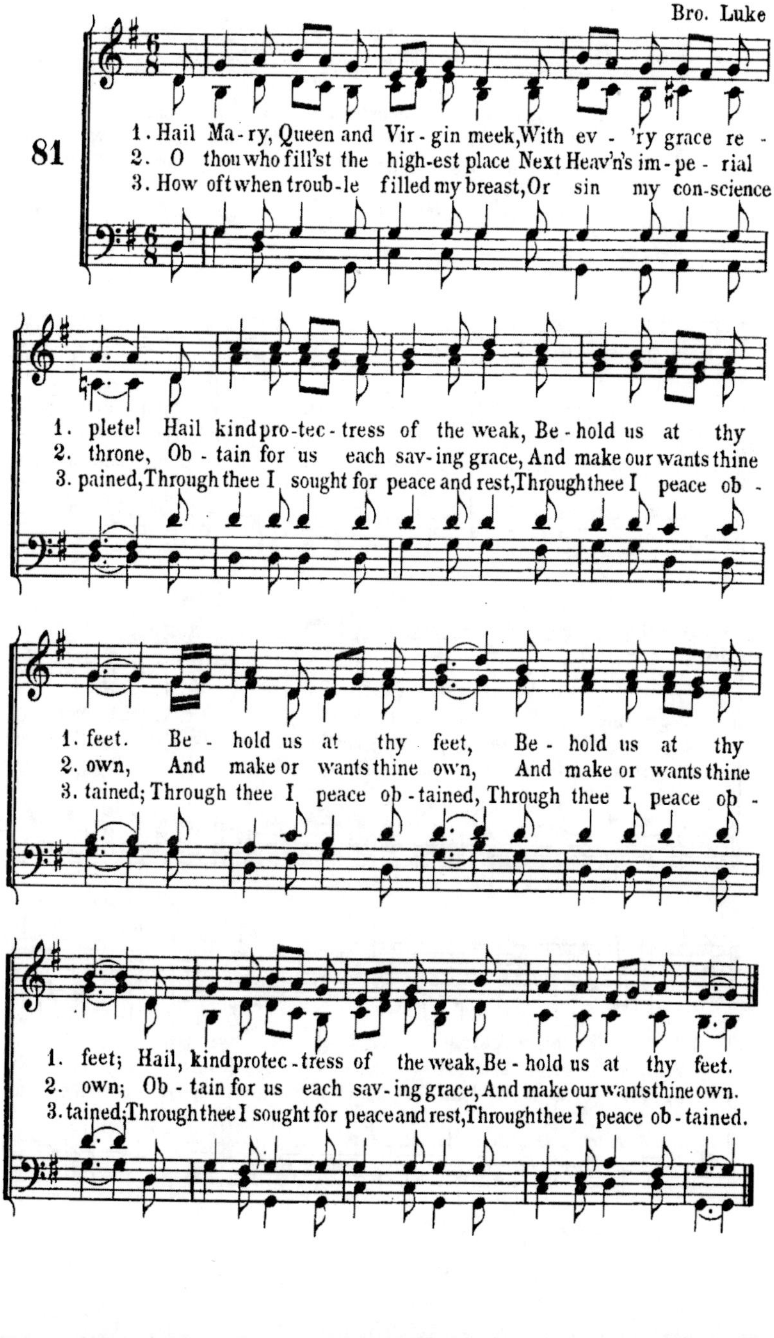
1. Hail Ma-ry, Queen and Vir-gin meek, With ev - 'ry grace re -
2. O thou who fill'st the high-est place Next Heav'n's im-pe - rial
3. How oft when troub-le filled my breast, Or sin my con-science
1. plete! Hail kind pro-tec-tress of the weak, Be-hold us at thy
2. throne, Ob - tain for us each sav-ing grace, And make our wants thine
3. pained, Through thee I sought for peace and rest, Through thee I peace ob -
1. feet. Be - hold us at thy feet, Be - hold us at thy
2. own, And make or wants thine own, And make or wants thine
3. tained; Through thee I peace ob-tained, Through thee I peace ob -
1. feet; Hail, kind protec-tress of the weak, Be-hold us at thy feet.
2. own; Ob - tain for us each sav-ing grace, And make our wants thine own.
3. tained; Through thee I sought for peace and rest, Through thee I peace ob-tained.

CAUSE OF OUR JOY

At a moderate pace — Rev. A. Schubiger, O. S. B.

mf SOLI
82
1. Our youth - ful hearts with joy are beat - ing And
2. Al - though on earth both toil and sor - row, Like
3. And when our day of life is set - ting, And
1. off-'ring praise with-out al - loy Our lov - ing hymn sends forth its
2. clouds a - round our souls may rise, We hope and trust, that on life's
3. earth fades from our dy - ing eyes, O then, our souls need not for -
CHORUS
1. greeting To Ma - ry cause of all our joy. We kneel, O Moth-er,
2. mor-row We'll reap great joy be-yond the skies. O "Morn-ing Star" that
3. get-ting, Give ear to our last fee-ble cries. Up - on thy gra-cious
SOLI
p dolce
1. at __ thy shrine And hail thee Moth - er all be - nign. Sweet Moth - er
2. shines so bright Thou art the cause of our de - light. Thy heav'n - ly
3. Vir - gin might We lean for help from heav-en's height. O Moth - er

ff
1. mild, oh hear each Child, O Cause of Joy, O Mother di-vine.
2. face, is full of grace And puts all gloom and woe to flight.
3. dear, be al-ways near To lead us all to end-less light.

VESPER HYMN

German Melody

83

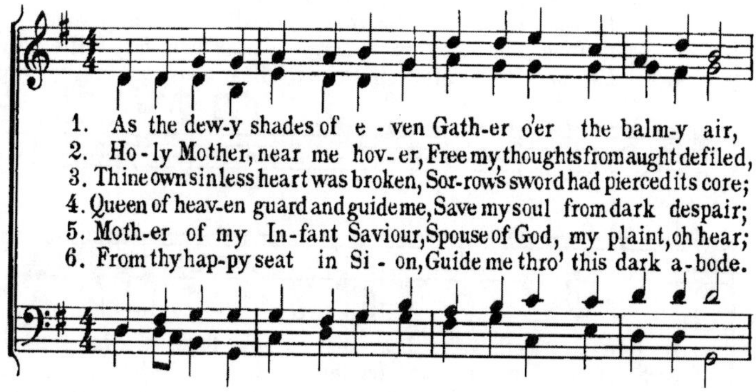
1. As the dew-y shades of e-ven Gath-er o'er the balm-y air,
2. Ho-ly Mother, near me hov-er, Free my thoughts from aught defiled,
3. Thine own sinless heart was broken, Sor-row's sword had pierced its core;
4. Queen of heav-en guard and guide me, Save my soul from dark despair;
5. Moth-er of my In-fant Saviour, Spouse of God, my plaint, oh hear;
6. From thy hap-py seat in Si-on, Guide me thro' this dark a-bode.

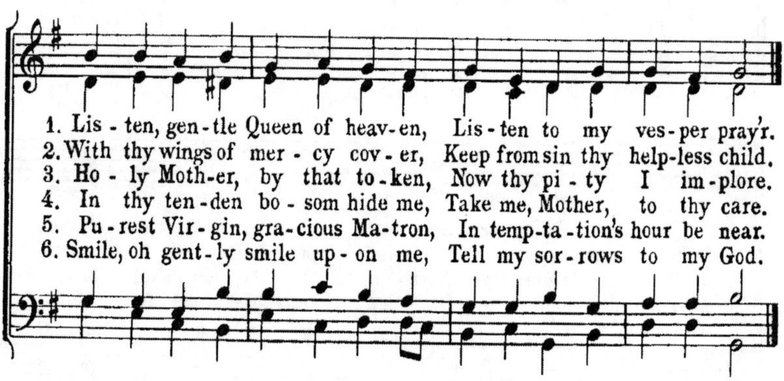
1. Lis-ten, gen-tle Queen of heav-en, Lis-ten to my ves-per pray'r.
2. With thy wings of mer-cy cov-er, Keep from sin thy help-less child.
3. Ho-ly Moth-er, by that to-ken, Now thy pi-ty I im-plore.
4. In thy ten-den bo-som hide me, Take me, Mother, to thy care.
5. Pu-rest Vir-gin, gra-cious Ma-tron, In temp-ta-tion's hour be near.
6. Smile, oh gent-ly smile up-on me, Tell my sor-rows to my God.

SNOW AND RAIN HAVE VANISHED

Labat

84

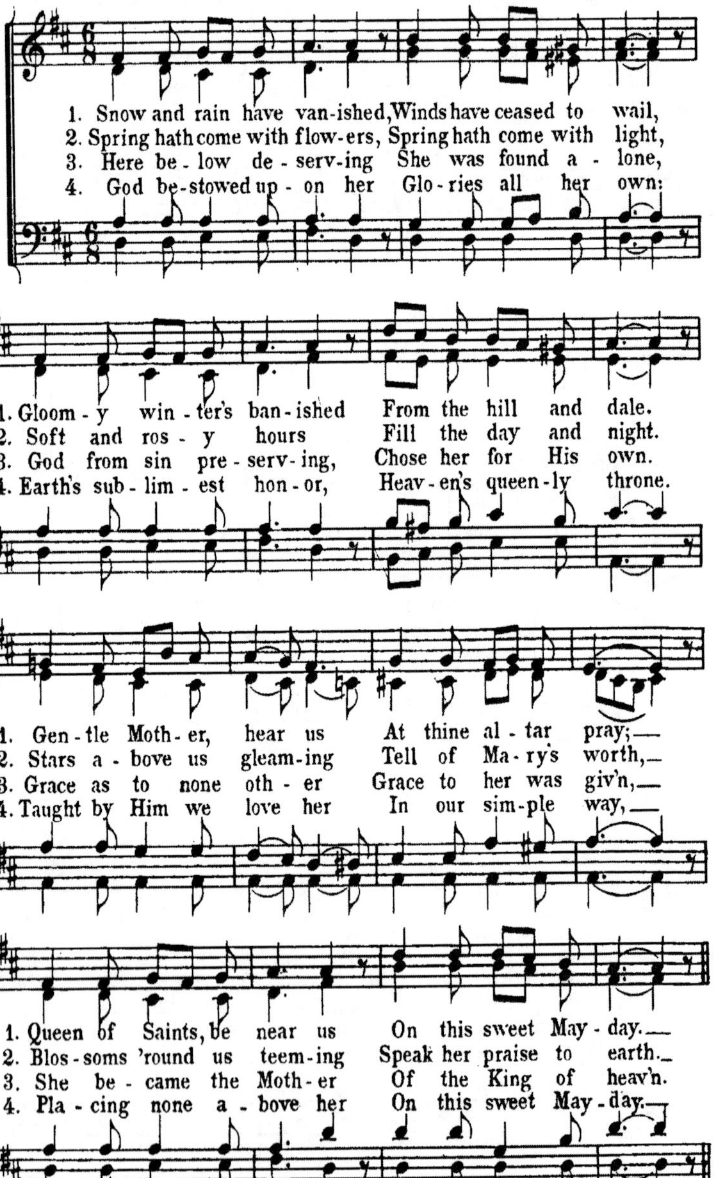
1. Snow and rain have van-ished, Winds have ceased to wail,
2. Spring hath come with flow-ers, Spring hath come with light,
3. Here be-low de-serv-ing She was found a-lone,
4. God be-stowed up-on her Glo-ries all her own:
1. Gloom-y win-ter's ban-ished From the hill and dale.
2. Soft and ros-y hours Fill the day and night.
3. God from sin pre-serv-ing, Chose her for His own.
4. Earth's sub-lim-est hon-or, Heav-en's queen-ly throne.
1. Gen-tle Moth-er, hear us At thine al-tar pray;—
2. Stars a-bove us gleam-ing Tell of Ma-ry's worth,—
3. Grace as to none oth-er Grace to her was giv'n,—
4. Taught by Him we love her In our sim-ple way,—
1. Queen of Saints, be near us On this sweet May-day.—
2. Blos-soms 'round us teem-ing Speak her praise to earth.—
3. She be-came the Moth-er Of the King of heav'n.
4. Pla-cing none a-bove her On this sweet May-day.—

CHORUS

Gen - tle Moth - er, hear us at thine al - tar pray;
Queen of Saints, be near us on this sweet May - day.

OH, TURN TO JESUS, MOTHER

♩ = 76

Webbe

85

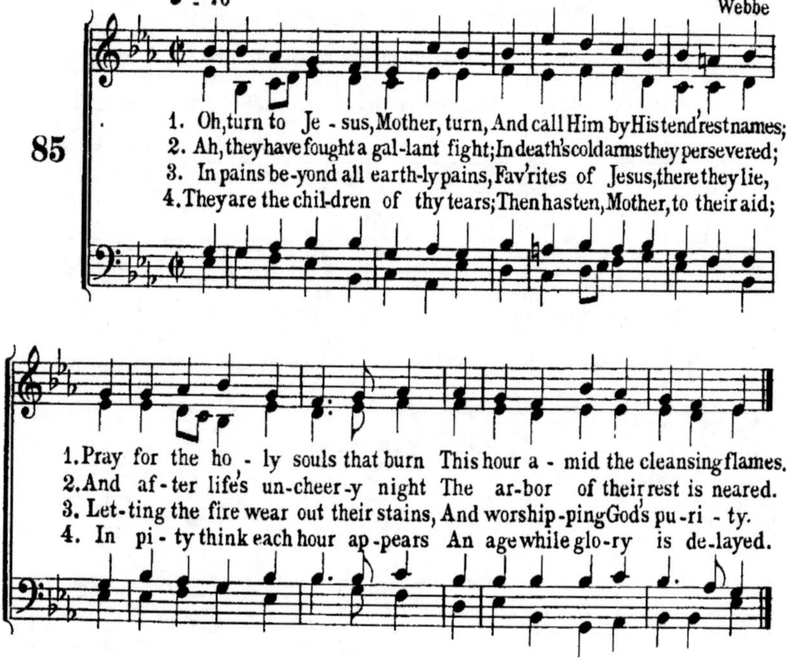
1. Oh, turn to Je - sus, Mother, turn, And call Him by His tend'rest names;
2. Ah, they have fought a gal-lant fight; In death's cold arms they persevered;
3. In pains be-yond all earth-ly pains, Fav'rites of Jesus, there they lie,
4. They are the chil-dren of thy tears; Then hasten, Mother, to their aid;
1. Pray for the ho - ly souls that burn This hour a - mid the cleansing flames.
2. And af - ter life's un-cheer-y night The ar-bor of their rest is neared.
3. Let-ting the fire wear out their stains, And worship-ping God's pu-ri - ty.
4. In pi - ty think each hour ap-pears An age while glo-ry is de-layed.

MOTHER DEAR, OH PRAY FOR ME

86

1. Moth-er dear, oh pray for me, Whilst, far from Heav'n and thee, I
2. Moth-er dear, oh pray for me, Should pleasure's si - ren lay E'er
3. Moth-er dear, oh pray for me, When all seems full of cheer, That
1. wan-der in a frag-ile bark O'er life's tem-pest-uous sea. O
2. tempt thy child to wan-der far From vir-tue's path a - way, Or
3. I may all my dan-ger see, For sure-ly then 'tis near. A
1. Vir-gin Moth-er, from thy throne, So bright in bliss a - bove, — Pro -
2. sorrow's gloom up-on me fall And dark-en all be - low, — Then,
3. Moth-er's help I, then, most need, For bale-ful is the ray, — That
1. tect thy child and cheer my path With thy sweet smile of love.
2. Ma - ry, aid thy weep-ing child, Thy-self a Moth-er show.
3. paints with gold the flow-'ry mead Which blossoms in my way.
CHORUS
Moth-er dear, re - mem-ber me, And nev-er cease thy care,

Till in heav-en e - ter-nal-ly, Thy love and bliss I share.

O GLORIOSA VIRGINUM

Jacobsen

87

1. O glori-ó-sa Vír-gi-num, Su-bli-mis in-ter si-de-ra, Qui
2. Tu Re-gis al-ti já-nu-a, Et au-la lu-cis fúl-gi-da; Vi -

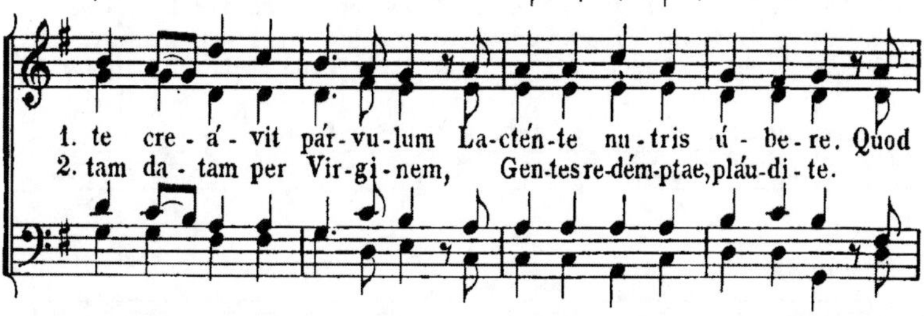
1. te cre-á-vit pár-vu-lum La-ctén-te nu-tris ú-be-re. Quod
2. tam da-tam per Vir-gi-nem, Gen-tes re-dém-ptae, pláu-di-te.

1. E-va tri-stis áb-stu-lit Tu red-dis al-mo gér-mi-ne: In
2. Je-su, ti-bi sit gló-ri-a, Qui na-tus es de Vír-gi-ne, Cum

1. trent ut as-tra flé-bi-les, Coe-li re-clú-dis cár-di-nes.
2. Pa-tre et al-mo Spí-ri-tu, In sem-pi-tér-na sáe-cu-la.
A-men.

'TIS THE MONTH OF OUR MOTHER

With dignity — French Air

88

1. 'Tis the month of our Moth-er, Whose blessed and beauti-ful days,
2. Oh what peace to her chil-dren, 'Mid sor-row and tri-als, to know
3. And what joy to the err-ing, The sin-ful and sor-row-ful soul,
4. Let us sing, then, re-joic-ing, That God hath so honored our race,
1. Move our lips and our spir-its To sing hymns of love and praise.
2. That the love of their moth-er Hath ev-er a sol-ace for woe!
3. That a trust in her guid-ance Will lead to a glo-ri-ous goal!
4. As to clothe with our na-ture Sweet Ma-ry, the Mother of grace.
CHORUS
All hail to our dear Moth-er, Who keeps us all in vir-tue's way!
ritardando
Hail to our im-mac-u-late Queen! Hail to Ma-ry, Queen of May!

SANCTORUM AGMINA

89

Somewhat lively
1. San-ctó-rum ág - mi - na Ex - cé - dens Dó - mi - na,
2. In val - le flé - bi - les Quó - ti - es éx - u - les,
3. Fac no-stra cór - po - ra Men - tes et pé - cto - ra
4. Vir - go te - nér - ri - ma, Ad - sis a - cér - ri - ma
5. Ut in-ter ág - mi - na San - cto-rum cár - mi - na
1. Ma - rí - a, sal - - ve! Dul - cé - do cór - di - um,
2. Heu, na - ti E - - vae! Ad te cla-má - vi - mus,
3. Sint pu - ra, Ma - - ter! Et ro - ga Fí - li - um
4. In mor-tis ho - - ra! Tu - úm-que Jé - su - lum,
5. De - o ca - ná - - mus: Ti - bí-que dé - bi - tas
1. Spes sup-pli - cán - ti - um. Ma - rí - a, sal - ve!
2. Et sus - pi - rá - vi - mus. Ma - rí - a, sal - ve!
3. Ut nos post ó - bi - tum A - gnó-scat Pa - ter!
4. Dul - cem pu - é - ru - lum Pro no - bis o - ra!
5. Per cun-cta grá - ti - as Sae - cla red - dá - mus!

ULTIMA IN MORTIS HORA

90

1. Úl - ti - ma in mor - tis ho - ra,
2. Vir - go ve - re be - ne - dí - cta,
3. Vir - go cle - mens, Vir - go pi - a,
1. Fí - li - um pro no - bis o - ra:
2. In - ter mun - das mun - da so - la:
3. Duc sa - lú - tis nos in vi a:
1. Bo - nam mor - tem ím - pe - tra,
2. A - scen - dí - sti sí - de - ra,
3. Nos, O Ma - ter, tu - é - re,
1. Vir - go Ma - ter, Dó - mi - na.
2. Scep - tra ge - ris, Dó - mi - na.
3. Vi - tae per ex - í - li - um.

AVE MARIS STELLA No. 1

91

Slowly
Lambillotte
1. A - ve, Ma - ris Stel - la, De - i Ma - ter al - ma,
2. Su - mens il - lud A - ve Ga - bri - e' - lis o - re,
3. Sol - ve vin - cla re - is, Pro - fer lu - men cae - cis,
4. Mon - stra te es - se Ma - trem, Su - mat per - te pre - ces,
5. Vir - go sin - gu - lá - ris, In - ter o - mnes mi - tis,
6. Vi - tam prae - sta pu - ram, I - ter pa - ra tu - tum,
7. Sit laus De - o Pa - tri, Sum - mo Christo de - cus,
1. At - que sem - per vir - go, Fe - lix coe li por - - ta;
2. Fun - da nos in pa - ce, Mu - tans He - vae no - - men;
3. Ma - la no - stra pel - le, Bo - na cun - cta po - - sce;
4. Qui pro no - bis na - tus Tu - lit es - se tu - - us;
5. Nos cul - pis so - lu - tos Mi - tes fac et ca - - stos;
6. Ut vi - dén - tes Je - sum Sem - per col - lae - té - - mur;
7. Spi - rí - tu - i San - cto, Tri - bus ho - nor u - - nus;
rall.
1. At - que sem - per vir - go, Fe - lix coe - li por - ta.
2. Fun - da nos in pa - ce, Mu - tans He - vae no - men.
3. Ma - la no - stra pel - le, Bo - na cun - cta po - sce.
4. Qui pro no - bis na - tus Tu - lit es - se tu - us. A - men.
5. Nos cul - pis so - lú - tos Mi - tes fac et ca - stos.
6. Ut vi - dén - tes Je - sum Sem - per col - lae - té - mur.
7. Spi - rí - tu - i San - cto, Tri - bus ho - nor u - nus.

AVE MARIS STELLA No. 2

Italian Melody

92

Slowly
1. A - ve, Ma - ris Stel - - la, De - i
2. Su - mens il - lud A - - ve Ga - bri - -
3. Sol - ve vin - cla re - - is, Pro - fer
4. Mon - stra te es - se Ma - - trem, Su - mat
5. Vir - go sin - gu - lá - - ris, In - ter
6. Vi - tam prae - sta pu - - ram, I - ter
7. Sit laus De - o Pa - - tri, Sum - mo
1. Ma - ter al - ma, At - que sem - per vir - -
2. é - lis o - re, Fun - da nos in pa - -
3. lu - men cae - cis, Ma - la no - stra pel - -
4. per - te pre - ces, Qui pro no - bis na - -
5. o - mnes mi - tis, Nos cul - pis so - lú - -
6. pa - ra tu - tum, Ut vi - dén - tes Je - -
7. Chri - sto de - cus, Spi - rí - tu - i san - -
rall.
1. go, Fe - lix coe - li por - ta.
2. ce, Mu - tans He - vae no - men.
3. le, Bo - na cun - cta po - sce.
4. tus Tu - lit es - se tu - us. A - men.
5. tos Mi - tes fac et ca - stos.
6. sum Sem - per col - lae - té - mur.
7. cto, Tri - bus ho - nor u - nus.

AVE MARIS STELLA No 3

Slowly Bro. Sixtus

93

1. A - ve, Ma - ris Stel - la, De - i Ma - ter
2. Su - mens il - lud A - ve Ga - bri - é - lis
3. Sol - ve vin - cla re - is, Pro - fer lu - men
4. Mon - stra te es - se Ma - trem, Su - mat per te
5. Vir - go sin - gu - lá - ris, In - ter o - mnes
6. Vi - tam prae - sta pu - ram, I - ter pa - ra
7. Sit laus De - o Pa - tri, Sum - mo Chri - sto
1. al - ma, At - que sem - per vir - go,
2. o - re, Fun - da nos in pa - ce,
3. cae - cis, Ma - la no - stra pel - le,
4. pre - ces, Qui pro no - bis na - tus
5. mi - tis, Nos cul - pis so - lú - tos
6. tu - tum, Ut vi - dén - tes Je - sum
7. de - cus, Spi - rí - tu - i San - cto,
1. Fe - lix coe - li por - ta.
2. Mu - tans He - vae no - men.
3. Bo - na cun - cta po - sce.
4. Tu - lit es - se tu - us. A - - men.
5. Mi - tes fac et ca - stos.
6. Sem - per col - lae - té - mur.
7. Tri - bus ho - nor u - nus.

THE MOST BLESSED VIRGIN

O SANCTISSIMA No 1

94

1. O san - ctís - si - ma, O pi - ís - si - ma,
2. To - ta pul - chra es, O Ma - rí - a,
3. Sic - ut lí - li - um in - ter spi - nas,
4. In mi - sé - ri - a, in an - gú - sti - a,
1. Dul - cis vir - go Ma - rí - a! Ma - ter a - má - ta,
2. Et má - cu - la non est in te. Ma - ter a - má - ta,
3. Sic Ma - rí - a in - ter fí - li - as. Ma - ter a - má - ta,
4. O - ra, vir - go, pro no - bis. In mor - tis ho - ra
p
1. in - te - me - rá - ta, O - ra, o - ra pro no - bis.
2. in - te - me - rá - ta, O - ra, o - ra pro no - bis.
3. in - te - me - rá - ta, O - ra, o - ra pro no - bis.
4. pro no - bis o - ra, O - ra, o - ra pro no - bis.

O SANCTISSIMA No. 2

Gordigiani

95

1. O san - ctís - si - ma, O pi - ís - si - ma,
2. To - ta pul-chra es, O Ma - rí - a,
3. Si - cut lí - li - um in - ter spi - nas,
4. In mi - sé - ri - a, in an - gú - sti - a,
1. O dul - cis vir - go Ma - rí - - a. Ma - ter a -
2. Et má - cu - la non est in te.
3. Sic Ma - rí - a in - ter fí - li - as.
4. O - ra vir - go pro no - - bis.
Ma - ter a - má - ta in - te - me -
má - - - - ta, in - te - me - rá - - -
Ma - ter a - má - ta in - te - me -
Ma - ter a - má - ta in - te - me -
rá - ta
- ta, O - ra pro no - bis, o - ra pro no - - bis.
rá - ta,
pp
mf
rá - ta

SANCTA MARIA

M. M. ♩ = 72

Arr. from J. B. Schweitzer

96

1. San - cta, san - cta, san - cta Ma - rí - a!
2. To - ta pul - chra es, Ma - rí - a!
1. San - cta De - i Gé - ni - trix! San - cta Vir - go,
2. Má - cu - la non est in te! Sal - ve Vir - go,
1. Vir - go vír - gi - num: O - ra, o - ra pro no - - bis.
2. Vir - go vír - gi - num: O - ra, o - ra pro no - - bis.

SUB TUUM PRAESIDIUM

Slowly

Lambillotte

97

Sub tu - um prae - sí - di - um con - fú - gi - mus, con - fú - gi - mus,

f
San-cta De-i Gé-ni-trix, San-cta De-i Gé-ni-trix.
Fine
pp
No-stras de-pre-ca-ti-ó- -nes ne de-spí-ci-as,
ne de-spí-ci-as in ne-ces-si-tá-ti-bus no- -stris.
Sed a pe-rí-cu-lis cun- -ctis lí-be-ra nos
sem-per, Vir-go glo-ri-ó-sa et be-ne-dí-cta.

SALVE MARIA SANCTISSIMA

Rev. A. Schubiger, O. S. B.

98

p
1. Sal-ve, Ma - rí - a, dul-cís-si - ma: Sal - ve, Re - gí - na
2. For-tis Bel - ló - na, pró-te - ge nos: Cle-mens Pa - tró - na,
3. Pre-ces be - ní - gne ex-áu - di - as: Nos de - pre - cán - tes
p
1. san-ctís-si - ma: Vir-go be - á - ta, Ma-ter a - má - ta! Sal-ve, Ma-
2. de-fén-de nos: In-gru-unt ho - stes Súf-fi - ce vi - res! Clemens Pa-
3. re-spí - ci - as! In mor-tis ho - ra Pro no-bis o - ra! Nos de - pre-
1. rí - a, dul - cís - si - ma: Sal-ve, Ma - rí - a, dul - cís - si - ma.
2. tró-na, de - fén - de nos: Clemens Pa - tró-na, de - fén - de nos.
3. cán-tes re - spí - ci - as: Nos de - pre - cán-tes re - spí - ci - as.

TOTA PULCHRA ES

Dom Pothier

99

CHANTERS
CHORUS.
To-ta pul-chra es Ma-rí - a! To-ta pul-chra es Ma-rí - a!

CHANT.
Et má-cu-la o-ri-gi-ná-lis non est in te.
CHOR.
Et má-cu-la o-ri-gi-ná-lis non est in te.
CHANT.
Tu glóri-a Je-rú-sa-lem.
CHOR.
Tu laetí-ti-a Is-ra-el.
CHANT.
Tu ho-no-ri-fi-cén-ti-a pó-pu-li no-stri.
CHOR.
Tu ad-vo-cá-ta pec-ca-tó-rum.
CHANT.
O Ma-rí-a!
CHOR.
O Ma-rí-a!
CHANT.
Vir-go pru-den-tís-si-ma.
CHOR.
Vir-go cle-men-tís-si-ma.
O-ra pro no-bis,
In-ter-cé-de pro no-bis ad Dó-mi-num Je-sum Christum. A-men.

LITANY No. 1

100

Ky - ri - e e - lé - i - son. Chri - ste e - lé - i - son.
Ky - ri - e e - lé - i - son.
Chri - ste au - di nos.
Chrì - ste ex - au - di nos.
1. Pa - ter de coe - lis De - us, mi - se - ré - re no - bis.
2. Fi - li Re - démptor mun - di De - us, mi - se - ré - re no - bis.
3. Spí - ri - tus San - cte De - us, mi - se - ré - re no - bis.
4. San - cta Tri - ni - tas, u - nus De - us, mi - se - ré - re no - bis.

By permission of J. Fischer & Bro.

San - cta Ma-rí - a,
San-cta De - i Gé-ni-trix,
San-cta Vir - go Vír-gi-num,
Ma - ter Chrí - sti,
Ma-ter di - ví-nae grá-ti-ae,
Ma - ter pu-rís si-ma,
Ma - ter ca-stís-si-ma,
Ma-ter in - vi - o - lá - ta,
Ma-ter in - te-me-rá - ta,
Ma - ter a - má-bi-lis,
Ma-ter ad-mi-rá-bi-lis,
Ma-ter bo - ni con-sí - li-i,
Ma-ter Cre - a - tó - ris,
Ma-ter Sal-va-tó - ris,
Vir-go pru-den-tís-si-ma,
Vir-go ve - ne-rán - da,
Vir-go prae-di-cán - da,
Vir-go po - tens,
Vir-go cle - mens,
Vir - go fi - dé - lis,
Spé-cu - lum ju-stí-ti-ae,
Se-des sa-pi-én-ti-ae,
Cau-sa no - strae lae-tí - ti-ae,
Vas spi - ri-tu-á - le,
Vas ho-no-rá-bi-le,
Vas insí-gne de - vo-ti-ó - nis,
Ro-sa mý-sti-ca,
Tur - ris Da-ví - di-ca,
Tur - ris e - búr-ne-a,
Do-mus aú - re-a,
Foé - de-ris ar - ca
Já - nu-a coe - li,
Stel-la ma-tu-tí - na,
Sa-lus in-fir-mó - rum,
Re-fú-gi-um pec-ca-tó - rum,
Con-so-lá-trix af-fli-ctó - rum,
Au-xí-li-um Chri-sti-a - nó-rum,
Re-gí-na An-ge-ló - rum,
Re-gí-na Pa - tri-ar-chá - rum,
Re-gí-na Pro-phe-tá - rum,
Re-gí-na A - po-sto-ló rum,
Re - gí - na Már-ty-rum,
Re-gí-na Con-fes-só - rum,
Re - gí - na Vír-gi-num,
Re-gí-na San - ctó-rum ó-mni-um,
Re-gí-na sine labe o-ri-gi-ná - li con-cé - pta,
Re-gí-na sa-cra-tís-si - mi Ro-sá-ri-i,

o - ra pro no-bis.

A-gnus De-i, qui tol-lis pec-cá-ta mun-di, par-ce no-bis Dó-mi-ne.
A-gnus De-i, qui tol-lis pec-cá-ta mun-di, ex-aú-di nos Dó-mi-ne.
A-gnus De-i, qui tol-lis pec-cá-ta mun-di, mi-se-ré-re no-bis.

LITANY No. 2

101

San-cta Ma-rí-a, San-cta De-i Gé-ne-trix,
San-cta Vir-go Vír-gi-num, O-ra pro no-bis.

For other invocations, see page 101

SAINT JOSEPH

SAINT JOSEPH DEAR WE PRAISE THEE

102

At a moderate pace
CHORUS
Saint Jo-seph dear, we praise thee and sing thy won-drous
pow'r. Oh, nev-er fail to aid us in ev-'ry need-y hour.
Fine
1. Thine aid canst thou re - fuse us, With Je-sus in thy arms, And
2. Sweet spouse of Ma - ry, teach us Thy ard-ent zeal and love, That
3. Let love of Je - sus on - ly Our as-pi-ra-tions fill; Be
1. all thy love o'er - flow - ing Up - on His In fant charms?
2. raise the heart's af - fec - tions All earth-ly things a - bove. Saint
3. it our tru - est pleas-ure To do His ho - ly will.

WITH GRATEFUL HEARTS

103

At a moderate pace
Monpou
1. With grate-ful hearts we raise to thee The tender accents of our love; We pledge our ut-most loy-al-ty To thee, great Saint in Heav'n a-bove.
2. More fa-vored than earth's great-est king Thou wast the guard-ian of that Child A-round whose crib great choirs did sing With ca-denced voic-es soft and mild.
3. All heav-en's hosts on that great night Looked on the Child, thy Spouse, and thee, And rav-ished with so fair a sight, Struck loud their harps with ju-bi-lee.
f
O Jo-seph dear, from thy bright throne, In-cline thine ear un-to our pray'r; And o'er us all, as o'er thine own, Ex-tend thy fond paternal care,
mf
Ex-tend thy fond paternal care.

HAIL SAINT JOSEPH, SPOUSE OF MARY

At a moderate pace F. S. C.

mf CHORUS
104
Hail Saint Jo - seph, Spouse of Ma - ry, Blest a -
bove all saints on high! When the death shades round us gath - er, Teach, oh
teach us how to die! Teach, oh teach us how to die.
Fine.
1. Dear Saint Jo - seph pure and gen - tle, Faith - ful guard - ian of the
2. He who rest - ed on thy bo - som, Is by count - less Saints a -
3. Now to thee no gift re - fus - ing, Je - sus stoops to hear thy
1. Child, Tread - ing with the Vir - gin Moth - er E - gypt's desert rough and wild.
2. dored; Pros - trate an - gels in His pres - ence Sing ho - sannas to their Lord.
3. pray'r; Then, dear Saint, from thy fair dwelling Give to us a fa - ther's care!
D.C.

SAINT JOSEPH

DEAR GUARDIAN OF MARY

105
Slowly
1. Dear Guard - ian of Ma - ry! dear nurse of her
2. For thou to the pil - grim art fa - ther and
3. God chose thee for Je - sus and Ma - ry; wilt
1. Child! Life's ways are full wea - ry, the des - ert is
2. guide, And Je - sus and Ma - ry felt safe at thy
3. thou For - give a poor ex - ile for choos - ing thee
1. wild; Bleak sands are all round us, no home can we
2. side. O Glo - ri - ous Pa - tron, se - cure shall I
3. now? There's no saint in heav - en, Saint Jo - seph, like
1. see; Sweet Spouse of our La-dy, we lean safe on thee.
2. be, Sweet Spouse of our La-dy, if thou stay with me!
3. thee. Sweet Spouse of our La-dy, do thou plead for me.

SAINT JOSEPH

HOLY PATRON, THEE SALUTING

Rather slowly — Tyrolese Melody

106

mf
1. Ho-ly Pa-tron, thee sa-lu-ting, Here we meet with hearts sin-cere; Good Saint Jo-seph, all u-nit-ing Call on thee to help our pray'r.
2. World-ly dangers for them fear-ing, Youth-ful hearts to thee we bring, Grant in vir-tue per-se-ver-ing, Vice may ne'er their bo-som sting.
3. Thou hast faith-ful-ly at-tend-ed Him whom heav'n and earth a-dore, And with pi-ous care de-fen-ed Ma-ry Vir-gin ev-er-more.
4. May our fer-vent pray'rs as-cend-ing Move thee for our souls to plead, And ob-tain for us thy chil-dren Ben-e-dic-tions in our need.
f CHORUS
Hap-py Saint, in bliss a-dor-ing Je-sus Sav-iour of man-kind, Hear thy chil-dren thee im-plor-ing; May we thy pro-tec-tion find.

SAINT JOSEPH

QUICUMQUE

107

1. Qui - cúm - que sa - nus ví - ve - re, Cur-
2. Hic spon - sus al - mae Vír - gi - nis, Pa-
3. Foe - no ja - cén - tem Párvu - lum Ad-
4. Mun - di su - pré - mus Ar - ti - fex E-
5. Ad - és - se mor - ti pró - xi - mus Cum
1. súm - que vi - tae claú - de - re, In fi - ne lae - tus
2. tér - que Je - su cré - di - tus, Ju - stus, fi - dé - lis,
3. ó - rat et post éx - u - lem So - lá - tur; in - de
4. jus la - bó - re pá - sci - tur; Sum - mi Pa - rén - tis
5. Ma - tre Je - sum cón - spi - cit, Et in - ter - i - psos
1. éx - pe - tit, O - pem Jo - sé - phi pó - stu - let.
2. ín - te - ger, Quod po - scit o - rans ím - pe - trat.
3. pér - di - tum, Quae - rit do - lens et ín - ve - nit.
4. Fí - li - us O - bé - dit il - li súb - di - tus.
5. jú - bi - lans, Dul - ci so - pó - re sól - vi - tur.

SAINT JOSEPH

TE JOSEPH CELEBRENT

108

1. Te, Jo - seph. cé - le - brent á - gmi-na coé - li - tum:
2. Al - mo cum tú - mi - dam gér - mi - ne cón - ju - gem
3. Tu na - tum Dó - mi - num strin-gis, ad éx - te - ras
4. Post mor - tem ré - li - quos mors pi - a cón - se - crat,
5. No - bis,_ sum - ma Tri - as, par - ce pre-cán - ti - bus:
1. Te cun-cti ré - so - nent Chri-stí - a - dum cho - ri, Qui cla - rus
2. Ad - mí - rans, dú - bi - o tán - ge-ris án - xi - us, Af - flá - tu
3. Ae - gý - pti pró - fu - gum tu sé-que-ris pla - gas: A - mís - sum
4. Pal - mam-que e-mé - ri - tos gló - ri - a sús - ci - pit: Tu vi - vens
5. Da Jo - seph mé - ri - tis sí - de-ra scán-de - re, Ut tan - dem
1. mé - ri - tis, jun-ctus es ín - cly - tae Casto foé - de-re Vír-gi - ni.
2. sú-pe-ri Flá-mi-nis An-ge - lús Con-cé - ptum pú-e-rum do-cet.
3. Só-ly-mis quae-ris, et ín - ve - nis, Mi-scens gaú - di-a flé-ti-bus. A - men.
4. sú-pe-ris par frú-e-ris De - o, Mi-ra sor - te be-á - ti - or.
5. lí-ce-at nos ti-bi pér-pe-tim Gra-tum pró-me-re cán-ti-cum.

1st Vespers R. Et príncipem omnis possessiónis suae.
2nd Vespers R. Et justítia ejus manet in saéculum saéculi.

ISTE QUEM LAETI

109

1. I - ste quem lae - ti có - li - mus fi - dé - les,
2. O ni - mis fe - lix, ni - mis O be - á - tus!
3. Er - go reg - nán - tem fla - gi - té - mus o - mnes
1. Cu - jus ex - cél - sos cá - ni - mus tri - úm - phos,
2. Cu - jus ex - tré - mam ví - gi - les ad ho - ram
3. Ad - sit ut no - bis ve - ni - ám - que no - stris
1. Be - á - tus Jo - seph mé - ru - it per - én - nis
2. Chri - stus et Vir - go si - mul a - sti - té - runt
3. Ob - ti - nens cul - pis, trí - bu - at su - pér - nae
1. Gaú - di - a vi - tae.
2. O - re se - re - no.
3. Mú - ne - ra pa - cis. A - men.

HOW KIND IT IS OF THEE

110

1. How kind it is of thee_ to stay,
2. How good and pure I ought to be,
3. O bless - ed guard - ian, kind_ and mild,
4. Thy pray'rs shall be my shield and spear,
1. Bright an-gel, far from heav'n a - way, And watch by night, and
2. Who al-ways live so near to thee; Be - neath thine eyes the
3. Have pit - y on a poor weak child, And pray that God may
4. Dear an-gel mine, when sin is near; Thine arms en - fold me
1. watch by day, Be - side a sin - ful_ child___ of
2. whole day round, Wher - e'er I tread is_ ho - ly
3. make me strong To do the right and_ shun___ the
4. when I die, And waft me home - ward to___ the
1. clay,_ Be - side a sin - ful child___ of clay!
2. ground,_ Where'er I tread is ho - ly ground!
3. wrong,_ To do the right and shun___ the wrong.
4. sky,_ And waft me home - ward to___ the sky.

HOLY GUARDIAN ANGEL

DEAR ANGEL, EVER AT MY SIDE

B. S.

111

1. Dear An - gel, ev - er at my side, How
2. But I have felt thy gra - cious pow'r, When
1. lov - ing must thou be, To leave thy home in
2. thou hast fought for me; And when my heart loves
1. Heav'n to guide A lit - tle child like me. Thy beau - ti - ful and
2. God, I know The sweet-ness is from thee. And when I pray, thou
1. shin - ing face I see not, though so near; The
2. pray - est too, Thy pray'r is all for me; But
1. sweet-ness of thy soft low voice I am too deaf to hear.
2. when I sleep, thou sleep - est not, But watch-est pa - tient - ly.

SAINT LA SALLE

GLORIOUS PATRON No. 1

W. A. R.

112

1. Glo-rious Pa-tron, low be-fore thee, Kneel thy sons with
2. Lov-er of our Queen and Moth-er, Thou to her didst
3. Mod-el of the Chris-tian Teacher, Pa-tron of the
4. In this life of sin and sor-row, Saint La Salle, oh,
1. hearts a - flame; And our voi-ces blend in mu-sic,
2. vow thy heart; Earth and all its joys for-sak-ing,
3. Chris-tian youth; Lead us all to heights of glo-ry,
4. guide our way; In the hour of dark temp-ta-tion,
1. Sing-ing prais-es to thy name. Saint John Bap-tist,
2. Thou didst choose the bet-ter part. Saint La Salle, our
3. As we strive, in ear-nest truth. Saint La Salle, thy
4. Fa-ther, be our spir-it's stay. Take our hand and
1. glo-rious Pa-tron, Saint La Salle, we sound thy fame.
2. glo-rious Fa-ther! Pierce our souls with love's own dart.
3. ways to fol-low, Help us in thy gen-tle ruth.
4. lead us home-ward, Saint La Salle, to Heav'n's bright day.

GLORIOUS PATRON No. 2

SAINT LA SALLE

GLORIOUS PATRON No. 3

114

GLORIOUS PATRON No. 4

J. Lewis Browne

115

Briskly ♩ = 104
1. Glorious Patron! low before thee Kneel thy sons, with hearts aflame! And our voices blend in music, Singing praises to thy name. Saint John Baptist! glorious Patron! Saint La Salle we sound thy fame.
2. Lover of our Queen and Mother, Thou to her didst vow thy heart; Earth, and all its joys, forsaking, Thou didst choose the better part. Saint La Salle, our glorious Father, Pierce our souls with love's own dart.
3. Model of the Christian Teacher! Patron of the Christian youth! Lead us all to heights of glory, As we strive in earnest ruth. Saint La Salle! oh, guard and guide us, As we spread afar the Truth!
4. In this life of sin and sorrow, Saint La Salle, oh, guide our way, In the hour of dark temptation, Father be our spirits' stay! Take our hand and lead us homeward, Saint La Salle, to Heaven's bright Day!

SAINT LA SALLE

WHILE HEART AND SOUL TO THEE WE RAISE

Bro. Romuald

116

1. While heart and soul to thee we raise, O Saint La
2. O Friend of youth, e'er bless and guide Thy chil - dren,
1. Salle, in hymns of praise, In - spire us with a no - ble zest To
2. who, on ev - 'ry side, Are sore be - set with sin and woe. Oh,
1. spend our lives in vir - tue's quest. Oh teach us day and night to
2. help them nev - er to fore - go The price - less gra - ces of the
p
1. seek The bless - ing of that Heart so meek Whose ev - 'ry
2. cross That purge a - way all earth - ly dross And fit the
1. fi - bre beats with love And lifts our thoughts to realms a - bove.
2. soul for par - a - dise, Its last - ing home be - yond the skies.

SAINT LA SALLE

E. Marzo

117

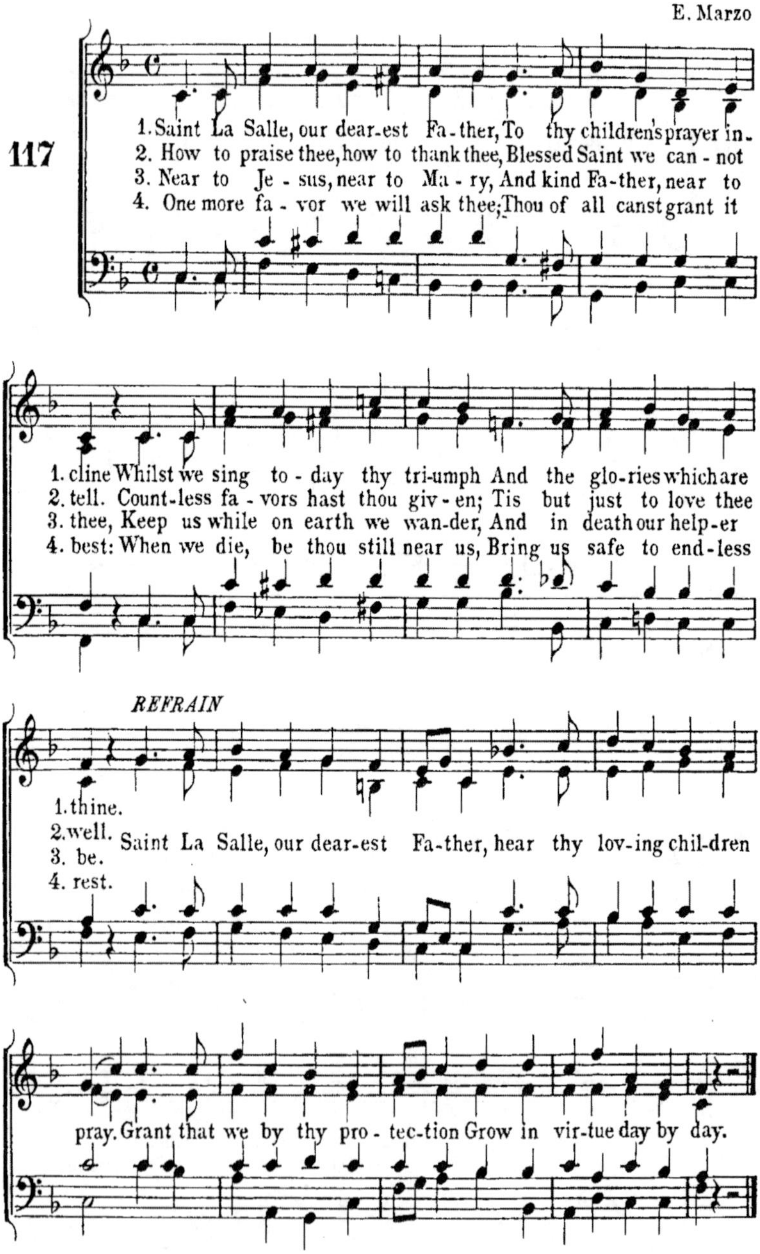
1. Saint La Salle, our dear-est Fa-ther, To thy children's prayer in-
2. How to praise thee, how to thank thee, Blessed Saint we can-not
3. Near to Je-sus, near to Ma-ry, And kind Fa-ther, near to
4. One more fa-vor we will ask thee; Thou of all canst grant it
1. cline Whilst we sing to-day thy tri-umph And the glo-ries which are
2. tell. Count-less fa-vors hast thou giv-en; Tis but just to love thee
3. thee, Keep us while on earth we wan-der, And in death our help-er
4. best: When we die, be thou still near us, Bring us safe to end-less
REFRAIN
1. thine.
2. well.
3. be.
4. rest.
Saint La Salle, our dear-est Fa-ther, hear thy lov-ing chil-dren
pray. Grant that we by thy pro-tec-tion Grow in vir-tue day by day.

SAINT LA SALLE

QUEM SION

118

1. Quem Si - on gau - dens cé - le - brat be - á - tum,
2. De - gis in ter - ris co - mes An - ge - ló - rum,
3. Dum te - nent cu - ræ ví - gi - les scho - lá - rum,
4. Te pi - um lau - dant pú - e - ri pa - tró - num,
5. Sit de - cus sum - mae Trí - a - di pe - rén - ne,
1. Hac di - e fe - sta de - cet, O Jo - án - nes, Nos tu - as
2. Qui stu - dent flo - ri ju - ve - ní - lis ae - vi, Sem - per in
3. Súb - le - vat men - tem fí - de - i vo - lá - tus; Pro De - o
4. Te du - cem sanc - tum ré - co - lunt ma - gí - stri, Te vo - cant
5. Quae dat in - fán - ti re - so - ná - re lau - dem In - te - gram;
rit.
1. dul - ci me - mo - rá - re sa - cras Cár - mi - ne lau - des.
2. coe - lis si - mul in - tu - én - tes Nú - mi - nis o - ra.
3. pu - gnans, á - ni - mas re - quí - ris, In - cly - tus he - ros. A - men.
4. cun - cti mé - ri - tis po - ten - tem: O - mni - bus ad - sis.
5. lin - guae fa - te - án - tur o - mnes Cun - cta re - gén - tem.
rit.

HIBERNIA'S PATRON SAINT, ALL HAIL

B. S.

119

1. Hi - ber - nia's Pa - tron Saint, all hail! With
2. Im - pelled by ap - os - tol - ic zeal Thou
3. When faith's bright camp the_ de - mons fled The
4. To_ God who sent thee to our isle Be
1. fade - less_ glo - ry_ crown'd; Thy chil-dren spread through
2. cam'st to_ E - rin's_ land; God's love for man thou_
3. path to_ heav'n was_ cleared; Re - li - gion raised her_
4. end less glo - ry_ giv'n! Oh!_ may He ev - er_
1. man - y lands This day thy prais - es sound.
2. didst re - veal And Sa - tan's hosts dis - band.
3. beau-teous head, An isle of saints ap - peared.
4. on it smile, And lead its sons to heav'n.
O Saint Pa - trick,
we pro - claim Thy heav'n - ly glo - ry far and wide.
Grant that, shielded by thy name, We may at last with thee a - bide.

FAITH OF OUR FATHERS

F. S. C.

120

1. Faith of our fa - thers! liv - ing still In spite of
2. Our fa - thers chained in pris-ons dark, Were still in
3. Faith of our fa - thers! Ma - ry's pray'rs Shall keep our
4. Faith of our fa - thers! days of old With - in our
1. dun - geon fire and sword; Oh how our hearts beat high with
2. heart and con-science free; How sweet would be their chil - dren's
3. coun - try fast to thee; And through the truth that comes from
4. hearts speak gal - lant ly; For a - ges thou hast stood by
1. joy When - e'er we hear that glo - rious word!
2. fate, If they, like them, could die for Thee.
3. God, Oh we shall pros - per and be free.
4. us, Dear Faith, and now we'll stand by thee.
CHORUS
Faith of our
fa - thers! Ho - ly Faith! We'll be true to thee till death, Faith of our
fa - thers! Ho - ly Faith! We'll be true to thee till death.

HAIL GLORIOUS SAINT PATRICK

At a moderate pace
Hemy
121
1. Hail, glo-rious Saint Pat-rick! dear saint of our
2. Hail, glo-rious Saint Pat-rick! thy words were once
3. In the war a - gainst sin, in the fight for the
4. Thy peo-ple, now ex-iles on ma - ny a
1. Isle! To us, thy poor chil-dren, be gra-cious the
2. strong A - gainst Sa - tan's wiles and a her - e - tic
3. faith, Dear saint, may thy chil-dren re - sist to the
4. shore, Shall love and re - vere thee till time be no
1. while, We pray to thee high in the man-sions a -
2. throng; Not less in thy might where in heav-en thou
3. death; Their strength be in meek-ness, in pen-ance, and
4. more; The fire thou hast kin - dled shall ev - er burn
1. bove, On E - rin's green val-leys to look down in love.
2. art; Oh, come to our aid, in our bat - tle take part.
3. prayer; Their ban - ner the cross which they glo - ry to bear.
4. bright, Its warmth un-di - min-ish'd, un - dy - ing its light.

SAINT AGNES

O HOLY MARTYR

Ph. Rohr

122

1. O ho - ly mar - tyr, spot - less dove, With joy we cel - e -
2. Thy cru - el suff-'rings all are past, A crown of glo - ry
3. Oh, pray that we may ev - er seek To be as free as
1. brate thy day; Thou dwell - est now in Heav'n a - bove, Where
2. decks thy brow, Ce les - tial light is round thee cast, And
3. thou from stain; As con - stant, fer - vent, pure and meek, Re -
CHORUS
1. ty - rants o'er thee have no sway.
2. God is thine for - ev - er now. Saint Ag - nes, let thy
3. gard - less of earth's fleet - ing pain.
plead - ing voice, For us at mer - cy's throne be heard, — Saint
Ag - nes, let thy plead - ing voice For us at mer - cy's throne be heard.

DEAREST SAINT

Jacobsen

123

1. Dear - est Saint, in praise un - end - ing,
2. For the Christ Child, who once sought thee,
3. Ah, while earth is still my dwell - ing,
1. Let me thank thee for thy care. At thy feet thy
2. In thy lov - ing arms Who lay, So much of His
3. Ev - 'ry day be thou my friend, Fill my soul with
1. love be - friend - ing, Dare I hope the Lord will spare?
2. Heart has taught thee, That He can - not say thee nay.
3. peace, fore - tell - ing Per - fect bliss that hath no end.

SAINT CECILIA

LET THE DEEP ORGAN SWELL THE LAY

Bro. Bonitus

124

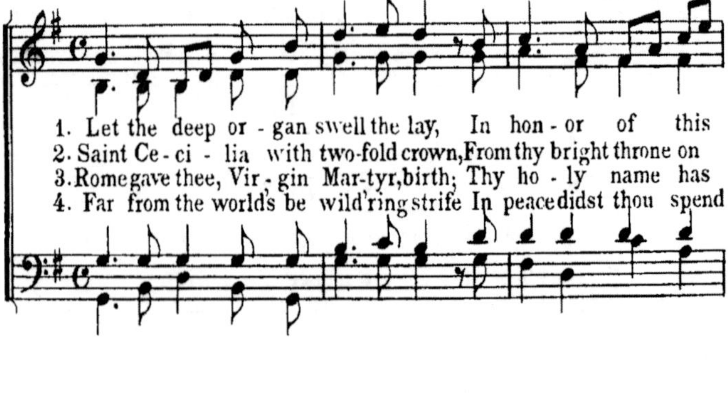
1. Let the deep or - gan swell the lay, In hon - or of this
2. Saint Ce - ci - lia with two-fold crown, From thy bright throne on
3. Rome gave thee, Vir - gin Mar-tyr, birth; Thy ho - ly name has
4. Far from the world's be wild'ring strife In peace didst thou spend

1. fes - tive day; Let the har - mo - nious choirs pro-claim Ce -
2. us look down; See all thy lov - ing cli - ents' care, And
3. filled the earth; And from the ver - y dawn of youth, Thou
4. all thy life, Teach - ing the or - gan to com - bine With
CHORUS
1. ci - lia's ev - er bless - ed name.
2. heark - en to their fer - vent pray'r.
3. gav'st thy heart to God and truth.
4. voice to praise the Lamb di - vine.
Let the har - mo - nious
choirs pro - claim Ce - ci - lia's ev - er bless - ed name,—
f
Let the har-mo-nious choirs pro-claim Ce-ci-lia's ev-er bless-ed name.

PRAY FOR THE DEAD

125

At a moderate pace
CHORUS
Pray for the dead at noon and eve, Lift up to God thy fond re - quest, Im-plore His goodness to re - lieve The suff'ring souls and grant them rest.
Fine
1. Pray for the dead! though sav - ed they Yet while the pen - al - ties re - main, Must suff - 'ring purge the debt a - way, And pen - ance cleanse their sin - ful stain.
2. Pray for the dead! thy pray'rs though weak, May yet be heard and bring them ease, For God will hear thy sighs if meek, Thy tears, if of - fered up for peace.
3. Pray for the dead! in ho - ly trust, Pray that their stains may be for - giv'n. Pray thou may'st leave thy bod - y's dust To en ter pure at once in heav'n.

HOLY GOD WE PRAISE THY NAME

P. Ritter

126

1. Ho - ly God, we praise thy name, Lord of all we
2. Hark! the loud ce - les - tial hymn An - gel choirs a -
3. Lo! the ap - os - tol - ic train Join Thy sa - cred
4. Ho - ly Fa - ther, Ho - ly Son, Ho - ly Spir - it,
1. bow be - fore Thee; All on earth Thy scep - tre claim,
2. bove are rais - ing; Cher - u - bim and Ser - a - phim,
3. name to hal - low; Pro - phets swell the loud re - frain,
4. Three we name Thee; While in es - sence on - ly one
1. All in heav'n a bove a - dore Thee; In - fi - nite Thy
2. In un - ceas - ing cho - rus prais - ing, Fill the heav'ns with
3. And with white - rob'd mar - tyrs fol - low; And from morn till
4. Un - di - vi - ded God, we claim Thee; And a - dor - ing
1. vast do - main, Ev - er - last - ing is Thy reign.
2. sweet ac - cord: Ho - ly, ho - ly, ho - ly Lord!
3. set of sun, Through the Church the song doth run.
4. bend the knee, While we own the mys - ter - y.

THE EARTH, O LORD, REJOICES

127

With spirit

f
1. The earth, O Lord, re - joic - es, And sings with glad ac-
2. Our ev - 'ry thought and ac - tion We of - fer up to
3. It pleased Thee, Lord, to make us That we may serve Thee
1. claim, A hymn of ma - ny voic - es In hon - or of Thy
2. Thee; From fol - ly and dis - trac - tion, We beg Thee keep us
3. here; Let not Thy grace for - sake us, But keep us in Thy
1. name. We join the hap - py cho - rus That hails the morn - ing
2. free. Let no pro - fane ex - am - ple, No cen - sure, no ap-
3. fear. Pre - serve our life, O Fa - ther, That we may serve Thee
1. light, And bless the Lord that o'er us Kept lov - ing watch all night.
2. plause, Lead us this day to tram - ple, O Lord, up - on Thy laws.
3. still, But let us lose it rath - er Than dis - o - bey Thy will.

OH COME, SWEET ANTHEMS LET US SING

Haydn

128

1. Oh come, sweet an - thems let us sing, Loud thanks to
2. In - to His pres - ence let us go, To crave His
3. The depths of earth are in His hand, Her se - cret
4. Oh let us to His courts re - pair, And bow with
1. our Al - might - y King; For we our voic - es high should
2. grace while here be - low; To Him ad - dress, in joy - ful
3. wealth at His com - mand; The strength of hills that reach the
4. ad - o - ra - tion there; Down on our knees de - vout - ly
CHORUS
1. raise, When our sal - va - tion's Rock we praise.
2. songs, The praise that to His name be - longs.
3. skies, Sub - ject - ed to His em - pire lies.
4. all, Be - fore the Lord, our Mak - er, fall.
Great is the
Lord! what tongue can frame An hon - or e - qual to His name?

DEAR CHILDREN, PRAISE THE LORD

Bro. Luke

129

1. Dear chil-dren,praise the Lord in all; Ear - ly and late, in
2. Praise Him for all His mer-cies giv'n In flow-ing streams,with
3. Praise Him,who in His Church hath sent Means to con-firm, re -
1. mirth and tears, Lift up your voice in earn - est call With
2. lav - ish hand; Who made you that your soul in heav'n Might
3. store, up - hold; Who stays your soul when it is faint, And
CHORUS
1. min - gled love and ho - ly fears.
2. ev - er in His pres - ence stand. Dear chil-dren,praise His
3. checks its course when o - ver bold.
ho - ly name, A - dore His pre - sence, fear His word; And

oh, in all, be this your aim, Still more and more to praise the Lord.

HEAR THY CHILDREN, GENTLE JESUS

German Melody

130

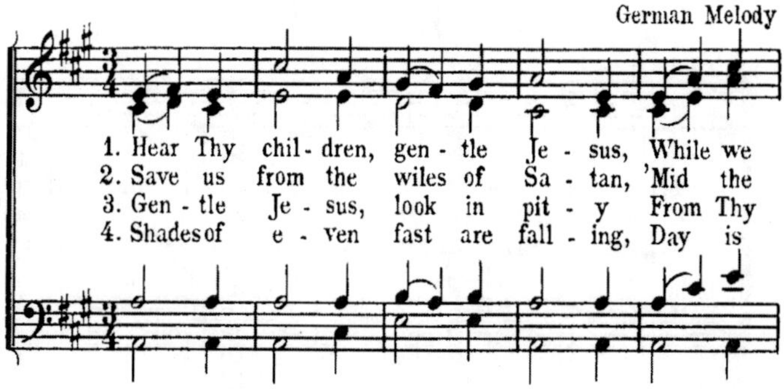
1. Hear Thy chil - dren, gen - tle Je - sus, While we
2. Save us from the wiles of Sa - tan, 'Mid the
3. Gen - tle Je - sus, look in pit - y From Thy
4. Shades of e - ven fast are fall - ing, Day is

1. breathe our ev' - ning pray'r; Save us from all
2. dark and dang - 'rous night; Sweet - ly may our
3. glo - rious throne a - bove; All the night Thy
4. fad - ing in - to gloom: When the shades of

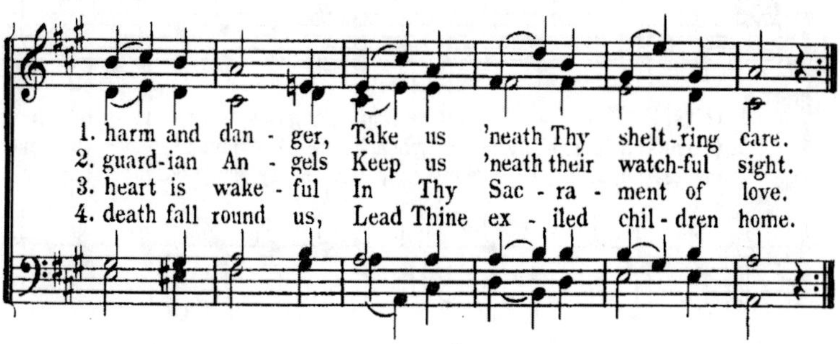
1. harm and dan - ger, Take us 'neath Thy shelt - 'ring care.
2. guard - ian An - gels Keep us 'neath their watch - ful sight.
3. heart is wake - ful In Thy Sac - ra - ment of love.
4. death fall round us, Lead Thine ex - iled chil - dren home.

ACTS OF THE THEOLOGICAL VIRTUES

131

f
1. Great God! what-ev - er through Thy Church Thou teachest to be
2. My God! I firm-ly hope in Thee, For Thou art great and
3. With all my heart and soul and strength, I love Thee, O my
1. true, I firm-ly do be - lieve it all And will con-fess it
2. good, And gav-est us Thine on - ly Son, To die up-on the
3. Lord, For Thou art per-fect, and all things Were made by Thy blest
p
1. too. Thou nev-er canst de-ceiv-ed be, Thou nev-er canst de -
2. Rood. I hope through Him for grace to live As Thy com-mand-ments
3. word. My neigh-bor to Thine im - age Thou, Like me, wast pleased to
1. ceive; For Thou art Truth it-self, and Thou Dost tell me to be - lieve.
2. teach; And through Thy mer-cy, when I die, The joys of Heav'n to reach.
3. make; And, as I love my-self, I love My neigh-bor for Thy sake.

JERUSALEM THE GOLDEN

At a moderate pace — Haller

132

1. Je - ru - sa - lem the gold - en! With milk and hon - ey
2. They stand, those halls of Si - on, All ju - bi - lant with
3. There is the throne of Da - vid, And bliss with-out al -
1. blest, Be - neath thy con - tem - pla - tion, Sink heart and voice op -
2. songs, And bright with ma - ny an an - gel And all the mar - tyr
3. loy, The shout of them that tri - umph, The song of fes - tal
CHORUS
1. pressed. I know not, Oh, I know not, What joys a - wait us
2. throngs. The Prince is ev - er in them, His light is al - ways
3. joy. And they who with their Lead - er Have con-quer'd in the
1. there; What ra-dian-cy of glo - ry, What bliss be-yond com - pare.
2. seen; The past-ures of the bless-ed Are deck'd in glo-rious sheen.
3. fight, For - ev - er and for - ev - er Are clad in robes of white.

JERUSALEM, MY HAPPY HOME

Mother Seton

133

1. Je - ru - sa - lem, my hap - py home, How do I sigh for
2. From ev - 'ry eye God wipes the tear, All sighs and sor - row
3. The thought of thee to us is giv'n, Our sor - rows to be -
1. thee! When shall my ex - ile have an end, Thy joys when shall I see?
2. cease; No more al - ter - nate hope and fear, But ev - er - last ing peace.
3. guile; To taste on earth the bliss of Heav'n In God's e - ter - nal smile.
CHORUS
rit
a tempo
Je - ru - sa - lem, Je - ru - sa - lem, Je - ru - sa -
lem, my hap - py home, How do I sigh for thee!

THE LORD HIMSELF THE MIGHTY GOD

F. S.C.

134

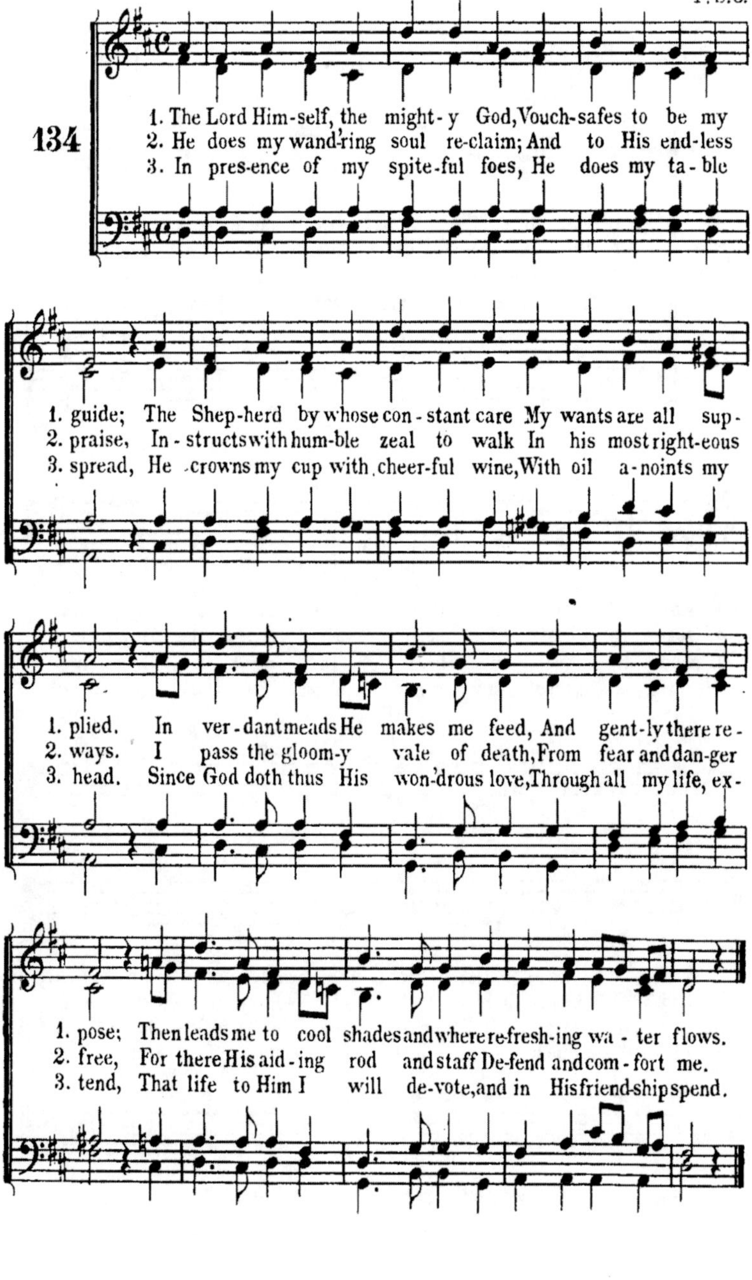
1. The Lord Him-self, the might-y God, Vouch-safes to be my
2. He does my wand'ring soul re-claim; And to His end-less
3. In pres-ence of my spite-ful foes, He does my ta-ble
1. guide; The Shep-herd by whose con-stant care My wants are all sup-
2. praise, In-structs with hum-ble zeal to walk In his most right-eous
3. spread, He crowns my cup with cheer-ful wine, With oil a-noints my
1. plied. In ver-dant meads He makes me feed, And gent-ly there re-
2. ways. I pass the gloom-y vale of death, From fear and dan-ger
3. head. Since God doth thus His won'drous love, Through all my life, ex-
1. pose; Then leads me to cool shades and where re-fresh-ing wa-ter flows.
2. free, For there His aid-ing rod and staff De-fend and com-fort me.
3. tend, That life to Him I will de-vote, and in His friend-ship spend.

LONG LIVE THE POPE

Words by
Rev. HUGH T. HENRY *Litt. D.*

Music by
H. G. GANSS

135

With dignity
1. Long live the Pope! His prais - es sound A- gain and yet a - gain: His rule is o - ver space and time; His throne the hearts of men: All
2. Be - lea - guered by the foes of earth, Be- set by hosts of hell, He guards the loy - al flock of Christ, A watch - ful sen - ti - nel: And
3. His sig - net is the Fish er - man's; No scep - tre does he bear; In meek and low - ly maj - es - ty He rules from Pe - ter's Chair: And
4. Then raise the chant, with heart and voice, In church and school and home: "Long live the Shep - herd of the Flock! Long live the Pope of Rome!" Al

By permission of J. Fischer & Bro.

1. hail, the Shep-herd-King of Rome, The theme of lov-ing
2. yet, a-mid the din and strife, The clash of mace and
3. yet from ev-'ry tribe and tongue, From ev-'ry clime and
4. might-y Fa-ther, bless his work, Pro-tect him in his
1. song: Let all the earth his glo-ry sing, And
2. sword, He bears a-lone the shep-herd staff, This
3. zone, Three hun-dred mill-ion voic-es sing, The
4. ways, Re-ceive his pray'rs ful-fil his hopes, And
rit. a tempo
1. heav'n the strain pro-long. Let all the earth his
2. cham-pion of the Lord. He bears a-lone the
3. glo-ry of his throne. Three hun-dred mill-ion
4. grant him "length of days!" Re-ceive his pray'rs ful
rit. a tempo
1. glo-ry sing, And heav'n the strain pro-long.
2. shep-herd staff, This cham-pion of the Lord.
3. voic-es sing, The glo-ry of his throne.
4. fil his hopes, And grant him "length of days."

BLEST IS THE FAITH

136

1. Blest is the Faith, di - vine and strong, Of thanks and praise, an end-less
2. Blest is the Hope that holds to God, In doubt and dark-ness still un-
3. Blest is the Love that can - not love Aught that earth gives of best and
1. fount-ain; Whose life is one per-pet - ual song, High up the
2. shak - en; And sings a - long the heav'n-ly road, Sweet-est when
3. bright-est; Whose rap-tures thrill like saints' a - bove, Most when its
CHORUS
1. Sav-ior's ho - ly moun - tain.
2. most it seems for sak - en. Oh, Si-on's songs are sweet to sing, With
3. earth-ly gifts are light - est.
mel - o-dies of glad-ness la-den; Hark! how the harps of an-gels ring:
Hail, Son of Man! Hail, Mother Maiden! Hail, Son of Man! Hail, Mother Maid - en!

AT THE RECEPTION OF A BISHOP

137

Sa - cér - dos et Pón - ti - fex
et vir - tú - tum Ó - pi - fex, Pa - stor bo - ne in pó - pu - lo,
sic pla - cu - í - sti Dó - mi - no. Al - le - lú - ia.

℣. Protéctor noster ádspice, Deus. ℟. Et réspice in fáciem Christi tui.
℣. Salvum fac servum tuum. ℟. Deus meus sperántem in te.
℣. Mitte ei, Dómine, auxílium de sancto. ℟. Et de Sion tuére eum.
℣. Nihil profíciat inimícus in eo. ℟. Et fílius iniquitátis non appónat nocére ei.
℣. Dómine exáudi oratiónem meam. ℟. Et clamor meus ad te véniat.
℣. Dóminus vobíscum. ℟. Et cum spíritu tuo.

ASPERGES ME

138

M.M. ♩ = 132
A - spér - ges me,* Dó - mi - ne, hys - só - po, et mun - dá - bor:
La - vá - bis me, et su - per ni - vem de - al - bá - bor.
(Ps. 50)
Mi - se - ré - re me - i, De - us, * se - cun - dum ma - gnam mi - se - ri -
cór - di - am tu - am. Gló - ri - a Pa - tri, et Fí - li - o,
et Spi - rí - tu - i San - cto: * Sic - ut e - rat in prin - cí - pi - o,
et nunc et sem - per, et in saé - cu - la sae - cu - ló - rum. A - men.

MASS

VIDI AQUAM

139

M. M. ♪ = 132
Vi - di a - quam* e - gre - di - én - tem de tem-
- plo, a lá - te - re dex - tro,
al - le - lú - ia: et o - mnes, ad quos
per - vé - nit a - qua i - sta
sal - vi fa - cti sunt, et di - cent, al - le-

lú - ia, al - le- - - lú - ia.
(Ps. 117)
Con-fi - té - mi-ni Dó-mi-no quó-ni - am bo - nus: * quó - ni - am in saé-cu -
lum mi-se-ri-cór - di - a e - jus. Gló-ri - a Pa-tri, et Fí - li - o,
et Spi - rí - tu - i San-cto. * Sic - ut e - rat in prin-cí - pi - o,
et nunc, et sem-per, et in saé-cu-la sae-cu - ló - rum. A - men.

MASS OF THE ANGELS

KYRIE

According to the Vatican Version

140

M.M. ♪ = 138
Ký-ri - e * e - lé-i-son, iij.
Chri-ste e- - lé - i - son, iij.
Ký-ri-e e- - lé - i - son. ij.
Ký-ri-e * **e - lé-i-son.

GLORIA

141

Et in ter - ra pax ho - mí - ni - bus bo - nae vo - lun - tá - tis.
Lau - dá - mus te. Be-ne - dí - ci - mus te. Ad - o - rá - mus te.
Glo - ri - fi - cá - mus te. Grá - ti - as á - gi - mus ti - bi
pro - pter ma - gnam gló - ri - am tu - am. Dó - mi - ne De -
us, Rex coe - lés - tis, De - us Pa - ter o - mní - po - tens.

Dó-mi-ne Fi-li u-ni-gé-ni-te, Je-su Chri-ste.
Dó-mi-ne De-us, A-gnus De-i, Fí-li-us Pa-tris.
Qui tol-lis pec-cá-ta mun-di, mi-se-ré-re no-bis.
Qui tol-lis pec-cá-ta mun-di, sús-ci-pe de-pre-ca-ti-ó-nem no-stram.
Qui se-des ad déx-te-ram Pa-tris, mi-se-ré-re no-bis.

Quó - ni - am tu so - lus san - ctus. Tu so - lus Dó - mi - nus.
Tu so-lus al - tís-si si - mus, Je - su Chri - ste, Cum San - cto Spí - ri - tu,
in gló - ri - a De - i Pa - tris. A - - - men.
Ped.

142 CREDO

Pa - trem o - mni - po - tén - tem, fa - ctó - rem coe - li et ter - rae,
vi - si - bí - li - um ó - mni - um, et in - vi - si - bí - li - um.

Et in u-num Dó-mi-num Je-sum Chri-stum, Fí-li-um De-i u-ni-gé-ni-tum.
Et ex Pa-tre na - tum an-te ó-mni-a saé - cu-la.
De-um de De-o, lu-men de lú-mi-ne, De-um ve-rum de De-o ve-ro.
Gé-ni-tum, non fa - ctum, con-sub-stan-ti-á-lem Pa-tri: per quem ómni-a fa-cta sunt.
Qui pro-pter nos hó-mi-nes et pro-pter no-stram sa-lú-tem de-scén-dit de coe-lis.

Et in-car-ná-tus est de Spí - ri - tu San-cto ex Ma-rí - a Vír - gi - ne:
Et ho-mo fa-ctus est. Cru - ci - fí - xus é - ti - am pro no - bis:
sub Pón - ti - o Pi - lá - to pas - sus et se - púl - tus est.
Et re - sur - ré - xit tér - ti - a di - e se - cún-dum Scri - ptú - ras.
Et as - cén - dit in coe - lum: se-det ad déx - te - ram Pa - tris.

Et í - te-rum ven-tú-rus est cum gló-ri - a ju-di-cá-re vi-vos et
mór-tu-os: cu-jus re-gni non e-rit fi-nis. Et in Spí-ri-tum San-ctum,
Dó-mi-num, et vi-vi-fi-cán-tum: qui ex Pa-tre Fi-li-ó-que pro-cé-dit.
Qui cum Pa-tre et Fí-li-o si-mul ad-o-rá-tur
et con-glo-ri-fi-cá-tur: qui lo-cú-tus est per Pro-phé-tas.

Et u - nam san - ctam ca - thó - li - cam et a - po - stó - li -
cam Ec - clé - si - am. Con - fí - te - or u - num ba - ptís - ma
in re - mis - si - ó - nem pec - ca - tó - rum. Et ex - spé - cto re -
sur - re - cti - ó - nem mor - tu - ó - rum. Et vi - tam ven -
tú - ri saé - cu - li. A - - - - - men.

SANCTUS

143

Sán- ctus,* Sán-ctus, San- -ctus
Dó - mi-nus Dé-us Sá- - ba-oth.
Ple-ni sunt coe- li et ter - ra gló-ri-a tu- a
Ho-sán-na in ex-cél - sis. Be-ne-dí - ctus qui ve - nit
in nó-mi-ne Dó-mi-ni. Ho-sán-na in ex-cél- - sis.

AGNUS DEI

144

A - gnus De - i,* qui tol - lis pec-cá - ta mun - di:
mi-se - ré-re no - bis. A-gnus De - i* qui tol - lis pec-cá-
ta mun - di: mi-se - ré-re no - bis. A - gnus De -
i* qui tol - lis pec-cá-ta mun - di: do-na no-bis pa - cem.

DEO GRATIAS

De - o grá-ti - as.

MASS IN HONOR OF SAINT LA SALLE

KYRIE

W.A.R.

145

f
Ký-ri-e e - lé-i-son.
Fine
Ký-ri-e e - lé-i-son. Ký-ri-e e - lé - i - son.
Fine
Chri-ste e - lé - i-son.

By permission of W. A. Raboch.

For two voices, use first staff.
For four voices, use second and third staves.

f
Chrí-ste e - lé - i - son. Chrí - ste e - lé - i - son.
D.C.
f

GLORIA

146 Briskly

p
Et in ter - ra pax ho - mí - ni - bus bo - nae vo - lun -
f
tá - tis. Lau - dá - mus te, Be - ne - dí - ci - mus te. Ad - o -
f
rá - mus te. Glo - ri - fi - cá - mus te. Grá - ti - as á - gi - mus

ti - bi pro-pter ma-gnam gló-ri-am tu - am. Dó-mi-ne De-us,
Rex coe-lé-stis, De-us Pa-ter o - mní - po-tens. Dó-mi-ne, Fi - li
u - ni-gé-ni-te, Je - su Chri-ste. Dó-mi-ne De-us, A - gnus De-i,
Fí - li-us Pa - tris.

p
Qui tol - lis pec-cá - ta mun - di, mi - se-ré - re no - bis. Qui
p
tol - lis pec-cá - ta mun - di, sús - ci - pe de-pre-ca - ti -
mf
ó - nem no - stram. Qui se-des ad déx-te-ram Pa - tris,
mf
pp
mi - se-ré-re no - bis.
pp

Tempo I.
Quó - ni - am tu so - lus san - ctus. Tu so - lus
Dó - mi - nus, Tu so - lus al - tís - si - mus,
Je - su Chri - ste. Cum San - cto Spí - ri -
tu in gló - ria De - i Pa - tris. A - men.

147

CREDO

f
Pa - trem o - mni - po - tén - tem, fa - ctó - rem coe - li et ter - rae, vi - si -
bí - li - um ó - mni - um et in - vi - si - bí - li - um. Et in u - num
Dó - mi - num Je - sum Chri - stum, Fí - li - um De - i u - ni - gé - ni -
tum. Et ex Pa - tre na - tum an - te ó - mni - a saé - cu - la.

ff
De - um de De - o, lu - men de lú - mi - ne, De-um ve - rum de
ff
mf
De-o ve-ro, Gé-ni-tum, non fa-ctum, Con-substan-ti - á - lem Pa-tri:
mf
Unison
cres - - cen -
per quem ó-mni-a fa - cta sunt. Qui pro-pter nos hó-mi-nes, et
Voices Unison
cres - - cen -
- do
ff Harmony
pro-pter no-stram sa - lú - tem de-scén-dit de coe - lis.
Harmony
- do
ff

Slowly
pp
poco
cres-
Et in-car-ná-tus est de Spí-ri-tu
Slowly
pp
-cen-
-do
San-cto ex Ma-rí-a Vír-gi-ne: Et ho-mo fa-ctus est.
mf
Cru-ci-fí-xus. é-ti-am pro no-bis: sub Pon-ti-o Pi-
lá-to pas-sus, et se-púl-tus est.

f
Et re-sur - ré - xit tér - ti - a di - e, se - cún - dum Scri-
f
ptú - ras. Et a - scén - dit in
coe - lum: se - det ad déx - te - ram Pa - tris. Et
í - te - rum ven - tú - rus est cum gló - ria ju - di - cá - re

ff
vi - vos et mór - tu - os: cu - jus
re - gni non e - rit fi - nis. Et in Spí - ri - tum
San - ctum, Dó-mi-num, et vi - vi - fi - cán - tem:
qui ex Pa - tre Fí - li - ó - que pro - cé - dit.

Unison
cres - - - -
Qui cum Pa - tre et Fí - li - o si - mul ad - o -
Voices Unison
cres- - - -
cen- - - do
rá - tur, et con - glo - ri - fi - cá - tur: qui lo - cú - tus
cen- - - do
Harmony
ff
f
est per Pro - phé - tas. Et u - nam san - ctam Ca -
ff
thó - li - cam et a - po - stó - li - cam Ec - clé - si - am. Con - fí - te - or

u - num ba - ptí - sma in re - mis - si - ó - nem pec - ca -
tó - rum. Et ex - spé - cto re - sur - re - cti -
grave
ó - nem mor - tu - ó - rum. Et vi - tam ven -
a tempo
pesante
tú - ri saé - cu - li. A - men.

148 SANCTUS

With dignity
Sanctus, Sanctus, Sanctus Dómi-nus De-us Sába-oth.
Pleni sunt coeli et terra glória tu-a. Hosánna in excelsis.

149 BENEDICTUS

Rather slowly
Be-ne-díctus qui venit in nómi-ne
Dómi-ni. Hosánna in excélsis.

AGNUS DEI

150

p
A - gnus De-i, qui tol-lis pec-cá-ta mun-di: mi-se-ré-re no -
p
bis.
mf
A - gnus De-i qui tol-lis pec-cá-ta mun-di:
mf
mi - se-ré-re no - bis.
p
A - gnus
p
De-i qui tol - lis pec-cá - ta mun-di: do-na no-bis pa - cem.
p
pp
p
pp

MASS FOR THE DEAD

INTROIT

Arranged by P. J. Jos. Vranken

VI
M.M. ♪ = 132
151
Ré - qui - em* ae - tér - - nam
dó - na é - is Dó - mi - - ne:
et lux per - pé - tu - a lú - ce - at é - is.
Ps. Te dé - cet hý - mnus Dé - us in Si - on,
et tí - bi red - dé - tur vó - tum in Je - rú - sa - lem:*
ex - áu - di o - ra - ti - ó - nem mé - am, ad te ó - mnis cá - ro vé - ni - et.

Repeat Requiem aeternam *to the Psalm*

By permission of J. Fischer & Bro.
A simplifed organ accompaniment is published by J. Fischer & Bro. New York

152

VI M.M. ♪ = 132

KYRIE

Ký - ri - e ___ * e - - - lé - i - son. *III.*
Chri - - ste ___ e - - - lé - i - son. *III.*
Ký - ri - e ___ e - - - lé - i - son. *II.*
Ký - ri - e ___ e - lé - i - son.

GRADUAL

II M.M. ♪ = 152

153

Ré - qui-em* ae-tér - - - nam do - na_
é - is ___ Dó - mi - ne: ___
et lux per-pé - - - - tu-a ___
lú - - ce-at é - is. ___
℣. In me-mó-ri-a ae-tér -
- - - na_

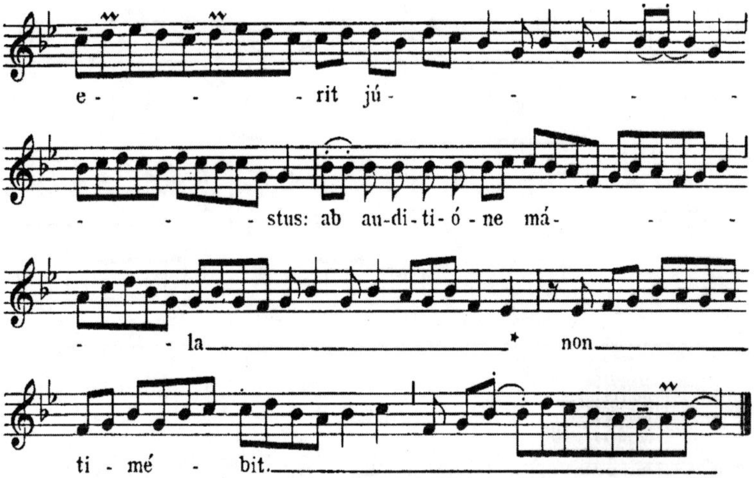
e - - - rit jú - - - -
- - - stus: ab au-di-ti-ó-ne má- - -
- - la * non
ti - mé - bit.

TRACT

VIII M.M. ♪ = 152

154

Ab-sól - ve, * Dó - mi-ne, á - ni-mas
ó-mni-um fi-dé - li-um de-fun-ctó - rum
ab ó - mni vín - cu-lo de-li - ctó - rum.
V. Et grá - ti - a tú - a íl - lis suc-cur - rén - - -
te, me-re-án - tur e - vá - de-re
ju-dí - ci-um ul - ti - ó - nis.

V. Et lú - cis ae - tér- - nae
be-a - ti - tú - di - ne* pér - fru - i.

SEQUENCE

I

155

M.M. ♪ = 160
Dí - es í - rae, di - es íl - la, Sól - vet saé - clum in fa - víl - la:
Tés - te Dá - vid cum Si - býl - la.
Quán - tus tré - mor est fu - tú - rus,
Quán - do jú - dex est ven - tú - rus, Cún - cta strí - cte dis - cus - sú - rus!
Tú - ba mi - rum spár - gens só - num Per se - púl - cra
re - gi - ó - num, Có - get ó - mnes an - te thró - num.
Mors stu - pé - bit et na - tú - ra, Cum re - súr - get
cre - a - tú - ra, Ju - di - cán - ti re - spon - sú - ra.

Li - ber scri - ptus pro - fe - ré - tur, In quo tó - tum
con - ti - né - tur, Un - de mún - dus ju - di - cé - tur.
Jú - dex ér - go cum se - dé - bit, Quíd - quid lá - tet
ap - pa - ré - bit: Nil in - úl - tum re - ma - né - bit.
Quid sum mí - ser tunc di - ctú - rus? Quem pa - tró - num ro - ga - tú - rus
Cum vix jú - stus sit se - cú - rus? Rex tre - mén - dae ma - je - stá - tis,
Qui sal - ván - dos sál - vas grá - tis, Sál - ve me, fons pi - e - tá - tis.
Re - cor - dá - re Je - su pí - e, Quod sum cáu - sa tú - ae ví - ae:
Ne me pér - das íl - la dí - e. Quáe - rens me, se - dí - sti lás - sus:
Red - e - mí - sti crú - cem pás - sus: Tán - tus lá - bor non sit cás - sus.

Jú-ste jú-dex ul - ti - ó - nis, Dó-num fac re-mis - si - ó - nis,
An-te dí - em ra - ti - ó - nis. In-ge - mí - sco, tám-quam ré - us:
Cúl-pa rú-bet vúl-tus mé-us: Sup-pli-cán - ti par - ce Dé-us.
Qui Ma-rí - am ab-sol - ví - sti, Et la - tró - nem ex - au - dí - sti,
Mí - hi quó - que spem de - dí - sti. Pré-ces mé-ae non sunt di-gnae:
Sed tu bó - nus fac be - ní - gne, Ne per - én - ni cré-mer í - gne.
In-ter ó - ves lo - cum praé - sta, Et ab hoé-dis me se-qués-tra, Stá-tu -
ens in par - te déx-tra. Con - fu - tá - tis ma - le - dí - ctis, Flám-mis á -
cri-bus ad-dí-ctis: Vó - ca me cum be-ne-dí-ctis. O - ro súp-plex et ac-cli -
nis, Cor con-trí - tum quá - si cí - nis: Gé-re cú - ram mé - i fí - nis.

La-cri-mó - sa dí-es íl-la, Qua re-súr-get ex fa-víl-la
Ju-di-cán-dus hó - mo ré-us: Hú-ic ér-go pár - ce Dé-us.
Pí-e Jé-su Dó-mi-ne, dó-na é - is ré-qui-em. A - men.

OFFERTORY

II M.M. ♪=144

156

Dó-mi - ne Jé - su Chrí - ste, * Rex
gló- - - ri - ae, lí - be - ra á - ni-mas
ó - mni - um fi - dé - li - um de - fun - ctó - rum
de poé - nis in - fér - ni et de pro-fún - do lá - cu:
lí - be - ra é - as de ó - re le - ó - nis,
ne ab - sór - be - at é - as tár - ta - rus,
ne cá - dant in ob - scú- - - rum:

sed sí - gni - fer sán - ctus Mí - cha - el
re-prae - sén - tet é- - as in lú-
cem sán - ctam: * Quam ó - lim A - bra - hae
pro - mi - sí - sti, et sé- - -
- - - - mi - ni é- - jus.
V. Hó-sti - as et pré - ces tí - bi, Dó - mi - - ne,
láu - dis of - fé - ri - mus: tu sús - ci - pe
pro a - ni - má - bus íl - lis, quá - rum hó - di - e
me - mó - ri - am fá - ci - mus: fac é - as, Dó - mi - ne,
de mór - te trans - í - re ad ví - tam.

* Quam ó - lim A - bra - hae pro - mi - sí - sti,
et sé - - - mi - ni é - jus.

SANCTUS

157

M.M. ♪ = 138
Sán - ctus, * Sán - ctus, Sán-ctus Dó-mi-nus Dé-us Sá-ba-oth.
Plé-ni sunt cóe-li et tér-ra glo-ri-a tú-a. Ho-sán-na in ex-cel-sis.
Be-ne-dí-ctus qui vé-nit in nó-mi-ne Dó-mi-ni. Ho-sán-na in ex-cél-sis.

AGNUS DEI

158

A - gnus Dé - i, * qui tól - lis pec - cá - ta mún - di:
dó - na é - is ré - qui - em. A - gnus Dé - i, *
qui tól - lis pec - cá - ta mún - di: dó - na é - is ré - qui - em.
A - gnus Dé - i, * qui tól - lis pec - cá - ta mún - di:
dó - na é - is ré - qui - em ** sem - pi - tér - nam.

COMMUNION

VIII.

159
Lux ae - tér - na* lú-ce-at é - is, Dó-mi - ne: *Cum san-ctis tú - is
in ae-tér-num, quí - a pi - us es. V. Ré - qui - em ae-tér - nam
dó - na é - is Dó-mi - ne, et lux per - pé - tu - a lú - ce - at é - is. *
Cum sán-ctis tú - is in ae - tér - num, quí - a pí - us es.

RESPONSORY

I.

M.M. ♪=144
160
Lí - be - ra me, Dó - - mi - ne,* de
mór - te ae - tér - - na, in dí - e íl - la
tre - mén - - da: * *Quán-do coé - li
mo - vén-di sunt et tér - ra: † Dum vé -
- - ne - ris ju - di - cá - re
saé - cu - lum per i - - gnem.

V. Tré-mens fá-ctus sum é - go, et tí - me - o,
dum dis-cús-si-o vé-ne - rit, át - que ven-tú - ra í - ra.
* Quán-do cóe - li mo - vén-di sunt et tér - ra.
V. Dí - es íl - la, dí - es í - rae, ca - la - mi - tá -
tis et mi - sé - ri - ae, dí - es má - gna
et a - má - ra vál - de. † Dum vé -
- ne - ris ju-di - cá - re
sáe - cu - lum per í - gnem.
V. Ré-qui - em ae - tér - nam dó - na é - is Dó - mi - ne:
et lux per - pé - tu - a lú - ce - at é - is.

Repeat Libera me *to* V. Tremens

1st Chorus
2nd Chorus
Ký-ri-e e-lé-i-son.
Chri-ste e-lé-i-son.
Jointly
Celebrant
Ký-ri-e e-lé-i-son.
Pa-ter no-ster....
V. Et ne nos in-dú-cas in ten-ta-ti-ó-nem. R. Sed lí-be-ra
nos a má-lo. V. A pór-ta ín-fe-ri. R. E-ru-e Dó-mi-ne
á-ni-mam é-jus. V. Re-qui-és-cat in pá-ce. R. A-men.
(á-ni-mas e-ó-rum.) (Re-qui-és-cant)
V. Dó-mi-ne ex-áu-di o-ra-ti-ó-nem mé-am.
R. Et clá-mor mé-us ad te vé-ni-at.
V. Dóminus vobíscum R. Et cum spíritu tú-o.
Oremus... R. Amen.
V. Réquiem aetérnam dóna ei Dómine. R. Et lux perpétua lúceat é-i.
(eis) (é-is.)
Chanters
Re-qui-és-cat in pá-ce. R. A-men.
(Re-qui-és-cant)

TONE OF THE PREFACE

161

Per ó-mni-a saé-cu-la sae-cu-ló-rum.
A-men.
Dó-mi-nus vo-bís-cum.
Et cum spí-ri-tu tú-o.
Súr-sum cor-da.
Ha-bé-mus ad Dó-mi-nun.
Grá-ti-as a-gá-mus Dó-mi-no Dé-o nó-stro.
Dí-gnum et jus-tum est.

162 AT THE PATER NOSTER

Et ne nos in-dú-cas in ten-ta-ti-ó-nem
Sed lí-be-ra nos a má-lo
Per ó-mni-a saé-cu-la sae-cu-ló-rum.
A-men.
Pax † Dó-mi-ni sit † sem-per vo-bis-† cum.
Et cum spí-ri-tu tú-o.

BENE-

163

Antiphon

E - go sum* re - sur - ré - cti - o et vi - ta:
et o - mnis qui vi - vit et cre - dit in me

1. Be-ne-dí - ctus Dóminus Deus Isra - - - el *
2. Et e - ré - xit, cornu salútis no - bis,*
3. Sic-ut lo - cútus est per os san - - - ctó - - rum,*
4. Sa-lú-tem ex inimícis no - stris,*
5. Ad fa-ci - éndam misericórdiam cum pátribus no - stris:*
6. Jus-ju-rán - dum, quod jurávit ad Abraham patrem no - strum,*
7. Ut si-ne timóre, de manu inimicórum nostrórum libe - rá - ti,*
8. In san-cti - táte et justítia coram i - pso,*
9. Et tu pu - er, prophéta Altíssimi vo - - - cá - be - ris:*
10. Ad dan-dam sciéntiam salútis plebi e - jus,*
11. Per ví-sce - ra misericórdiae Dei no - stri:*
12. Il - lu-mi - náre his qui in ténebris et in umbra mortis se - dent:*
13. Réqui-em ae - - - - tér - nam *
14. Et lux per - - - - pé - tu - a *

V. Kyrie eléison, etc., as on p. 178

DICTUS

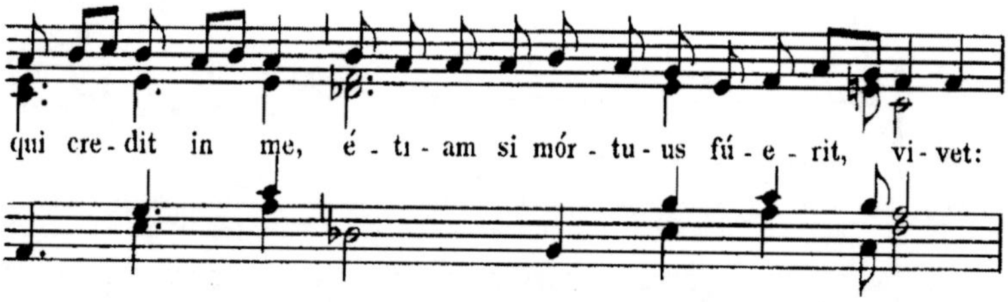
qui cre - dit in me, é - ti - am si mór - tu - us fú - e - rit, vi - vet:

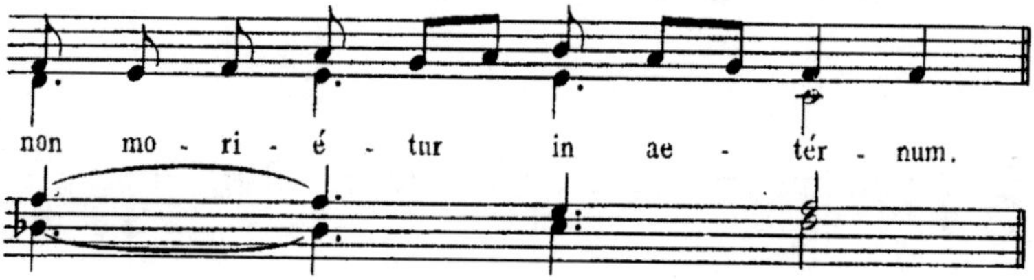
non mo - ri - é - tur in ae - tér - num.

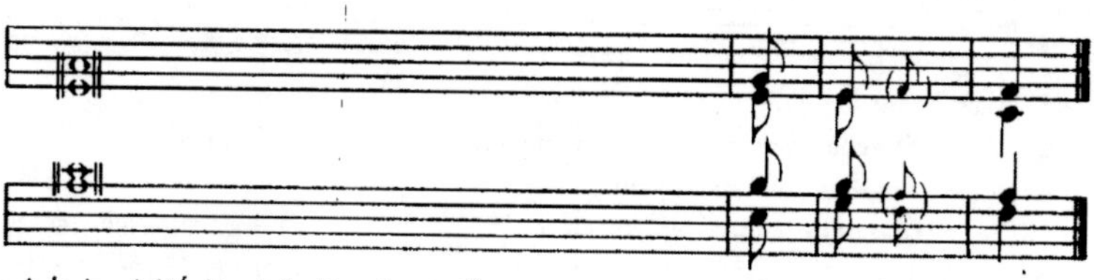

1. quia visitávit, et fecit redemptiónem ple - bis su - ae.
2. in domo David púe - - - - ri su - i:
3. qui a saéculo sunt, prophetá - - - rum e - jus:
4. et de manu ómnium qui o - dé - runt nos:
5. et memorári testaménti su - - - i - san - cti.
6. datúrum se no - bis:
7. serviá - - - - - mus il - li:
8. ómnibus dié - - - - bus - no - stris.
9. praeíbis enim ante fáciem Dómini paráre vi - as e - jus:
10. in remissiónem peccatórum e - ó - rum:
11. in quibus visitávit nos, oriens ex al - to:
12. ad dírigéndos pedes nostros in vi - - - am pa - cis.
13. dona e - - - - - is, Dó - mí - ne.
14. lúce - - - - - at e - is.

Repeat Antiphon, Ego sum

MISE-

Antiphon 1. *F*

164

1.	Mi-se - rére	me - i De - us,*
2.	Et secúndum multitúdinem miserati -	- ónum tu - á - rum;*
3.	Amplius lava me ab iniqui - -	- tá - te me - a:*
4.	Quóniam iniquitátem meam	e-go co-gnó - sco:*
5.	Tibi soli peccávi, et malum	coram te fe - ci:*
6.	Ecce enim in iniquitáti - - -	- bus con-cé-ptus sum:*
7.	Ecce enim veritátem	di - le - xí - sti:*
8.	Aspérges me hyssópo,	et mun-dá - bor:*
9.	Audítui meo dabis gaúdium	et lae-tí-ti - am:*
10.	Avérte fáciem tuam a pec - -	- cá - tis me - is:*
11.	Cor mundum crea	in me De - us:*
12.	Ne projícias me a	fá-ci-e tu - a:*
13.	Redde mihi laetítiam salu - -	- tá - ris tu - i:*
14.	Docébo iníquos	vi - as tu - as:*
15.	Líbera me de sanguínibus, Deus, Deus sa -	lú - tis me - ae:*
16.	Dómine, lábia	me-a a - pé-ri - es:*
17.	Quóniam si voluísses sacrifícium, de -	- dís - sem ú-ti que:*
18.	Sacrifícium Deo spíritus con - -	- tri - bu - lá - tus:*
19.	Benígne fac, Dómine, in bona voluntáte	tu - a Si - on:*
20.	Tunc acceptábis sacrifícium justítiae, oblatiónes et	ho - ló-caú - sta:*
21.	Réqui - - - - - -	- em ae-tér - nam:*
22.	Et	lux per-pé-tu - a.*

RERE

os sa hu - mi - li - á - ta

1. secúndum magnam misericór - - - di - am tu - am.
2. dele iniqui - - - - - - tá - tem me - am.
3. et a peccáto me - o mun-da me.
4. et peccátum meum contra me est sem - per.
5. ut justificéris in sermónibus tuis, et vincas cum ju - di - cá - ris.
6. et in peccátis concépit me ma - ter me - a.
7. incérta et occúlta sapiéntiae tuae manife - - stá - sti mi - hi.
8. lavábis me, et super nivem de - al - bá - bor.
9. et exsultábunt ossa hu - - - - - mi - li - á - ta.
10. et omnes iniquitátes me - as de - le.
11. et spíritum rectum ínnova in viscé - - - ri - bus me - is
12. et spíritum sanctum tuum ne áu - - - fe - ras a - me.
13. et spíritu principá - - - - li con - fír - ma me.
14. et ímpii ad te con - ver - tén - tur.
15. et exsultábit lingua mea justí - - - ti - am tu - am.
16. et os meum annúntiábit lau - dem tu - am.
17. holocaústis non de - le - ctá - be - ris.
18. cor contrítum et humiliátum, Deus, non de - spí - ci - es.
19. ut aedificéntur mu - - - - ri Je - rú - sa - lem.
20. tunc impónent super altáre tu - um ví - tu - los.
21. dona e - is Dó - mi - ne.
22. lú - - - - - - - ce - at e - is.

DE PR

Antiphon

Si in - i - qui - tá - tes * ob - ser - vá - ve - ris,

165

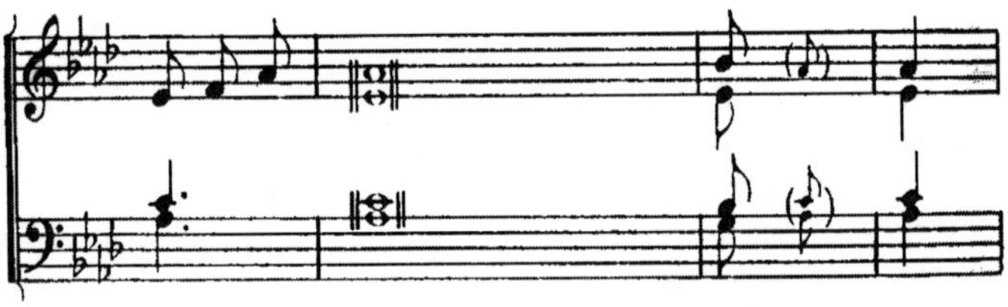

1. De pro-fún- dis clamávi ad te, Dó - mi - ne: *
2. Fiant aures tuae inten - dén - tes *
3. Si iniquitátes observáveris, Dó - mi - ne: *
4. Quia apud te propitiáti - o est: *
5. Sustínuit ánima mea in verbo e - jus: *
6. A custódia matutína usque ad no - ctem, *
7. Quia apud Dóminum miseri- cór - di - a: *
8. Et ipse rédimet Isra - el ________ *
9. Réquiem ae - - - tér - nam *
10. Et lux per - - - pé - tu - a *

FUNDIS

Do - mi - ne: Do - mi - ne, quis su - sti - né - bit?

1. Dómine, exaúdi	vo	-	cem		me		-	am
2. in vocem deprecati -	- ó	-	nis		me		-	ae.
3. Dómine, quis	sus	-	ti	-	né		-	bit?
4. et propter legem tuam sustínu -	i		te,		Dó -	mi	-	ne.
5. sperávit ánima me -	- a		in		Dó -	mi	-	no.
6. speret Isra - - -	- el		in		Dó -	mi	-	no.
7. et copiósa apud e - -	- um		red	-	ém -	pti	-	o.
8. ex ómnibus iniquitá -	- ti	-	bus		e		-	jus.
9. dona	e	-	is,		Dó -	mi	-	ne.
10. lú - - -	- ce	-	at		e		-	is.

Repeat Antiphon, Si iniquitátes

DEUS IN ADJUTORIUM

166

Dó-mi-ne, ad adjuvándum me fe-stí - na. Glória Pátri, et Fílio,

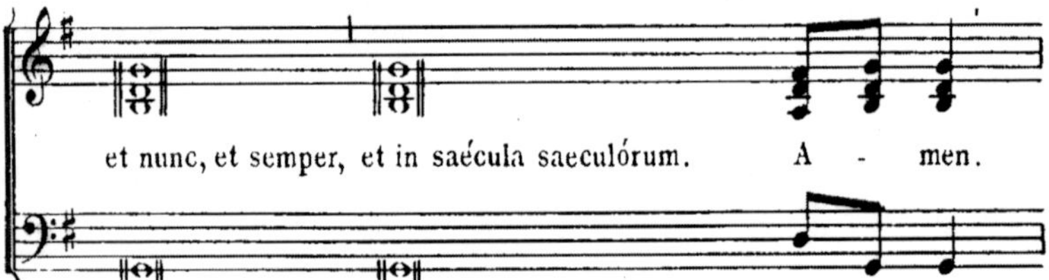
et nunc, et semper, et in saécula saeculórum. A - men.

167

1. Antiphon VII. C 2

DIXIT

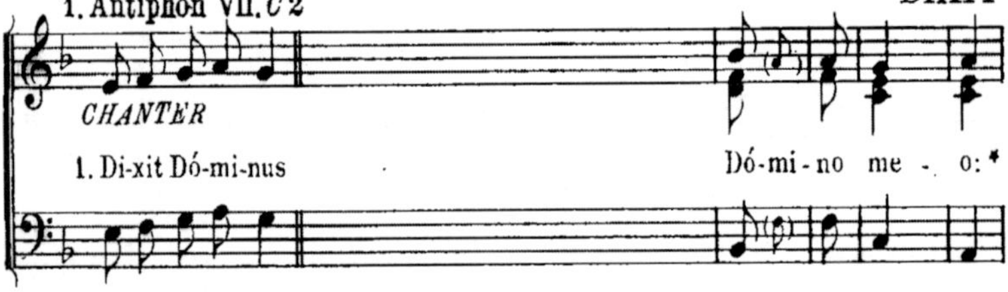
CHANTER
1. Di-xit Dó-mi-nus Dó-mi-no me - o:*

2. Donec ponam ini - - mí - cos tú - os.*
3. Virgam virtútis túae emíttet Dómi-nus ex Sí - on:*
4. Técum princípium in die virtútis
túae in splendóri-bus san-ctó - rum:*
5. Jurávit Dóminus, et non poeni - té - bit e - um:*
6. Dóminus a déx - tris tu - is,*
7. Judicábit in natiónibus, im - plé-bit ru - í - nas:*
8. De torrénte in ví - a bi - bet:*
9. Glória Pá-tri, et Fí-li - o,*
10. Sicut érat in princípio, et nunc, et sém - per,*

MEUM INTENDE

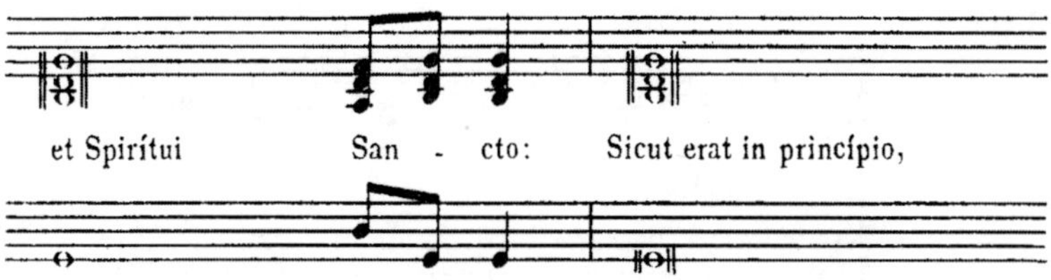
et Spirítui San - cto: Sicut erat in princípio,

T.P. *From Septuagesime Sunday until Holy Thursday*

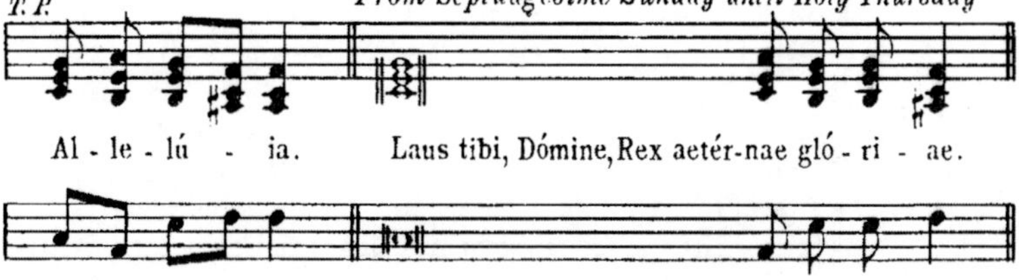
Al - le - lú - ia. Laus tibi, Dómine, Rex aetér-nae gló - ri - ae.

DOMINUS

1. Sede a dex - tris me - is.

2. scabéllum pé - dum tu - ó - rum.
3. domináre in médio inimi - - có - rum tu - ó - rum.

4. ex útero ante lucíferum gé - nu - i te.
5. Tu es sacérdos in aetérnum secúndum órdi-nem Mel - chí - se - dech.
6. confrégit in díe írae sú - ae ré - ges.
7. conquassábit cápita in tér - ra mul - tó - rum.
8. proptérea exal - - - - tá - bit cá - put.
9. et Spi - - - - - rí - tu - i Sán - cto.
10. et in saécula saec - - ló - rum. A - men.

Antiphon

Di - xit Dó - mi - nus Dó - mi - no

CONFI-

2. Ant. III. *B*

168

Ma-gna ó-pe-ra Dó-mi-ni.

1. Con-fi - tébor tibi Dómine in tóto
2. Mágna
3. Conféssio et magnificéntia
4. Memóriam fécit mirabílium suórum,† miséricors et mise- -
5. Mémor érit in saéculum testa-
6. Ut det íllis haeredi- -
7. Fidélia ómnia mandáta éjus: † confirmáta in
8. Redemptiónem misit
9. Sánctum et terríbile
10. Intelléctus bónus ómnibus faci-
11. Glória
12. Sicut érat in princípio, et

Antiphon

Ma - gna ó - pe - ra Dó - mi - ni,

me - o: Se - de a dex - tris me - is.

TEBOR

1. cór - de mé - o:* in consílio justórum, et congre - ga - ti - ó - ne.
2. ó - pe-ra Dó-mi - ni:* exquisíta in ómnes volun - - tá - tes é - jus.
3. o - pus é - jus:* et justítia éjus mánet in saé-cu-lum saé-cu-li.

4. rá - tor Dó-mi-nus:* escam dedit ti - - - mén - ti - bus se.
5. mén - ti sú - i:* virtútem óperum suórum annuntiábit pó-pu - lo sú - o.
6. tá - temgén-ti - um:* ópera mánuum éjus véritas et ju - dí-ci-um.

7. saé-cu-lum saé-cu - li:* fácta in veritáte et ae - qui - tá - te.
8. pó-pu-lo sú - o:* mandávit in aetérnum testa - mén - tum sú - um.
9. nó - men e - jus:* inítium sapiéntiae tí - mor Dó-mi-ni.
10. én-ti-bus é - um:* laudátio éjus mánet in saé-cu-lum saé-cu-li.
11. Pa-tri, et Fí-li - o,* et Spi - - - rí-tu - i Sán - cto.
12. núnc, et sem-per,* et in saécula saecu - - - ló - rum. A - men.

ex - qui - sí - ta in o - mnes vo - lun - tá - tes é - jus.

BEATUS

3. Ant. IV. *G*

169

Qui ti-met Dó-mi-num.

1. Be-á - tus vir, qui
2. Pótens in térra érit
3. Glória, et divítiae in
4. Exórtum est in ténebris
5. Jucúndus hómo qui miserétur et cómmodat, † disponet sermones súos
6. In memória aetérna
7. Parátum cor éjus speráre in Dómino, † confirmátum
8. Dispérsit, dedit paupéribus: † justítia éjus mánet in saé-
9. Peccátor vidébit, et irascétur, † déntibus súis frémet
10. Gloria Pa- -
11. Sicut érat in princípio, et

Qui ti - met Dó - mi - num, in man - -

N. B.— † indicates pause

VIR

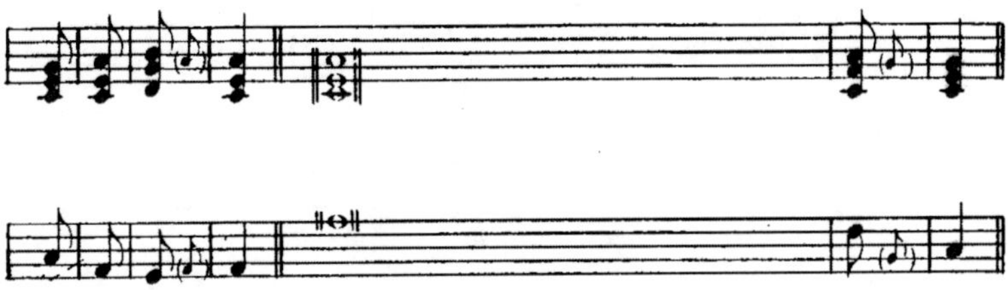

1. tí-met Dó-mi-num:*	in mandátis éjus vólet	ní - mis.
2. sé-men é - jus:*	generátio rectórum benedi - -	- cé - tur.
3. dó-mo é - jus:*	et justítia éjus mánet in saéculum	saé-cu - li.
4. lú-men ré - ctis:*	mísericors, et miserátor, et	ju - stus.
5. in ju - dí-ci - o:*	quia in aetérnum non commo -	- vé-bi - tur.
6. é - rit jú - stus:*	ab auditióne mála non ti - -	- mé - bit.
7. ést cor é - jus:*	non commovébitur donec despíciat inimícos	sú - os.
8. cu - lum saé-cu - li:*	córnu éjus exaltábitur in	gló-ri - a.
9. et ta - bé - scet:*	desidérium peccatórum pe -	- rí - bit.
10. tri, et Fí-li - o,*	et Spirítui	Sán - cto.
11. nunc, et sém - per,*	et in saécula saeculórum.	A - men.

dá - tis é - jus cu - pit ni - mis.

LAUDATE

4. Ant. VII. *c*

170

Sit no-men Dó-mi-ni.

1. Lau-dá - te
2. Sit nómen Dómini
3. A sólis órtu usque
4. Excélsus super ómnes
5. Quis sicut Dóminus Déus noster, qui in
6. Súscitans a
7. Ut cóllocet éum
8. Qui habitáre fácit stéri -
9. Glória
10. Sicut érat in princípio, et

Antiphon

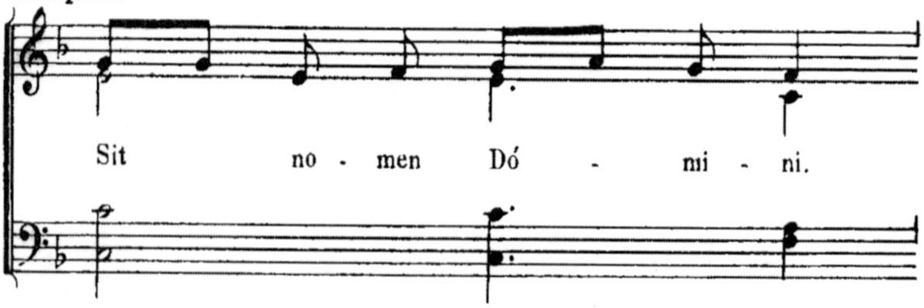
Sit no - men Dó - mi - ni.

PUERI

1. pú-e - ri Dó-mi-num:* laudáte nó - men Dó-mi-ni.
2. be - ne - dí - ctum,* ex hoc nunc, et ús-que in saé-cu-lum.
3. ad oc - cá - sum,* laudábile nó - men Dó-mi-ni.
4. gén - tes Dó-mi-nus,* et super coélos gló-ri - a é - jus.

5. ál - tis há-bi - tat,* et humília réspecit in coélo et in tér - ra?
6. tér - ra ín-o - pem,* et de stércore é-ri-gens páupe - rem.
7. cum prin - cí-pi - bus,* cum princípibus pó-pu - li sú - i.
8. lem in dó - mo,* mátrem fili - - - - ó-rum lae - tán - tem.
9. Pá-tri, et Fí-li - o,* et Spi- - - rí-tu - i Sán - cto.
10. núnc, et sém - per,* et in saécula saecu- - ló - rum. A - men.

be - ne - dí - ctum in saé - cu - la.

IN

5 Ant. *Foreign Tone*

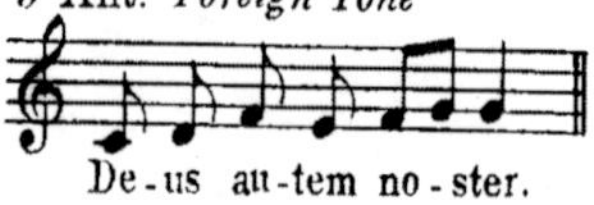
De-us au-tem no-ster.

171

1. In ex - itu Isra-el de Ae - gý - pto,*
2. Facta est Judaé-a sanctificá - ti - o e - jus:*
3. Mare vi - - - -dit, et fu - git:*
4. Montes exsulta-vérunt ut a - rí - e - tes,*
5. Quid est tibi, mare, quod fu - gí - sti:*
6. Montes exsultástis sic - - ut a - rí - e - tes,*
7. A fácie Dómini mo - - - ta est ter - ra:*
8. Qui convértit petram in sta - gna a - quá - rum,*
9. Non nobis, Dómi - - -ne, non no - bis,*
10. Super misericórdia tua et veri - tá - te tu - a:*
11. Deus autem no - - -ster in coe - lo:*
12. Simu-lácra génti-um argén - tum et au - rum:*
13. Os habent, et non lo - quén - tur:*
14. Aures habent, et non aú - di - ent:*
15. Manus habent, et non *a*(palpá- bunt:) † pedes habent, et non am - bu - lá - bunt:*
16. Sími-les illis fiant qui fá - ci - unt e - a:*
17. Domus Israel sperá - - - vit in Dó-mi - no:*
18. Domus A-a-ron sperá - - vit in Dó-mi - no:*
19. Qui timent Dóminum, speravé-runt in Dó-mi - no:*
20. Dóminus memor fu - it no - stri,*
21. Benedíxit dómui *b*(I - sra - el:)*
22. Benedíxit ómnibus qui ti - ment Dó - mi - num:*
23. Adjíciat Dóminus *c* (su - per vos:)*
24. Benedícti vos a Dó-mi - no:*
25. Coelum coe - li Dó-mi - no:*
26. Non mórtui laudá - - - bunt te, Dó-mi - ne:*
27. Sed nos qui vívimus, benedí - ci - mus Dó-mi - no:*
28. Gló-ria Pa - - -tri, et Fí - li - o,*
29. Sicut erat in princípio, et nunc, et sem - - per,*

Alternative reading

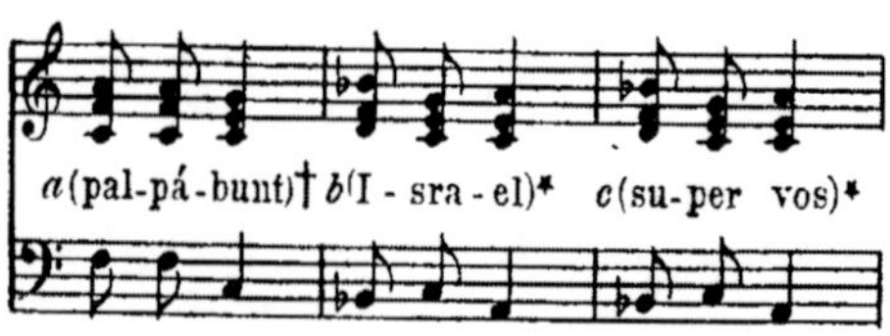
a(pal-pá-bunt)† *b*(I - sra - el)* *c*(su-per vos)*

EXITU

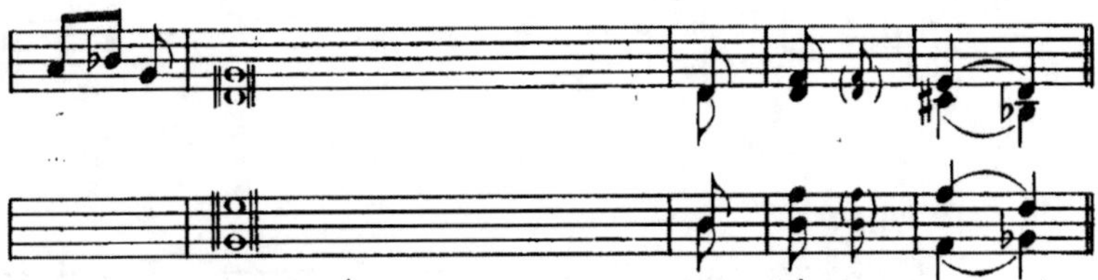

1. do - mus Jacob de pópu - - - lo bár - ba - ro:
2. Israel poté - - - - stas e - - jus.
3. Jordánis convérsus est re - trór - sum.
4. et colles sicut a - - - gni ó - vi - um.
5. et tu Jordanis, quia convérsus es re - trór - sum?
6. et colles sicut a - - - gni ó - vi - um?
7. a fácie De - - - - i Ja - - cob.
8. et rupem in fontes a - quá - rum.
9. sed nómini tuo da gló - ri - am.
10. nequándo dicant gentes: Ubi est Deus e - ó - rum?
11. ómnia quaecúmque vólu - - -it, fe - cit.
12. ópera mánu - - - - um hó - mi - num.
13. oculos habent, et non vi - dé - - bunt.
14. nares habent, et non o - - - do - rá - - bunt.
15. non clamábunt in gúttu - - - re su - - o.

16. et omnes qui confídunt in e - - is.
17. adjútor eórum et protéctor e - ó - rum est.
18. adjútor eórum et protéctor e - ó - rum est.
19. adjútor eórum et protéctor e - ó - rum est.
20. et benedí - - - - xit no - - bis.
21. benedíxit dómu - - - i A - a - ron.
22. pusíllis cum ma - jó - ri - bus.
23. super vos, et super fíli - - - os ve - - stros.
24. qui fecit coelum et ter - - ram.
25. terram autem dedit fíli - - - is hó - mi - num.
26. neque omnes qui descéndunt in in - fér - num.
27. ex hoc nunc, et usque in saé - cu - lum.
28. et Spirí - tu - - - - i San - cto.
29. et in saécula saeculó - - - rum. A - - men.

Antiphon

De-us au-tem no-ster in coe-lo ó-mni-a quae-cúm-que vó-lu-it fe-cit.

MAGNI-

VIII. G

172

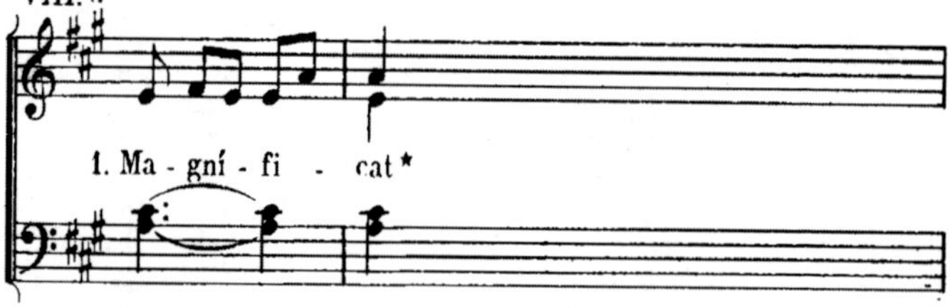
1. Ma - gní - fi - cat *

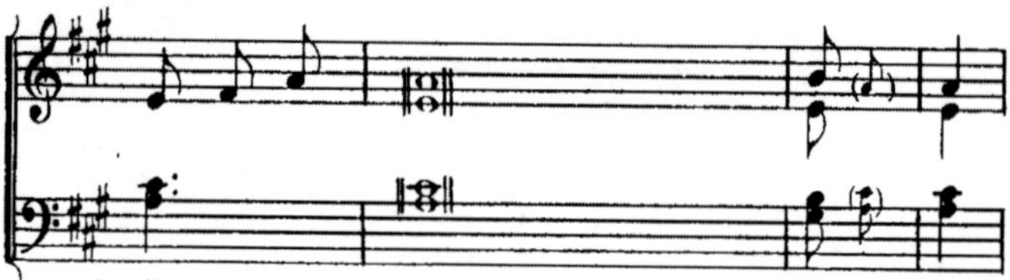

2.	Et	ex - sul -	távit spíritus	mé	-	us *
3.	Qui - a	re -	spéxit humilitátem ancíllae	sú	-	ae:*
4.	Qui - a	fé -	cit mihi mágna qui	po-tens		est:*
5.	Et	mi - se -	ricórdia éjus a progénie in pro -	gé - ni	-	es *
6.	Fé - cit	po -	téntiam in bráchio	su	-	o: *
7.	De - pó - su -		it poténtes de	se	-	de,*
8.	E - su - ri -		éntes implévit	bo	-	nis:*
9.	Sus - cé - pit		Israel púerum	su	-	um,*
10.	Sic - ut	lo -	cútus est ad pátres	no	-	stros,*
11.	Gló - ri - a		Pátri, et	Fí - li	-	o,*
12.	Sic - ut	é -	rat in princípio, et nunc, et	sem	-	per,*

On Ordinary Sundays during the Year

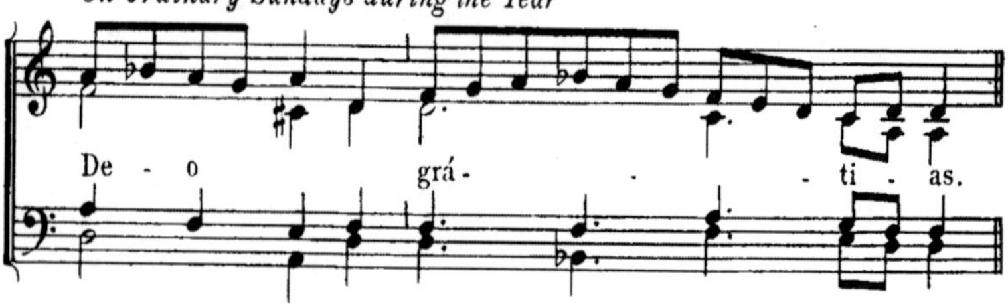
De - o grá - - ti - as.

Ant. *T. P.*
Al - le - lú - ia, al - le - lú - ia, al - le - lú - ia. R. De - o grá - ti - as.

FICAT

1. ánima me - a Dó - mi - num.

2. in Déo salu- - - - - tá - ri me - o.
3. ecce enim ex hoc beátam me dícent ómnes gene - ra - ti - ó - nes.
4. et sanctum no - men e - jus.
5. timén - - - - - ti - bus e - um.
6. dispérsit supérbos mente cór - dis su - i.
7. et exal - - - - - tá - vit hú - mi - les.
8. et dívites dimí sit in - á - nes.
9. recordátus misericór - - - - di - ae su - ae.
10. Abraham et sémini e - - - - jus in saé - cu - la.
11. et Spirí - - - - - tu - i Sán - cto.
12. et in saécula saecu - - - - ló - rum. A - men.

For Advent and Lent

De - o grá - ti - as. R. Et vitam aetérnam. A - men.

For Vesper Hymns see pages 212-216

DIXIT

1. Ant. III. *A*

173

Dum es - set Rex* in ac-cú-bi-tu su - o,

1. Di-xit Dóminus Dó-mi-no mé - o: *
2. Donec ponam ini- - mí - cos tú - os, *
3. Virgam virtútis túae emíttet Dómi-nus ex Si - on: *
4. Técum princípium in die virtútis túae in splendóri-bus san - ctó - rum: *
5. Jurávit Dóminus, et non poeni - té - bit é - um: *
6. Dóminus a déx - tris tú - is: *
7. Judicábit in natiónibus, im - - plé-bit ru - í - nas: *
8. De torrénte in vi - a bi - bet: *
9. Glória Pa-tri, et Fí-li - o, *
10. Sicut érat in princípio, et núnc et sem - per, *

LAUDATE

2. Ant. IV. *A*

174

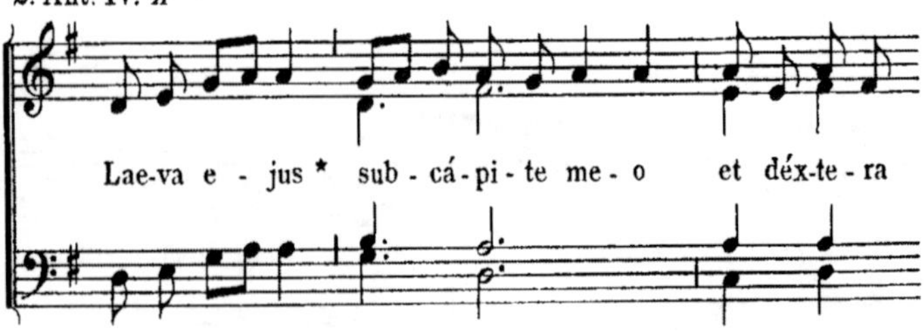
Lae-va e - jus * sub - cá - pi - te me - o et déx-te - ra

DOMINUS

T.P.
nar-dus me-a de - dit o-dó-rem su - a - vi - tá - tis. Al-le - lú - ia.

1. Séde a dex - tris me - is:
2. scabellum pe - - - - dum tu - ó - rum.
3. domináre in médio inimicó - - rum tu - ó - rum.

4. ex útero ante lucíferum gé - nu - i te.
5. Tu es sacérdos in aetérnum secúndum órdi-nem Mel - chí - se - dech.
6. confrégit in die irae su - ae ré - ges.
7. conquassábit cápita in tér - - ra mul - tó - rum.
8. proptérea exal - - tá - bit ca - put.
9. et Spirí - - tu - i San - cto.
10. et in saécula saecu - - ló - rum. A - men.

Repeat 1. Antiphon

PUERI

T.P.
il - li - us am-ple-xá - bi-tur me. Al - le - lú - ia.

1. Lau-dá - te pú - - - e - ri Dó-mi-num:*
2. Sit nómen Dómini be - ne - dí - ctum,*
3. A solis órtu usque ad oc - cá - sum,*
4. Excélsus super ómnes gén - tes Dó-mi-nus,*
5. Quis sicut Dóminus Déus nóster, qui in ál - tis há-bi-tat,*
6. Súscitans a ter - ra ín-o-pem,*
7. Ut cóllocet éum cum prin - cí-pi-bus,*
8. Qui habitáre fácit stéri - - lem in dó - mo,*
9. Glória Pá - - tri, et Fí-li - o,*
10. Sicut érat in princípio, et nunc, et sem - per,*

LAETATUS

3. Ant. III. *B*

175

Ni-gra sum sed for-mó-sa,* fí-li-ae Je-rú-sa-lem: í-de-o di-

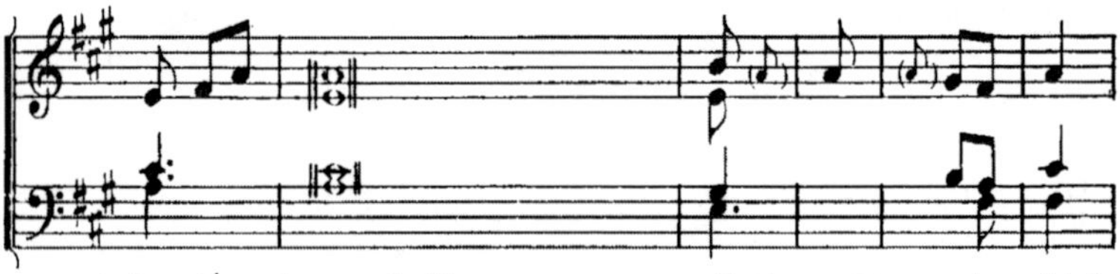

1. Lae-tá - tus sum in his quae dí-cta sunt mi - hi:*
2. Stántes erant pe - des nó - stri,*
3. Jerúsalem quae aedifi - - cá-tur ut cí-vi - tas:*
4. Illuc enim ascendérunt tribus, tri - bus Dó-mi - ni:*
5. Quia illic sedérunt sedes in ju - dí-ci - o,*
6. Rogáte quae ad pácem sunt Je - rú-sa - lem:*
7. Fiat pax in vir - - tú - te tú - a:*
8. Propter frátres méos et pró-xi - mos mé - os,*
9. Propter dómum Dómini De - i nó - stri,*
10. Glória Pá-tri, et Fí-li - o,*
11. Sicut érat in princípio, et núnc, et sem - per,*

1. laudá - - - te nó - men Dó - mi - ni.
2. ex hoc nunc, et us - que in saé - cu - lum.
3. laudábi - - - le nó - men Dó - mi - ni.
4. et super coélos gló - ri - a é - jus.
5. et humília réspicit in coé - lo et in tér - ra?
6. et de stércore é - ri - gens paú - pe - rem:
7. cum princípibus pó - pu - li sú - i.
8. mátrem fili - - - ó - rum lae - tán - tem.
9. et Spi - - - rí - tu - i Sán - cto.
10. et in saécula sae - - - cu - ló - rum. A - men.

Repeat 2. Antiphon

SUM

T.P.
lé-xit me Rex et in-tro-dú-xit me in cu-bí - cu - lum su-um. Al-le - lú-ia.

1. In dómum Dó - - - mi - ni í - bi - mus.
2. in átriis tú - - - is, Je - rú - sa - lem.
3. cujus participátio éjus in id - í - psum.
4. testimónium Israel ad confiténdum nó - mi - ni Dó - mi - ni.
5. sedes super dó - mum Dá - vid.
6. et abundántia dili - - - gén - ti - bus te.
7. et abundántia in túr - - - ri - bus tú - is.
8. loquébar pá - cem de te:
9. quaesívi bó - na ti - bi.
10. et Spirí tu - i Sán - cto.
11. et in saécula saecu - - - ló - rum. A - men.

Repeat 3. Antiphon

NISI

4. Ant. VIII. G

176

Jam hi - ems trán - si - it * im-ber áb - i - it et re-cés - sit:

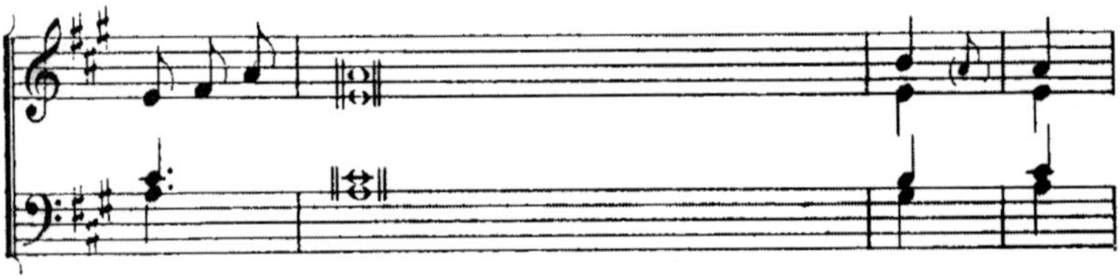

1. Ni - si Dó - minus aedificáverit do - mum,*
2. Nisi Dóminus custodíerit civi - - tá - tem,*
3. Vánum est vóbis ante lucem súr - ge - re: *
4. Cum déderit diléctis súis só - mnum:*
5. Sicut sagíttae in mánu po - - -tén - tis:*
6. Beátus vir qui implévit desidérium súum ex i - psis:*
7. Glória Pátri, et Fí - li - o,*
8. Sicut érat in princípio, et nunc, et sem - per,*

LAUDA

5. Ant. IV. A*

177

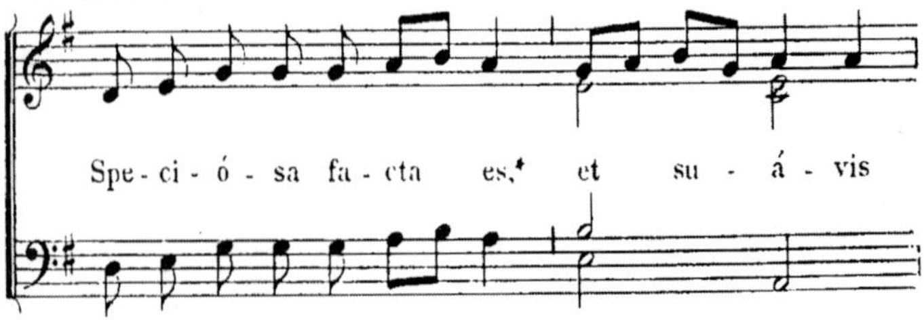
Spe - ci - ó - sa fa - cta es,* et su - á - vis

DOMINUS

T.P.
sur - ge a - mí - ca me - a, et ve - ni. Al - le - lú - ia.

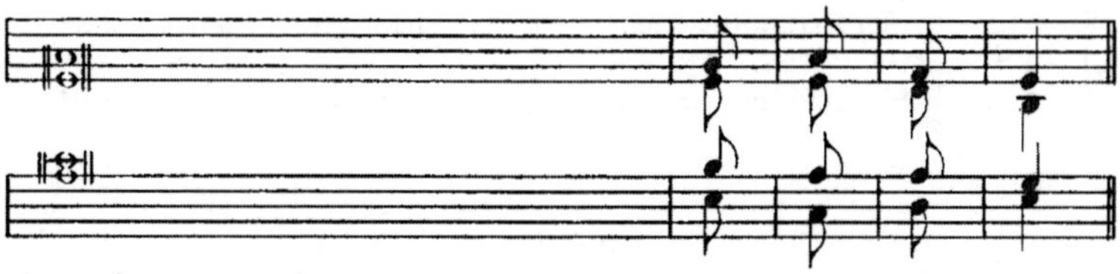

1. in vánum laboravérunt qui aedí - - fi - cant é - am.
2. frustra vígilat qui cu - - - stó - dit é - am.
3. súrgite postquam sedéritis, qui manducátis pá - nem do - ló - ris.
4. ecce haeréditas Dómini, fílii: mérces, frú - ctus vén - tris.
5. ita fílii ex - cus - só - rum.
6. non confundétur cum loquétur inimícis sú - is in pór - ta.
7. et Spirí - - - - tu - i Sán - cto.
8. et in saécula saecu - - - ló - rum. A - men.

Repeat 4. Antiphon

JERUSALEM

T.P.
in de-lí - ci - is tu - is, San-cta De-i Gé-ni-trix. Al - le - lú - ia.

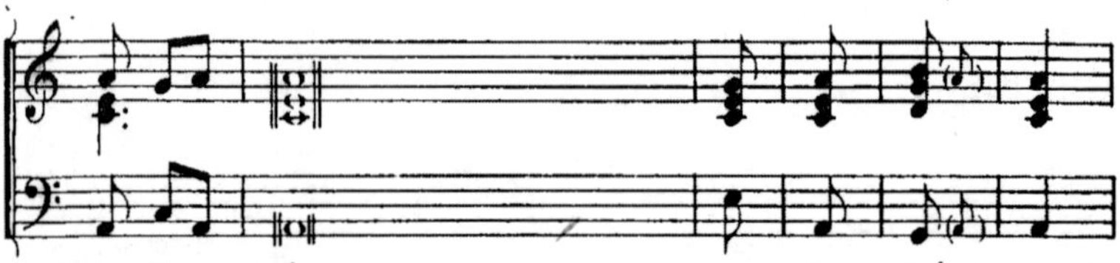

1. Lau-da	Jerú - -	- sa	- lem	Dó-mi	-	num:*
2.	Quóniam confortávit séras portá -	rum	tu -	á	-	rum:*
3.	Qui pósuit fines	tú	- os	pá	-	cem:*
4.	Qui emíttit elóquium	sú	- um	tér	-	rae:*
5.	Qui dat nívem	sic	- ut	lá	-	nam:*
6.	Mittit crystállum súam sic -	ut	buc -	cél	-	las:*
7.	Emíttet vérbum súum, et liquefá -	ci	- et	é	-	a:*
8.	Qui annúntiat vérbum	sú	- um	Ja	-	cob:*
9.	Non fécit táliter ómni	na	- ti -	ó	-	ni:*
10.	Glória Pá - -	- tri,	et	Fí-li	-	o,*
11.	Sicut érat in princípio, et	nunc,	et	sém	-	per,*

Chapter

Ab inítio et ante saécula creáta sum, et usque ad futúrum saéculum non désinam, et in habitatióne sancta coram ipso ministrávi.

AVE MARIS STELLA

M. M. ♪.= 144 According to the Vatican Version

178

1. A - ve ma - ris stel - la, De - i Ma - ter al - ma,
2. Su-mens il - lud A - ve Ga-bri - é - lis o - re,
3. Sol - ve vin - cla re - is, Pro-fer lú - men cae - cis,
4. Mon-stra te es - se ma - trem: Su-mat per te pre - ces,
5. Vir - go sin - gu - lá - ris, In - ter o - mnes mi - tis,
6. Vi - tam prae - sta pu - ram, I - ter pá - ra tu - tum:
7. Sit laus De - o Pa - tri, Sum-mo Chri-sto de - cus,

V. Dignáre me laudáre te, Virgo sacrá - ta.
R. Da mihi virtútem contra hostes tu - os.

1. láuda Dé - - - um tú - um Si - on.
2. benedíxit fíli - - is tú - is in te.
3. et ádipe frumén - - ti sá - ti - at te.
4. velóciter cúr - - - rit sér - mo é - jus.
5. nébulam sicut cí - ne - rem spár - git.
6. ante fáciem frígoris éjus quis sus - ti - né - bit?
7. flábit spíritus éjus et flú - ent á - quae.
8. justítias et judíci - - a sú - a Is - ra - el.
9. et judícia súa non mani - fe - stá - vit e - is.
10. et Spi - - - rí - tu - i Sán - cto.
11. et in saécula sae - - cu - ló - rum. A - men.

Repeat 5 Antiphon

R.

1. At-que sem-per Vir - go, Fe - lix coe-li por-ta.
2. Fun-da nos in pa - ce, Mu-tans He-vae no-men.
3. Ma-la no-stra pel - le, Bo - na cun-cta po-sce.
4. Qui pro no-bis na - tus, Tu-lit es-se tu-us.
5. Nos cul-pis so - lú - tos, Mi-tes fac et ca-stos.
6. Ut vi-dén-tes Je - sum, Sem-per col-lae-té-mur.
7. Spi-rí-tu-i San-cto, Tri-bus ho-nor u-nus. A - men.

N.B. Other melodies for Ave Maris Stella will be found on pages 91, 92, 93.

MAGNIFICAT

Antiphon IV. *E*

179

San - cta Ma - rí - a * suc - cúr - re mí - se - ris,
ju - va pu - sil - lá - ni - mes ré - fo - ve flé - bi - les:
o - ra pro pó - pu - lo, in - tér - ve - ni pro clé - ro,
in - ter - cé - de pro de - vó - to fe - mí - ne - o se - xu:

sén-ti - ant o - mnes tu - um ju - vá-men, qui-cúm-que cé - le-brant+
+ tu-am san-ctam fe - sti - vi - tá-tem.
T. P.
Al - le - lú - ia.

On the Feast of Our Lady of Mount Carmel

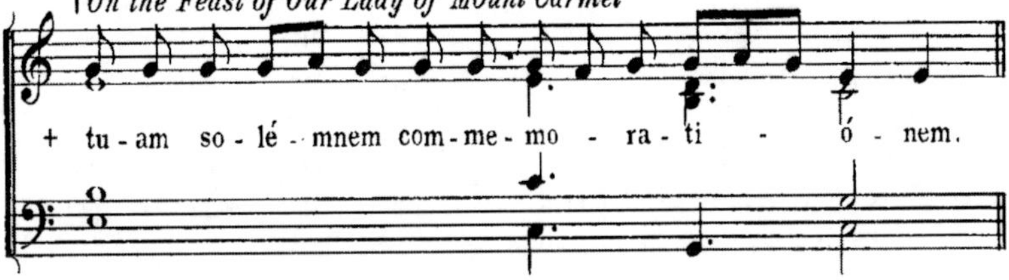
+ tu - am so - lé - mnem com-me-mo - ra - ti - ó - nem.

On the Feast of the Holy Name of Mary

+ tu - i san-cti nó - mi-nis com-me-mo - ra - ti - ó - nem.

Votive office Immac. Conception M. B. V. Mary

+ tu-am san-ctam Im-ma-cu - lá - tam Con - ce - pti - ó - nem.

1. Ma - gní - ficat
2. Et ex - sultávit spí - - - ri - tus mé - us *
3. Qui - a respéxit humilitátem an - cíl - lae sú - ae: *
4. Qui - a fécit mihi má - · - - gna qui po - tens est: *
5. Et mi - sericórdia éjus a progénie in pro - gé - ni - es *
6. Fé - cit poténtiam in brá - - chi - o sú - o: *
7. De - pó - suit potén - - - tes de sé - de, *
8. E - su - riéntes im - - - plé - vit bó - nis: *
9. Sus - cé - pit Israel pú - - - e - rum sú - um, *
10. Sic - ut locútus est ad pá - tres nó - stros, *
11. Gló - ri - a Pá - - - - tri, et Fí - li - o, *
12. Sic - ut érat in princípio, et nunc, et sém - per, *

V. Be - ne-di-cá-mus Do - - - mi-no.
R. De - - - o grá - ti - as.

MOST BLESSED VIRGIN

1. áni- - - - - ma mé - a Dó-mi - num.
2. in Déo sa - - - - lu - tá - ri mé - o.
3. ecce enim ex hoc beátam me dicent omnes ge-ne - ra - ti ó - nes.
4. et sán- - - - - ctum nó - men é - jus.
5. ti - - - - - mén - ti - bus é - um.
6. dispérsit supérbos mén - - - te cór - dis súi - i.
7. et ex- - - - - al - tá - vit hú-mi - les.
8. et dívites di - - - - mí - sit in - - á - nes.
9. recordátus miseri - - - cór - di - ae sú - ae.
10. Abraham et sémini é - jus in saé-cu - la.
11. et Spi- - - - - rí - tu - i Sán - cto.
12. et in saécula sae - - - cu - ló - rum. A - men.

Repeat Antiphon

V. Dóminus det nobis suam pa - cem.
R. Et vitam aetérnam. A - men.

SECOND

All as in First Vespers

MAGNI-

Antiphon VIII. *G*

180

Be-á - tam me di-cent * o-mnes ge-ne-ra-ti-ó-nes,

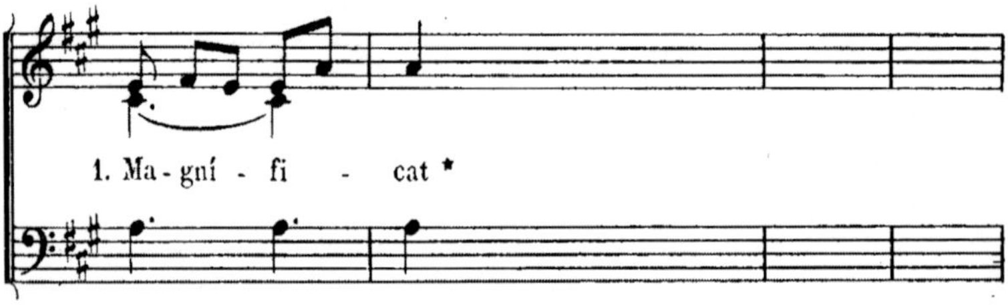
1. Ma-gní - fi - cat *

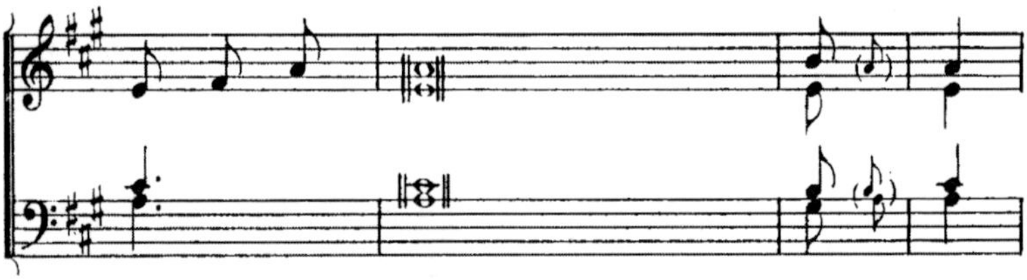

2. Et	ex -	sul -	távit spíritus	mé	-	us *
3. Qui -	a	re -	spéxit humilitátem ancíllae	sú	-	ae: *
4. Qui -	a	fé -	cit míhi mágna qui	pó - tens		est: *
5. Et	mi -	se -	ricórdia ejus a progénie in pro -	gé - ni	-	es *
6. Fé -	cit	po -	téntiam in bráchio	sú	-	o: *
7. De -	pó -	su -	it poténtes de	sé	-	de, *
8. E -	su -	ri -	éntes implévit	bo	-	nis: *
9. Sus -	cé -	pit	Israel púerum	sú	-	um, *
10. Sic -	ut	lo -	cútus est ad pátres	nó	-	stros, *
11. Gló -	ri -	a	Pátri, et	Fí - li	-	o, *
12. Sic -	ut	é -	rat in princípio, et nunc, et	sém	-	per, *

VESPERS

except the Magnificat

FICAT

T.P.
qui-a an-cíl-lam hú-mi-lem re-spé-xit De-us. Al-le-lú-ia.

1. á - ni - ma me - a Dó-mi - num.

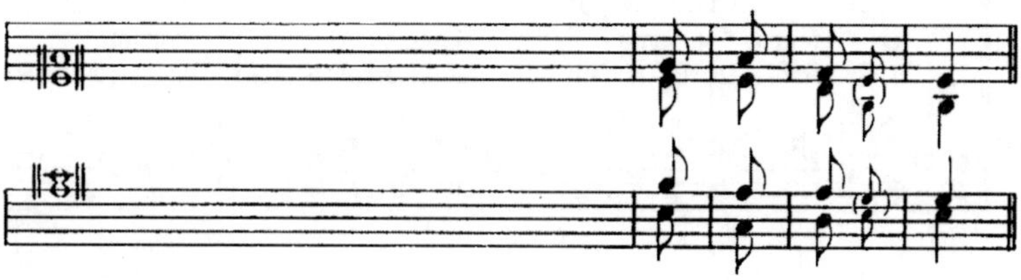

2. in Déo salu- - - - tá - ri mé - o.
3. ecce enim ex hoc beátam me dícent ómnes gene - ra - ti - ó - nes.
4. et sánctum nó - men é - jus.
5. timén - - - - - ti - bus é - um.
6. dispérsit supérbos ménte cór - dis sú - i.
7. et exal- - - - - tá - vit hú-mi - les.
8. et dívites dimí - - - - sit in - á - nes.
9. recordátus misericór- - - - di - ae sú - ae.
10. Abraham et sémini é- - - - jus in saé-cu - la.
11. et Spirí- - - - - tu - i Sán - cto.
12. et in saécula saecu- - - - ló - rum. A - men.

Repeat Antiphon

LUCIS CREATOR (For Sundays)

Solesmes

M.M. ♪ = 144

181

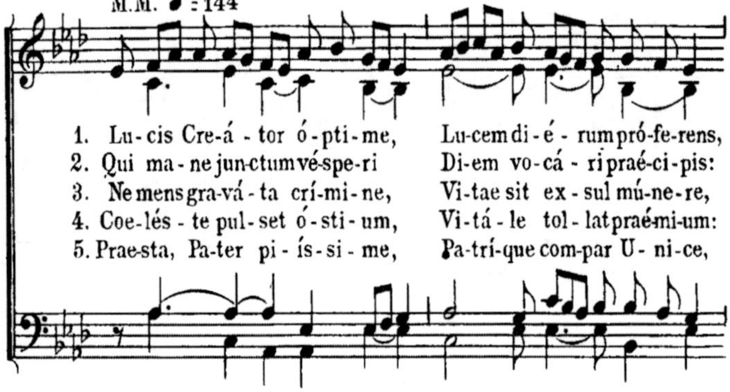
1. Lu - cis Cre-á - tor ó-pti-me, Lu-cem di-é - rum pró-fe-rens,
2. Qui ma - ne jun-ctum vé-spe-ri Di-em vo-cá - ri praé-ci-pis:
3. Ne mens gra-vá - ta crí-mi-ne, Vi-tae sit ex - sul mú-ne-re,
4. Coe-lés - te pul-set ó-sti-um, Vi-tá - le tol-lat praé-mi-um:
5. Prae-sta, Pa-ter pi - ís-si - me, Pa-trí-que com-par U - ni-ce,

1. Pri-mór-di-is lu-cis no-vae Mun-di pa-rans o - rí - gi-nem:
2. Il - lá - bi-tur te-trum cha-os, Au-di pre-ces cum flé-ti-bus.
3. Dum nil per-én-ne có - gi-tat, Se-sé-que cul-pis íl - li-gat.
4. Vi-té-mus o-mne nó - xi-um, Pur-gé-mus o-mne pés-si-mum.
5. Cum Spí-ri-tu Pa-rá - cli-to, Reg-nans per o-mne saé-cu-lum. A - men.

V. Dirigátur, Domine, orátio me - a.
R. Sicut incénsum in conspéctu tu - o.

ISTE CONFESSOR (For Confessors)

182

1. Iste Confésor Dómini, coléntes
2. Qui pius, prudens, húmilis, pudícus,
3. Cujus ob praestans méritum frequénter
4. Noster hinc illi chorus obsequéntem
5. Sit salus illi, decus atque virtus,
1. Quem pie laudant pópuli per orbem, Hac die laetus méru-
" " " " "
2. Sóbriam duxit sine labe vitam, Donec humános ani-
3. Aegra quae passim jacuére membra, Víribus morbi dómi-
4. Cóncinit laudem celebrésque palmas, Ut piis ejus préci-
5. Qui super coeli sólio corúscans, Totíus mundi séri-
1. it beátas Scándere sedes.
" (suprémos Laudis honóres.) m.t.v.
2. mávit aurae Spíritus artus.
3. tis, salúti Restitúntur.
4. bus juvémur Omne per aevum.
5. em gubérnat, Trinus et unus. Amen.

1st Vespers R. Stolam glóriae índuit eum.
2nd Vespers R. Et osténdit illi regnum Dei.

EXSULTET No. 1 (For Apostles and Evangelists)

I Mode (Dorian) M.M. ♪=152

Solesmes.

183

1. Ex - súl - tet or - bis gaú-di - is, Coe-lum re - súl-tet laú-di -
2. Vos sae - cu - ló - rum jú - di - ces, Et ve - ra mun-di lú - mi-
3. Qui tem-pla coe - li claú-di - tis, Se - rás-que ver - bo sól - vi -
4. Prae-cé - pta quo-rum pró-ti - nus Lan-guor sa - lús-que sén-ti -
5. Ut cum red - í - bit ár - bi - ter In fi - ne Christus saé-cu-
6. Pa - tri, si - múl-que Fí - li - o, Ti - bí - que, Sancte Spí - ri -
1. bus: A - po - sto - ló - rum gló - ri - am
2. na: Vo - tis pre - cá - mur cór - di - um,
3. tis: Nos a re - á - tu nó - xi - os
4. unt, Sa - ná - te men-tes lán-gui - das,
5. li, Nos sem - pi - tér - ni gaú - di - i
6. tus, Sic - ut fu - it, sit jú - gi - ter
1. Tel - lus et a - stra cón - ci - nunt.
2. Au - dí - te vo - ces súp - pli - cum.
3. Sol - vi ju - bé - te, quaé - su - mus.
4. Au - gé - te nos vir - tú - ti - bus;
5. Con - cé - dat es - se cóm - po - tes.
6. Sae - clum per o - mne gló - ri - a. A - men.

1st Vespers ℟. Et in fines orbis terrae verba eórum.
2nd Vespers ℟. Et facta ejus intellexérunt.

EXSULTET No. 2 (For Apostles and Evangelists)

IV Mode (Phrygian) M.M. ♪ = 144

184

Ex - súl - tet or - bis gaú - di - is,
Coe - lum re - súl - tet láu - di - bus:
A - po - sto - ló - rum gló - ri - am
Tel - lus et a - stra cón - ci - nunt. A - men.

JESU CORONA VIRGINUM (For Virgins)

185

1. Je - su, co - ró - na Vír - gi - num, Quem Ma - ter
2. Qui per - gis in - ter lí - li - a, Sep - tus cho -
3. Quo - cúm - que ten - dis, Vir - gi - nes Se - quún - tur
4. Te de - pre - cá - mur súp - pli - ces No - stris ut
5. Vir - tus, ho - nor, laus, gló - ri - a De - o Pa -
1. il - la cón - ci - pit, Quae so - la vir - go pár - tu -
2. ré - is Vír - gi - num, Spon - sus de - có - rus gló - ri -
3. at - que láu - di - bus Post te ca - nén - tes cúr - si -
4. ad - das sén - si - bus Ne - scí - re pror - sus ó - mni -
5. tri cum Fí - li - o, San - cto si - mul Pa - rá - cli -
1. rit, Haec vo - ta cle - mens ác - ci - pe.
2. a, Spon - sís - que red - dens praé - mi - a.
3. tant, Hym - nós - que dul - ces pér - so - nant. A - men.
4. a Cor - ru - pti - ó - nis vúl - ne - ra.
5. to, In sae - cu - ló - rum saé - cu - la.

ALMA

(FROM ADVENT TILL THE PURIFICATION)

186

M.M. ♪=126
Al - ma* Re-demp-to-ris Ma-ter, quae pér-vi-a coe-li por-ta
ma-nes, et stel-la ma-ris, suc-cúr-re ca-dén-ti, súr-ge-re qui cu-rat
pó-pu-lo: Tu quae ge-nu-í-sti, na-tú-ra mi-rán-te, tu-um san-ctum
Ge-ni-tó-rem, Vir-go pri-us ac po-sté-ri-us: Ga-bri-é-lis ab o-re
su-mens il-lud A - ve, pec-ca-tó-rum mi-se-ré - re

(In Advent)

V. Angelus Dómini nuntiávit Maríae.
R. Et concépit de Spíritu Sancto.

(From Christmas to Purification)

V. Post partum Virgo invioláta permansísti.
R. Dei Génitrix intercéde pro nobis.

AVE REGINA COELORUM

(FROM THE PURIFICATION TILL EASTER)

187

M.M. ♪=126
A - ve * Re - gí - na coe - ló - rum, A - ve Dó - mi -
na An - ge - ló - rum: Sal - ve ra - dix, sal - ve por - ta, Ex
qua mun - do lux est or - ta: Gau - de Vir - go glo - ri - ó - sa,
Su - per o - mnes spe - ci - ó - sa: Va - le, o val - de de -
có - ra Et pro no - bis Chri - stum ex - ó - ra.

V. Dignáre me laudáre te, Virgo sacráta.
R. Da mihi virtútem contra hostes tuos.

REGINA COELI No. 1

(From Easter Till Trinity Sunday)

A. Lotti

188

Re-gí-na coe-li, lae-tá - re, Al-le - lú - ia! lae
tá - re, Al-le - lú - ia! Qui - a quem me-ru-ís-ti por - tá - re,
Al-le-lú - ia, Al-le - lú - ia! Re-sur-réx - it si-cut di - xit,
Al-le-lú-ia! Al - le - lú - ia!
O - ra pro
O - ra pro no-bis
O - ra pro no - bis De- -
O - ra pro no - bis De- -
no-bis De - um.
De- - - um.
Al-le-lú-ia! Al-le-lú-ia! Al-le-lú - ia!
- - - - um.
- - - um.

V. Gaude et laetáre, Virgo María, Allelúia. R. Quia surréxit Dóminus vere, Allelúia.

REGINA COELI No. 2

(FROM EASTER TILL TRINITY SUNDAY)

189

M.M. ♪ = 126
Re - gi - na coe - li,* lae - tá - re, al - le - lú - ia:
Qui - a quem me-ru - í - sti por - tá - re, al - le - lu - ia: Re - sur - ré - xit,
sic - ut di - xit, al - le - lú - ia: O - ra pro no - bis De - um, al - le - lú - ia.

V. Gaude et laetáre Virgo María, allelúia.
R. Quia surréxit Dóminus vere, allelúia.

SALVE REGINA

(FROM TRINITY SUNDAY TILL ADVENT)

190

M.M. ♪ = 126
Sal - ve, Re - gí - na,* Ma - ter mi - se - ri - cór - di - ae: vi - ta, dul - cé -
do, et spes no - stra, sal - ve. Ad te cla - má - mus, éx - su - les, fí - li - i He - vae.

Ad te su-spi-rá-mus, ge-mén-tes et flen-tes, in hac la-cri-má-rum val-le.
E-ia er-go, Ad-vo-cá-ta no-stra, il-los tu-os mi-se-ri-
cór-des ó-cu-los ad nos con-vér-te. Et Je-sum, be-ne-dí-ctum
fru-ctum ven-tris tu-i, no-bis post hoc ex-sí-li-um o-stén-de.
O cle-mens: O pi-a: O dul-cis Vir-go Ma-rí-a.

V. Ora pro nobis, sancta Dei Génitrix.
R. Ut digni efficiámur promissiónibus Christi.

O SALUTARIS № 1

M.M. ♪ = 132

Solesmes

191

1. O sa - - lu - tá - ris Hó - sti - a,
2. U - ni tri - nó - que Dó - mi - no
1. Quae coe - li pan - dis ó - sti - um: Bel - la pre - munt ho - stí - li - a,
2. Sit sem - pi - tér - na gló - ri - a, Qui vi - tam si - ne tér - mi - no
1. Da ro - bur, fer au - xí - li - um.
2. No - bis do - net in pá - tri - a. A - men.

O SALUTARIS № 2

A. J. Weiss

192

1. O sa - lu - tá - ris Hó - sti - a, Quae coe - li
2. U - ni tri - nó - que Dó - mi - no Sit sem - pi -

1. pan - dis ó - sti - um, Bel - la pre - munt ho - stí - li -
2. tér - na gló - ri - a, Qui vi - tam si - ne tér - mi -
1. a, Da ro - bur, fer au - xí - li - um.
2. no No - bis do - net in pá - tri - a. A - men.

O SALUTARIS No. 3

Webbe

193

1. O sa - lu - tá - ris Hó - sti - a, Quae
2. U - ni tri - nó - que Dó - mi - no Sit
1. coe - li pan - dis ó - sti - um, Bel - la pre -
2. sem - pi - tér - na gló - ri - a, Qui vi - tam
p
1. munt ho - stí - li - a, Da ro - bur, fer au - xí - li - um.
2. si - ne tér - mi - no No - bis do - net in pá - tri - a. A - men.

O SALUTARIS Nº 4

C. Wondell

194

1. O sa-lu - tá - ris Hó - sti - a, Quae coe-li pan-dis
2. U - ni tri - nó - que Dó - mi - no Sit sem-pi - tér-na
1. ó - sti - um; Bel - la pre-munt ho - stí - li - a, Da ro - bur,
2. gló - ri - a, Qui vi - tam si - ne tér - mi - no No - bis do -
p
1. fer au - xí - li - um, Da ro-bur, fer au - xí - li - um.
2. net in pá - tri - a, No-bis do-net in pá - tri - a. A - men.
f

O SALUTARIS Nº 5

At a moderate pace

Werner

195

f
1. O sa-lu - tá - ris Hó - sti - a, Quae coe - li pan - dis
2. U - ni tri - nó - que Dó - mi - no Sit sem-pi - tér - na

p
1. ó - sti - um, Bel - la pre - munt ho - stí - li - a,
2. gló - ri - a, Qui vi - tam si - ne tér - mi - no,
p
1. Bel - la pre - munt ho -
. Qui vi - tam si - ne
cresc.
1. Bel - la - pre - munt ho - stí - li - a Da
2. Qui vi - tam si - ne tér - mi - no, No -
cresc.
1. stí - li - a Bel - la pre - munt ho - stí - li - a.
2. tér - mi - no, Qui vi - tam si - ne tér-mi-no.
1. ro - bur, fer au - xí - li - um.
2. bis do - net in pá - tri - a. A - men.

O SALUTARIS Nº 6

Werner

196

1. O sa - lu - tá - ris Hó - sti - a Quae coe - li
2. U ni tri - nó - que Dó - mi - no Sit sem - pi -

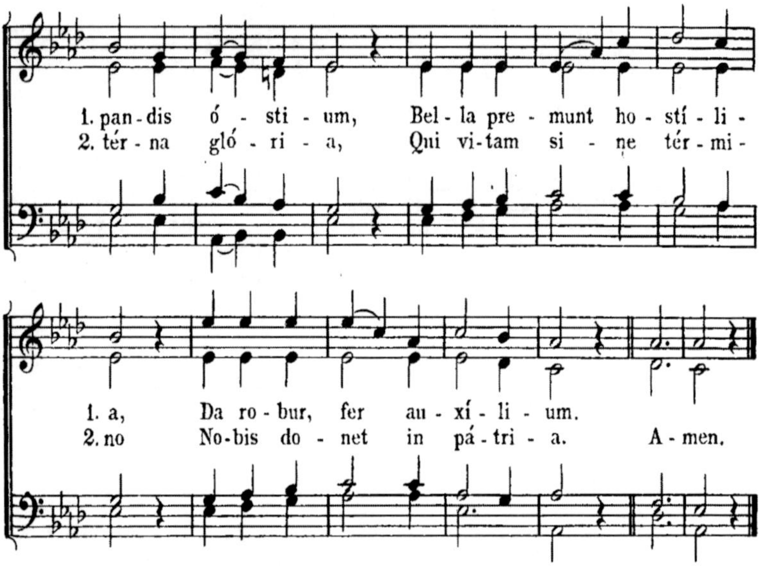
1. pan-dis ó - sti - um, Bel - la pre - munt ho - stí - li -
2. tér - na gló - ri - a, Qui vi-tam si - ne tér - mi -
1. a, Da ro - bur, fer au - xí - li - um.
2. no No-bis do - net in pá - tri - a. A - men.

O SALUTARIS No. 7

197

f
1. O sa - lu - tá - ris Hó - sti - a Quae coe - li
2. U - ni tri - nó - que Dó - mi - no Sit sem - pi -
1. pan - dis ó - sti - um, Bel - la pre - munt ho - stí - li -
2. tér - na gló - ri - a, Qui vi - tam si - ne tér - mi -

p
1. a, Da ro bur, fer au - xí - li - um.
2. no No - bis do - net in pá - tri - a. A - men.

O SALUTARIS No. 8

198

Slowly
1. O sa - lu - tá - ris Hó - sti - a, Quae coe - li
2. U - ni tri - nó - que Dó - mi - no Sit sem - pi -

1. pan - dis ó - sti - um, Bel - la pre - munt ho - stí - li -
2. tér - na gló - ri - a, Qui vi - tam si - ne tér - mi -

1. a, Da ro - bur, fer au - xí - li - um.
2. no No - bis do - net in pá - tri - a. A - men.

TANTUM ERGO Nº 1

Solesmes

199

M.M. ♪ = 120
1. Tan-tum er-go Sa-cra-mén-tum Ve - ne-ré-mur cér-nu-i:
2. Ge-ni-tó-ri Ge-ni-to-que Laus et ju-bi-lá-ti-o;
1. Et an-tí-quum do-cu-mén-tum No-vo ce-dat rí-tu-i:
2. Sa-lus, ho-nor, vir-tus quo-que Sit et be-ne-dí-cti-o:
rall.
1. Prae-stet fi-des sup-ple-mén-tum Sen-su-um de-fé-ctu-i.
2. Pro-ce-dén-ti ab u-tró-que Com-par sit lau-dá-ti-o. A-men.

TANTUM ERGO Nº 2

Minard

200

Slowly
pp
1. Tan-tum er-go Sa-cra-mén-tum Ve-ne-ré-mur cér-nu-i,
2. Ge-ni-tó-ri Ge-ni-tó-que Laus et ju-bi-lá-ti-o,

f
1. Et an - tí - quum do - cu - mén - tum No - vo ce - dat
2. Sa - lus, ho - nor, vir - tus quo - que Sit et be - ne -
p
1. rí - tu - i, Prae - stet fi - des sup - ple - mén - tum
2. dí - cti - o; Pro - ce - dén - ti ab u - tró - que
ff rall. pp
1. Sén - su - um de - fé - ctu - i.
2. Com - par sit lau - dá - ti - o. A - men, A - men.

TANTUM ERGO No 3

201

With dignity

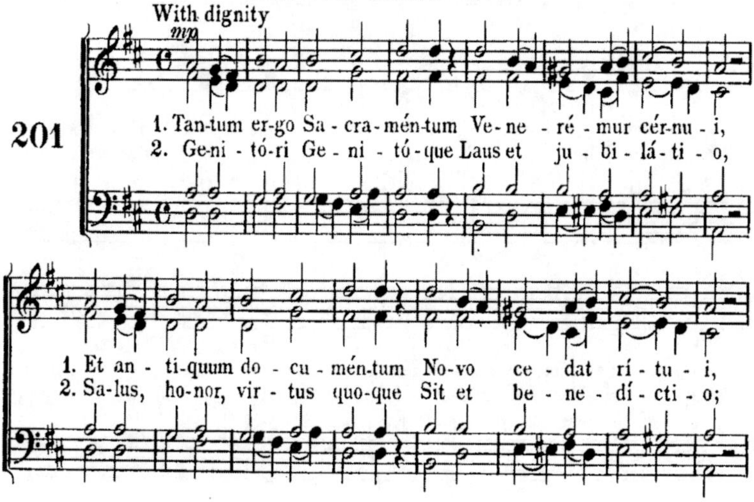
mp
1. Tan - tum er - go Sa - cra - mén - tum Ve - ne - ré - mur cér - nu - i,
2. Ge - ni - tó - ri Ge - ni - tó - que Laus et ju - bi - lá - ti - o,
1. Et an - ti - quum do - cu - mén - tum No - vo ce - dat rí - tu - i,
2. Sa - lus, ho - nor, vir - tus quo - que Sit et be - ne - dí - cti - o;

p
cresc.
1. Prae-stet fi-des sup-ple - mén-tum Sén-su - um de - fé-ctu - i.
2. Pro-ce - dén-ti ab u - tró - que Com-par sit lau-dá-ti - o. A - men.

TANTUM ERGO Nº 4

F.S.C.

202

1. Tan-tum er - go Sa-cra-mén - tum Ve - ne ré-mur
2. Ge - ni - tó - ri Ge - ni - tó - que Laus et ju - bi -
1. cér - nu - i, Et an - tí - quum do - cu - mén - tum
2. lá - ti - o, Sa - lus, ho - nor, vir - tus quo - que
1. No - vo ce - dat rí - tu - i, Prae - stet fi - des
2. Sit et be - ne - dí - cti - o; Pro - ce dén - ti
1. sup-ple-mén - tum Sén - su - um de - fé - ctu - i.
2. ab u - tró - que Com - par sit lau - dá - ti - o. A - men.

TANTUM ERGO No. 5

A. J. Weiss

203

1. {Tan-tum er-go Sa-cra-mén-tum Ve-ne-ré-mur cér-nu-i,
Et an-ti-quum do-cu-mén-tum No-vo ce-dat rí-tu-i,
2. {Ge-ni-tó-ri Ge-ni-tó-que Laus et ju-bi-lá-ti-o,
Sa-lus, ho-nor, vir-tus quo-que Sit et be-ne-dí-cti-o;
1. Prae-stet fi-des sup-ple-mén-tum, Sén-su-um de-fé-ctu i.
2. Pro-ce-dén-ti ab u-tró-que Com-par sit lau-dá-ti-o.
A-men.

TANTUM ERGO No. 6

Limagne

At a moderate pace

204

1. Tan-tum er-go Sa-cra-mén-tum Ve-ne-ré-mur
2. Ge-ni-tó-ri Ge-ni-tó-que Laus et ju-bi-
1. cér-nu-i, Et an-tí-quum do-cu-mén-tum
2. lá-ti-o, Sa-lus, ho-nor, vir-tus quo-que

1. No - vo ce - dat rí - tu - i, Prae - stet fi - des
2. Sit et be - ne - dí - cti - o; Pro - ce - dén - ti
1. sup - ple - mén - tum Sén-su - um de - fé - ctu - i.
2. ab u - tró - que Com-par sit lau - dá - ti - o. A - men.

TANTUM ERGO Nº 7

Webbe

205

1. Tan-tum er - go Sa-cra-mén - tum Ve - ne - ré-mur cér - nu - i,
2. Ge - ni - tó - ri Ge-ni - tó - que Laus et ju - bi - lá - ti - o,
1. Et an - tí - quum do - cu - mén - tum No - vo ce - dat rí - tu - i,
2. Sa - lus, ho - nor, vir - tus quo - que Sit et be - ne - dí - cti - o;
1. Prae-stet fi - des sup-ple-mén - tum Sén-su - um de - fé - ctu - i.
2. Pro - ce - dén-ti ab u - tró - que Com-par sit lau - dá - ti - o. A-men.

TANTUM ERGO No. 8

206

Gently
pp
f
1. Tan-tum er-go Sa-cra-mén-tum Ve-ne-ré-mur cér-nu-i, Et an-tí-quum do-cu-mén-tum No-vo ce-dat rí-tu-i, Prae-stet fi-des sup-ple-mén-tum Sén-su-um de-féc-tu-i.
2. Ge-ni-tó-ri Ge-ni-tó-que Laus et ju-bi-lá-ti-o, Sa-lus, ho-nor, vir-tus quo-que Sit et be-ne-dí-cti-o; Pro-ce-dén-ti ab u-tró-que Com-par sit lau-dá-ti-o. A-men.

TANTUM ERGO No. 9

207

1. Tan-tum er - go Sa-cra-mén-tum, Ve - ne - ré - mur
2. Ge - ni - tó - ri Ge - ni - tó - que Laus et ju - bi -
1. cér - nu - i, Et an - tí - quum do - cu - mén - tum No - vo
2. lá - ti - o, Sa-lus, ho - nor, vir - tus quo - que Sit et
p
1. ce - dat rí - tu - i, Prae-stet fi-des sup-ple-mén - tum
2. be - ne - dí - cti - o, Pro - ce - dén-ti ab u - tró - que
f
1. Sén - su - um de - fé - ctu - i. Prae - stet fi - des
2. Com-par sit lau - dá - ti - o. Pro - ce - dén - ti
1. sup-ple-mén-tum Sén-su - um de - fé - ctu - i.
2. ab u - tró-que Com-par sit lau - dá - ti - o. A - men.

INVOCATIONS

208

1. Cor Je-su sa-cra- - - - tís - si mum:
2. Cor Ma-rí-ae im-ma-cu- - - lá - tum:
3. San-cte Jo-seph, Pa-trone no-ster di-le - ctís - si - me:
4. San-cte Jo-an-nes Ba - - - ptí - sta:
5. Vi- vat Je-sus in cór-di-bus no - stris:
1. mi - se - ré - re no - - bis.
2. o - - ra pro no - - bis.
3. o - - ra pro no - - bis.
4. o - - ra pro no - - bis.
5. in ae - - tér - - num.

PARCE DOMINE

209

Par-ce Dó-mi - ne, — par-ce pó-pu-lo - tu - o: —
ne in ae - tér - num i - ra - scá - ris no - bis.

THE DIVINE PRAISES[1]

J. H. Schloeder

210

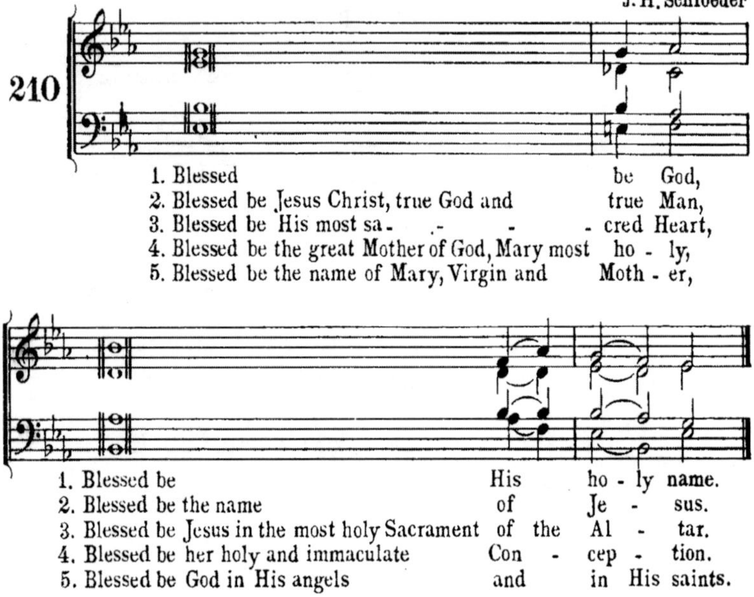
1. Blessed be God,
2. Blessed be Jesus Christ, true God and true Man,
3. Blessed be His most sa - - - - cred Heart,
4. Blessed be the great Mother of God, Mary most ho - ly,
5. Blessed be the name of Mary, Virgin and Moth - er,
1. Blessed be His ho - ly name.
2. Blessed be the name of Je - sus.
3. Blessed be Jesus in the most holy Sacrament of the Al - tar.
4. Blessed be her holy and immaculate Con - cep - tion.
5. Blessed be God in His angels and in His saints.

LAUDATE DOMINUM

211

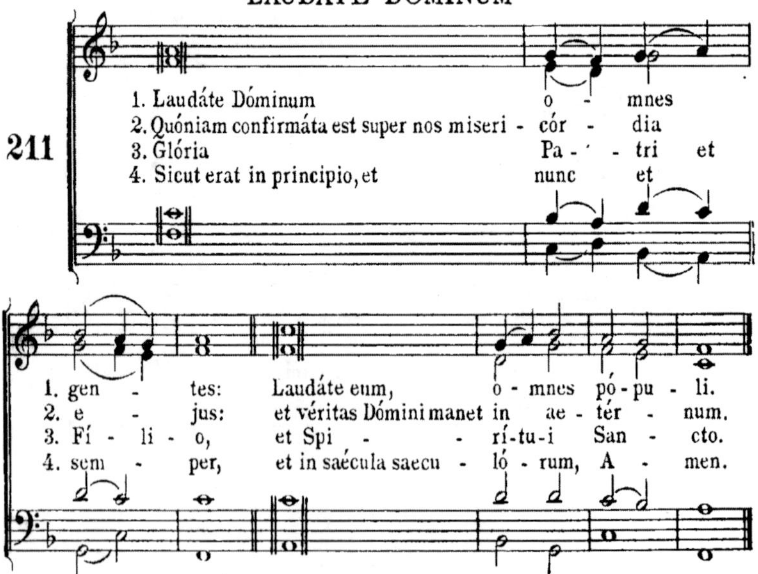
1. Laudáte Dóminum o - mnes
2. Quóniam confirmáta est super nos miseri - cór - dia
3. Glória Pa - - tri et
4. Sicut erat in principio, et nunc et
1. gen - tes: Laudáte eum, o - mnes pó - pu - li.
2. e - jus: et véritas Dómini manet in ae - tér - num.
3. Fí - li - o, et Spi - - rí-tu-i San - cto.
4. sem - per, et in saécula saecu - ló - rum, A - men.

[1] By permission of J. Fischer & Bro.

TE DEUM

212

M.M. ♪ = 160
Te De-um lau-dá - mus: * te Dó-mi-num con-fi - té-mur.
Te ae-tér-num Pa - trem o-mnis ter-ra ve-ne-rá - tur.
Ti-bi o-mnes An-ge-li, ti-bi Coe-li et u-ni-vér-sae Po-te-stá-tes:

Ti - bi Ché - ru - bim et Sé - ra - phim in - ces - sá - bi - li
vo - ce pro - clá - mant: San - ctus: San - ctus:
San - ctus Do-mi-nus De - us Sá - ba - oth. Ple-ni sunt coe - li et
ter - ra ma - je - stá - tis gló - ri - ae tu - ae.

Te glo - ri - ó - sus A - po - sto - ló - rum cho - rus:
Te Pro - phe - tá - rum lau - dá - bi - lis nú - me - rus:
Te Már - ty - rum can - di - dá - tus lau - dat ex - ér - ci - tus.
Te per or - bem ter - rá - rum san - cta con - fi - té - tur Ec - clé - si - a:

Pa - trem im-mén-sae ma-je - stá - tis: Ve-ne-rán-dum tu-um
ve - rum et ú - ni - cum Fí - li - um: San-ctum quo-que
Pa - rá - cli - tum Spí - ri - tum. Tu Rex
gló - ri - ae, Chri - ste. Tu Pa-tris sem-pi-tér-nus es Fí - li - us.

Tu ad li - be - rán - dum sus - ce - ptú - rus hó - mi - nem,
non hor - ru - í - sti Vir - gi - nis ú - te - rum. Tu de - ví - cto mor -
tis a - cú - le - o a - pe - ru - i - sti cre - dén - ti - bus re - gna coe - ló - rum.
Tu ad déx - te - ram De - i se - des, in gló - ri - a Pa - tris.

Ju-dex cré-de-ris es-se ven-tú-rus. Te er-go quaé-su-mus,
tu-is fá-mu-lis súb-ve-ni, quos pre-ti-ó-so
sán-gui-ne re-de-mí-sti. Ae-tér-na fac
cum San-ctis tu-is in gló-ri-a nu-me-rá-ri.

Sal-vum fac pó-pu-lum tu-um Dó-mi-ne, et bé - ne-dic hae-re - di -
tá - ti tu - ae. Et re - ge e - os,
et ex - tól - le il - los us - que in ae - tér - num.
Per sín - gu - los di - es, be - ne - dí - ci - mus te.

Et lau - dá - mus no - men tu - um in saé - cu - lum,
et in saé - cu - lum saé - cu - li.
Di - gná - re Dó - mi - ne
di - e i - sto
si - ne pec - cá - to nos cu - sto - dí - re.
Mi - se - ré - re no - stri Dó - mi - ne,
mi - se - ré - re no - stri.

Fi - at mi - se - ri - cór - di - a tu - a Dó - mi - ne su - per nos,
quem ád - mo - dum spe - rá - vi - mus in te. In te Dó - mi - ne
spe - rá - vi: non con - fún - dar in ae - tér num.

V. Confírma hoc, Deus, quod operátus es in nobis.
R. A templo sancto tuo quod est in Jerúsalem.
V. Benedicámus Patrem et Fílium cum Sancto Spíritu.
R. Laudémus et superexaltémus eum in saecula.

V. Benedíctus es, Domine, in firmaménto coeli.
R. Et laudábilis, et gloriósus, et superexaltátus in saécula.

V. Dómine exaudi orationem meam.
R. Et clamor meus ad te véniat.

V. Dominus vobiscum.
R. Et cum spíritu tuo.

V. Oremus: Deus - - - - nostrum. R. Amen.
V. Jesus Christus fáciat nos unánimes.
R. Nunc et semper et in saécula saeculórum, Amen.

ALL PRAISE TO SAINT PATRICK

Irish Melody

213

1. All praise to Saint Pat-rick who brought to our moun-tains The
2. There is not a Saint in the bright courts of heav - en More
3. Then what shall we do for thee, heav - en sent Fa - ther? What
1. gift of God's faith, the sweet light of His love! All hail to the shepherd who
2. faith-ful than he to the land of his choice; Oh, well may the na-tion to
3. shall the proof of our loy - al - ty be? By all that is dear to our
1. showed us the fount-ains That rise in the Heart of the
2. whom he was giv - en, In the feast of their Sire and A -
3. hearts, we would rath - er Be mar-tyred, sweet Saint! than bring
1. Sav - iour a-bove! For hun-dreds of years, In smiles and in tears, Our
2. pos - tle re-joice! In glo - ry a - bove True to his love, He
3. shame up - on thee! But oh, he will take The prom-ise we make, So to

1. Saint has been with us, our shield and our stay; All else may have gone, Saint
2. keeps the false faith from his chil-dren a-way; The dark false faith, Far
3. live that our lives by God's help may dis-play The light that he bore To
ritard
a tempo
1. Patrick a-lone, He hath been to us light when earth's lights were all set, For the
2. worse than death, Oh, he drives it far off from the green sun-ny shore, Like the
3. E-rin's shore. Oh yes, Fa-ther of Ire-land! no child wilt thou own Whose
1. glo-ries of faith they can nev-er de-cay; And the best of our glo-ries is
2. rep-tiles that fled from his curse in dis-may; And E-rin, when er-ror's proud
3. life is not light-ed by grace on its way; For they are true I-rish, Oh
ritard
1. bright with us yet, In the faith and the feast of Saint Pat-rick's Day.
2. tri-umph is o'er, Will still be found keep-ing Saint Pat-rick's Day.
3. yes! they a-lone, Whose hearts are all true on Saint Pat-rick's Day.

THE MEMORARE

Lambillotte

214

CHORUS
mf
Oh, be thou mind-ful, Moth-er most ten-der, Ne'er was thine
aid im - plored in - vain. Faint in the com-bat,
Lest we sur-ren-der, Do thou our falt-'ring hearts sus -
tain, Do thou our falt-'ring hearts sus - tain.
Fine

In the a - ges gone by, as all rec - ords de -
clare, Not e'en once hast thou slight - ed the
sup - pli - ant's cry; Nor shall a - - ges that fol - low, thy
mer - cies im - pair! To all that in - voke thee, Sweet
Moth - - er, be nigh, Sweet Moth - - er, be nigh.

THE ANGELUS 1

215

TENOR SOLO
An - ge-lus Dó-mi-ni an - nun - ti - á vit Ma-
rí - ae, et con cé - pit, de Spí - ri - tu San - cto.
SOPRANO SOLO
A - ve Ma - rí - a grá - ti - a ple - na Dó-mi-nus te-cum be-ne-
dí-cta tu in mu-li - é - ri-bus et be-ne-dí-ctus fructus ventris tui Je-sus.
SOP. San - cta Ma - rí - a
ALTO
TENOR San - cta Ma - rí - a Ma - ter De - i, o - ra pro
pp
BASS
San - cta Ma - ter De - i
no-bis pec-ca - tó - ri-bus nunc et in ho-ra mor-tis no-strae.

1 From St. Basil's Hymnal, but arranged by W. A. Rabock.

o - ra pro no - - bis pec - - ca - -
A - - men, O-ra pro no-bis, San-cta Ma-rí-a, Ma-ter
tó - ri - bus nunc et in
De - i; o - ra pro no-bis pec-ca-tó-ri-bus nunc
ho - ra mor-tis no strae. A - men.
et in ho-ra mor-tis no-strae. A - men.
Fine
SOPRANO SOLO
Ec-ce ancil-la Dómi-ni; fi-at mi-hi secundum verbum tu - um.
BASS SOLO
Et Ver-bum ca-ro fa-ctum est et ha-bi-tá-vit in
no - bis, et ha-bi-tá-vit in no - - bis.

INDEX[1]

ENGLISH NUMBERS

Nº	Title, or First Words of Hymn	Page	Source of Words	Source of Air
2	A Glorious Voice	2		Ancient Hymn
60	A Message from the Sacred Heart	60	Rev. M. Russell, S.J.	J. Hayden
*131	Acts of the Theological Virtues	132	"Hymns for the Year," 1867	
122	Agnes, Hymn to St.	123		Ph. Rohr
213	All Praise to St. Patrick	246	Rev. F. W. Faber	Irish Air
*6	Angels We Have Heard on High	6	Bishop Chadwick	Old French Air
123	Anthony, Hymn to St.	124		Jacobsen
83	As the Dewy Shades of Even	83		German Air 1715
*23	At the Cross Her Station Keeping	23	Rev. E. Caswall, Tr.	Mainz Gesangbuch, 1661
74	Ave Maria	74		
*75	Ave Sanctissima	74	Mrs. Hemans & Sister	
137	Bishop, At the Reception of a	139	Roman Ritual	Plain Chant
*136	Blest is the Faith	138	Rev. F. W. Faber	
82	Cause of Our Joy	82	Benedictine Hymn	Rev. A. Schubiger, O.S.B.
*124	Cecilia, Hymn to St.	124	Rev. C. Pise	Bro. Bonitus
*27	Christ the Lord is Risen To-Day	27	Miss Leeson, Tr.	
*17	Christians Who of Jesus' Sorrows, Nº1	17	From the French	Pergolesi
*18	" " " " " Nº2	18	" " "	
*5	Come, All Ye Faithful	5	From the Latin	Lerler
*31	Come, Holy Ghost, Creator Blest	31	Rev. E Caswall, Tr.	Lambillotte
*32	Come, Holy Ghost, Creator Come	32	John Dryden	Holy Face Hymnal
*76	Daughter of a Mighty Father	76		
*111	Dear Angel Ever At My Side	112	Rev. F. W. Faber	B.S.
*129	Dear Children, Praise the Lord	130		Bro. Luke
*105	Dear Guardian of Mary	106	Rev. F. W. Faber	Bro. Bonitus
123	Dearest Saint (St. Anthony)	124		Jacobsen
210	Divine Praises	236	Roman Ritual	J.H. Schloeder
13	Epiphany Hymn	13	R. Campbell, Tr.	C. Schmidt
*72	Fading, Still Fading	72		T.V. Wiesenthal
*120	Faith of Our Fathers	121	Rev. F. W. Faber	F. S. C.
48	First Communicants, Processional of	48	Rev. P. Wetzelsperger, O.S.B. Tr.	St. Gall Hymnal
*64	Glorious Mother	64		
112	Glorious Patron (St. La Salle) Nº1	113	"Mercedes"	W.A. Raboch
113	" " " Nº2	114	"	W.A. Raboch
114	" " " Nº3	115	"	French Hymnal
115	" " " Nº4	116	"	Dr. J.L. Browne
*131	Great God, Whatever thro' thy Church	132	"Hymns for the Year," 1867	

[1] An asterick * before the Hymn Number indicates that the melody is taken from the *Catholic Youth's Hymn Book*, the predecessor of the *De La Salle Hymnal*.

No	Title or First Words of Hymn	Page	Source of Words	Source of Air
121	Hail Glorious St. Patrick	122	Sister Agnes	H.F. Hemy
*81	Hail Mary, Queen and Virgin Meek	81		Bro. Luke
77	Hail Queen of Heaven	77	Rev. Dr. Lingard	English Air
*68	Hail Queen of the Heavens	68		
104	Hail St. Joseph Spouse of Mary	105	Sodality Manual	P. Basuian
*65	Hail Virgin Dearest Mary	65		Lambillotte
*37	Have Mercy on Us, God Most High	36	Rev. F. W. Faber	Bro. Luke
*130	Hear Thy Children, Gentle Jesus	131	Rev. F. Stanfield	German Air
*119	Hibernia's Patron Saint, All Hail	120		B.S.
*126	Holy God, We Praise Thy Name	127	Rev. C Walworth	P. Ritter, 1792
71	Holy Mary, Mother Mild	71		W. Dressler
*106	Holy Patron, Thee Saluting	107		Tyrolese Air
*110	How Kind It is of Thee	111		
14	How Sweet the Name of Jesus Sounds	14	Rev. J. Newton *(A)*[2]	W.A. Raboch
57	I Need Thee, Gracious Jesus	57	"Hymns for the Year" 1867	J.G. Marcks
66	Immaculate Mother We Come	66	From the French	Lourdes Pilgrims
39	In This Sacrament, Sweet Jesus	39		French Hymnal
133	Jerusalem, My Happy Home	134	Fr. L. Anderson	Mother Seton
132	Jerusalem the Golden	133	Rev. J. M. Neale, Tr.	Haller
28	Jesus Christ is Risen	28	Tate & Brady, Tr.	Lyra Davidica, 1708
45	Jesus, Gentlest Saviour	45	Rev. F. W. Faber	Adapted
*22	Jesus! Jesus! Behold at Length	22		
41	Jesus, Jesus, Come to Me	41		Prussian Air
*38	Jesus, My Lord, My God, My All	38	Rev. F. W. Faber	Swiss Air
*124	Let the Deep Organ Swell	124	Rev. C. Pise	Bro. Bonitus
135	Long Live the Pope	136	Rev. H.T. Henry, Litt.D	Rev. H.G. Ganss
63	Look Down, O Mother Mary	63	Rev. E. Vaughan, C.SS.R., Tr.	J.B. Schweitzer
42	Lord Jesus, Whom by Power Divine	42	From the Latin	Holy Face Hymnal
*67	Loved Heart, All Mild, All Meek	66		Lambillotte
*76	Macula Non est in Te	76		
69	Mary, Mildest Queen, Remember [3]	69	Tr. from G. Görres	Schubiger's Hymnal
*79	Mary, Star of the Sea	79		B.S.
214	Memorare	248	Father. Bernard *(A)*	Lambillotte
*86	Mother Dear, Oh Pray for Me	86		
73	Mother Mary, At Thine Altar	73	Rev. F. W. Faber	Lambillotte
19	O Come and Mourn with Me	19	Rev. F. W. Faber	French Air
3	O Come, Divine Messiah	3	From the French	French Hymnal
*128	O Come, Sweet Anthems Let Us Sing	129	Tate & Brady *(A)*	J. Haydn
24	O Happy Time of Blessed Tears	124	Rev. F. W. Faber	J.G. Marcks
80	O Heart of Mary, Pure and Fair	80	Oratorian Hymnal	Piel
122	O Holy Martyr, Spotless Dove	123		
8	O Holy Night	8		A. Adam
*15	O Jesus Dear, the Thought of Thee	15	Rev. E. Caswall, Tr.	

[2] *A* = adapted. [3] Also known as Memorare

Nº	Title, or First Words of Hymn	Page	Source of Words	Source of Air
*59	O Jesus, Jesus, Dearest Lord	59	Rev. F. W. Faber	
*38	O Jesus, Lord, My God, My All	38	Rev. F. W. Faber	Swiss Air
*46	O Lord, I am not Worthy	46		Burns
70	O Purest of Creatures	70	Rev. F. W. Faber	L. Selle
36	O Thou Immortal Light Divine	36	Rev. E. Caswell, Tr.	C. Gounod
85	O Turn to Jesus, Mother, Turn	85	Rev. F. W. Faber	S. Webbe
66	Our Lady of Lourdes	66	From the French	Lourdes Pilgrims
*30	Our Lord is Risen from the Dead	30	C. Wesley *(A)*	French Air
82	Our Youthful Hearts	82	Benedictine Hymn	Rev. A. Schubiger, O.S.B.
135	Pope, Hymn for the	136	Rev. H.T. Henry, Litt. D.	Rev. H.G. Ganss
*125	Pray for the Dead	126		
48	Processional of First Communicants	48	Rev. P. Wetzelsperger, O.S.B., Tr.	St. Gall Hymnal
102	St. Joseph Dear, We Praise Thee	103	Oratorian Hymnal *(A)*	Oratorian Hymnal
117	St. La Salle Our Dearest Father	118	F. S. C.	E. Marzo
47	Salutation of the Blessed Sacrament	47	Rev. A. Bachofen, O.S.B., Tr.	German Hymnal
11	See Amid the Winter's Snow	41	Rev. E. Caswell, Tr.	
*1	See He Comes	1		
33	See the Paraclete Descending	32		Prussian Air
7	Silent Night	7	From the German of J. Mohr	F. Gruber
*84	Snow and Rain Have Vanished	84	Rev. J. C. Cummings	Labat
*44	Soul of My Saviour	44	Tr. of "Anima Christi"	
*23	Stabat Mater	23	Rev. E. Caswall, Tr. *(A)*	Mainz Gesangbuch, 1661
21	Station Hymn	21	Rev. P. Cummins, O.S.B.	Schubiger's Hymnal
70	Star of the Sea	70	Rev. F. W. Faber	L. Selle
48	The Blessed Hour is Coming	48	Rev. P. Wetzelsperger, O.S.B., Tr.	St. Gall Hymnal
*127	The Earth, O Lord, Rejoices	128		
*134	The Lord Himself, the Mighty God	135	Metrical Version of Ps. 23	F. S. C.
9	The Snow Lay on the Ground	9	Old English Carol	Traditional Air
20	Thou Loving Maker of Mankind	20	Rev. E. Caswall, Tr.	St. Basil's Hymnal
21	Thy Slayers, Dear Jesus	21	Rev. P. Cummins, O. S. B.	Schubiger's Hymnal
*88	'Tis the Month of Our Mother	88		
83	Vesper Hymn	83		German Air, 1715
13	What Beauteous Sun-Surpassing Star	13	R. Campbell, Tr.	C. Schmidt
*10	What Lovely Infant Can This Be?	10	Children's Carol	
43	When at Thy Altar, Lord, I Kneel	43		English Air
*79	When Ev'ning Shades are Falling	79		B.S.
40	When Our Saviour Wished to Prove	40	St. Basil's Hymnal	Stevenson
58	When Softly Dawns the Golden Light	58	Messenger of the Sacred Heart	Oratorian Hymnal
116	While Heart and Soul to Thee We Raise	117	Bro. Romuald	Bro. Romuald
*103	With Grateful Hearts	104		Monpou
*78	With Holy Choirs of Angels	78		German Air

INDEX
LATIN NUMBERS

Nº	Title, or First Words of Hymn	Page	Source of Words	Source of Air
62	Ad Sacratissimum Cor Jesu	62	Church Hymn	Piel
*4	Adeste Fideles	4	Cistercian Gradual	Traditional Air
56	Adoremus in Aeternum	56		Plain Chant, Arr. by W.A.R.
186	Alma Redemptoris	217	Antiphonary	Vatican Version
140-144	Angels, Mass of the	143	Kyriale	Vatican Version
215	Angelus, The	250	Breviary	St. Basil's Hymnal
138	Asperges	140	Kyriale	Vatican Version
137	At the Reception of a Bishop	139	Antiphonary	Plain Chant
*91	Ave Maris Stella, Nº 1	91	Breviary	Lambillotte
92	" " " Nº 2	92	"	Italian Air
93	" " " Nº 3	93	"	Bro. Sixtus
178	" " " Nº 4	204	"	Solesmes Chant
187	Ave Regina Coelorum	218	"	Solesmes Chant
137	Bishop, At the Reception of	139	Antiphonary	Plain Chant
34	Confirma Hoc, Deus	34	Ritual	Gregorian Chant
34	Confirmation, Holy	34	"	" "
61	Cor Jesu	61		Frank
62	Cor Jesu, Ad Sacratissimum	62	Church Hymn	Piel
183	Exsultet, Nº 1	214	Breviary	Vatican Version
184	" Nº 2	215	"	" "
26	Gethsemane et Golgotha	26	Old Latin Hymn	Rev. P. Stöcklin, O.S.B.
12	In Nativitate Domini	12	Old Latin Hymn	Rev. A. Schubiger, O.S.B.
208	Invocations	235		Plain Chant
182	Iste Confessor	213	Breviary	Vatican Version
109	Iste Quem Laeti	110	"	" "
*185	Jesu Corona Virginum	216	Breviary	Traditional Air
16	Jesu Dulcis Memoria	16	St. Bernard (?)	
211	Laudate Dominum	236	Vesperal	Plain Chant
100	Litany of the Most Blessed Virgin Nº 1	100	Liturgic Prayer	Vatican Version
101	" " " " " " Nº 2	102	" "	
182	Lucis Creator	212	Breviary	Solesmes Chant
140-144	Mass of the Angels	143	Kyriale	Vatican Version
145-150	Mass in Honor of St. La Salle	153	"	W. A. Raboch
151-165	Mass for the Dead	167	Officium et Missa pro Defunctis	Vatican Version (Arr. by P. T. Jos. Varken)
62	O Cor Jesu, Fons Amoris	62	Rev. A. Bachofen, O.S.B., Tr.	Piel
52	O Esca Viatorum, Nº 1	52	Old Latin Hymn	Cantata Catholica
53	" " " Nº 2	53	" " "	Rev. A. Schubiger, O.S.B.
29	O Filii et Filiae	29	Breviary	
87	O Gloriosa Virginum	87	Liturgic Hymn	Jacobsen
50	O Mi Jesu	50	Old Latin Hymn	Schubiger's Hymnal

Nº	Title, or First Words of Hymn	Page	Source of Words	Source of Air
191	O Salutaris, Nº 1	222	St. Thomas Aquinas	Solesmes Chant
192	" Nº 2	222	" "	A.J. Weiss
193	" Nº 3	223	" "	S. Webbe
*194	" Nº 4	224	" "	C. Wondell
195	" Nº 5	224	" "	A. Werner
*196	" Nº 6	225	" "	A. Werner
197	" Nº 7	226	" "	
198	" Nº 8	227	" "	Gregorian Chant
*94	O Sanctissima, Nº 1	94	Liturgic Hymn	Sicilian Air
95	" Nº 2	95	" "	Gordigiani
*55	Pange, Lingua	55	St. Thomas Aquinas	Solesmes Chant
*209	Parce, Domine	235	Breviary	Ancient
161	Pater Noster, Tone of	179	Kyriale	Vatican Version
162	Preface, Tone	179	"	" "
118	Quem Sion	119	Breviary	Plain Chant
*107	Quicumque	108	Liturgic Hymn	Traditional Air
*51	Quod in Coena	51	St. Thomas Aquinas	German Air
188	Regina Coeli, Nº 1	219	Breviary	A. Lotti
189	" " Nº 2	220	"	Solesmes Chant
12	Resonet in Laudibus	12	Old Latin Hymn	Rev. A. Schubiger, O.S.B.
98	Salve Maria Sanctissima	98	Old Latin Hymn	Rev. A. Schubiger, O.S.B.
190	Salve Regina	220	Breviary	Solesmes Chant
96	Sancta Maria	96	Church Hymn	J.B. Schweitzer
89	Sanctorum Agmina	89	Rev. L. Janssens, O.S.B.	Ancient Hymnals
*24	Stabat Mater, Nº 1	25	Rev. E. Caswall, Tr. *(A)*	Mainz Gesangbuch, 1661
25	" " Nº 2	25	Jacopone da Todi	Solesmes Chant
*97	Sub Tuum Pracoidium	96	Breviary	Lambillotte
199	Tantum Ergo, Nº 1	228	St. Thomas Aquinas	Solesmes Chant
200	" " Nº 2	228	" "	Minard
*201	" " Nº 3	229	" "	
202	" " Nº 4	230	" "	F.S.C.
203	" " Nº 5	231	" "	A.J. Weiss
204	" " Nº 6	231	" "	Limagne
205	" " Nº 7	232	" "	S. Webbe
206	" " Nº 8	233	" "	
207	" " Nº 9	234	" "	
212	Te Deum	237	SS. Augustine & Ambrose (?)	Vatican Version
108	Te Joseph Celebrent	109	Breviary	" "
99	Tota Pulchra	98	Church Hymn	Dom Pothier, O.S.B., Arr.
90	Ultima in Mortis Hora	90	Old Latin Hymn	Ancient Hymnal
*49	Veni, Jesu	49		Cherubini
54	Verbum Supernum	54	St. Thomas Aquinas	Luxemburg Hymnal *(A)*
166-172	Vespers for Sundays	186	Antiphonary	Vatican Version
173-180	Vespers of the Most Blessed Virgin	198	" "	" "
139	Vidi Aquam	141	Kyriale	" "